KEEPING KASSIE

CASSIE COLTON

Published by Mystic Marigold Publishing, LLC

Williamsburg, VA

Cassiecoltonbooks.com

Copyright © 2023 Cassie Colton

Cover by Scott Carpenter

Edited by Eileen Troemel

Dedication

The story of the marigold:
Ever since I was a little girl, my grandmother would plant marigolds along the front edge of her sidewalk. In the fall, she'd gather the seeds, dry them and place them in a paper bag. Over the years our family took for granted the love she poured into the flowers. They were always a constant in our lives, much like my grandmother.

When my gram became too frail to stay at her home, my aunt took her in and I'd fly to visit and help care for her. The last year she was alive, she called to tell me that she couldn't find any marigold seeds. The day before I left to see her, I found a box.

Since it was too early to plant, I left them with her, and my aunt helped her plant them. Six weeks later, I lost my gram. Our family was devastated.

A few weeks later, we lost my wonderful Aunt June. She could light up a room with her smile and I still hear her laugh. It didn't matter when she saw you, she'd always beam in joy and never left without saying, "I love you, Baby." She could make your heavy heart feel better by one of her hugs alone. She taught her family the meaning of love by her actions. She was one of the strongest women I have ever known.

My Aunt Judy sent me the seeds from the last marigolds my grandmother sowed. I planted them shortly after losing these two women who taught me about love, loyalty and going after my dream. When I was researching flowers for Chase to send to Kassie, I found an article on how marigolds can survive in the toughest of climates. They can make it through wet seasons and dry and still retain their beauty. I cried as I planted and asked for some sign, they were there with me. That summer, my marigolds grew over three feet tall and bloomed until December. I sent pictures to my family and they were in awe of how big these flowers grew as none of us had seen them get to that height before. I knew that was my sign. My gram and Aunt June are here with me today. They remind me that we are together through thick and thin. We have to keep faith in ourselves and each other. They were our marigolds.

If you look closely on my logo, the burgundy rose is for my grandmother and the butterfly on the leaf is my Aunt June. They are always with me.

This story contains elements of each of them and I hope when you read the conclusion of Chase and Kassie, you know love can withstand anything as long as you have faith.

I love you, Gram. I love you, Aunt June.
Love,
Cassie

CHAPTER ONE

"Kassie, I need you to sit down. I have a few things we need to discuss." Jake stood in rumpled clothes with red brimmed eyes and his hair in disarray. He held a handful of yellow packets. He waited for Kassie to take a seat at the table before sitting across from her. "Before the team left, they each left a sealed packet if something unforeseeable happened. Chase didn't want to worry you about this because he planned to stay stateside after this mission. We need to face facts. There isn't any way they survived the crash."

Kassie took the bundles from his hand and spread them out. Chase's handwriting scrawled across the first one with her name. Opening the seal, she found a bunch of legal documents and a letter to her.

Princess,

If you're reading this, I didn't make it back home. I transferred the ownership of the mountain to you in hopes you'll continue to build the hospital for me. As you've written to me before, make something good out of something terrible.

I can't think of anything worse than losing us. No matter what sweetheart, I'll always be with you on the mountain. I want you and Emma to be happy. Continue counseling with Claire and go on with your life. This may be the hardest letter I've ever written because I know how much I have to lose. My parents taught me about love and loyalty, yet I didn't understand the difference until I met you. You are my life, Princess. I'll live through you and the hospital. Make sure Ladybug knows how much I love her. Please keep an eye on Jake for me, you'll be the only family he has left.

Don't ever forget how much I love you. You are everything I wanted and most importantly everything I needed. I'm proud of you, baby. Don't let my death derail you from life. Find love, find joy, find yourself, and know I'm watching over you. I love you, Princess.

Love,
Chase

Kassie set the letter down and placed all the legal documents back in the envelope. Peering at Jake, she knew he grappled with Chase's disappearance.

Keeping Kassie

"I'm not ready for this, Jake. Chase asked me to not give up. He'd walk through hell to get back to me," Kassie whispered.

"I know it's hard to believe. Darlin', no amount of wishful thinking can bring Chase or the team back. Two of the teammate's families have planned funerals for them. We need to attend."

Surprised by the families acceptance of the men's deaths without questioning the details or length of the search, Kassie furrowed her brows and shook her head.

"The crash occurred only a couple of weeks ago. We don't even know what happened. It's like pulling teeth to get any information. They might still be out there waiting for us to help them. What if they're hurt or hiding? I don't know. I think if Chase died, I'd feel...something."

Jake nodded his head. "I understand. You haven't really lived the military life. We live with this possibility. Every time someone goes out on deployment, this lingers in the back of their family's mind. In a way, we prepare emotionally for it. It still hurts, but we know we must accept it."

Kassie stood. "No. I don't have to accept it. I won't stop searching until some sort of evidence is found to prove without a doubt, Chase and the team are gone."

"Taco and Shadow's families planned funerals for next week." Jake quietly stated. Holding his hat, he stared at the floor. "I want to have a memorial for Chase at the top of the mountain in his family's cemetery. Chase wanted to be buried there if anything happened. We'll do it the week after next. I'll take care of everything."

"What?" Kassie turned to glare at him. "How can you give up without a question? You raised him! You, better than anyone, know Chase. If an opportunity presented itself,

3

Chase would fight his way back to us. I don't want to throw him a memorial. I'm not giving up!"

"The town wants to say their goodbyes. I know it's excruciating. Chase wouldn't want you to struggle with his death after everything you've faced down. We need closure, sweetheart. It'll help us accept he's gone." Jake gently persisted.

"I'm not doing it." Kassie pursed her lips. "I'll go to the other team member's funerals and pay my respects, but I'm certainly not planning Chase's memorial anytime soon."

Rebecca Rhodes, the CIA agent who Leo worked with, had called Kassie with the official report. The helo crashed over the Caspian Sea. Search and rescue found a couple of personal items from the team. They only found the pilot's and the new corpsman's bodies. After a week, they stopped the search, presuming the rest of the team perished in the sea.

Jake frowned. "The men put instructions in those packets. They trusted you to follow their last wishes, I'll let you get to it."

Kassie watched him leave, made a cup of tea with Bear's honey, and headed to Chase's room. Sitting in her favorite reading nook overlooking Serenity Mountain and the lake, she watched the sun set. She closed her eyes and said the prayer she had chanted every day since they learned of the crash. Kassie knew her friends and family felt she was in denial, especially after her recovery process from Roger kidnapping her. Chase and the team saved her life. She owed it to them to search out all possibilities no matter how small. She persisted in holding on to her faith in Chase until evidence proved otherwise.

CHAPTER TWO

Settling Emma upstairs in her room with Rollo, Kassie made her way back to the kitchen where the three men assigned to her and Emma's security, waited. Taking a seat at the head of the table, she watched as the men exchanged glances around her.

Leo's new tech specialist and Kassie's friend, Matthew Cartwright cleared his throat. "I saw Jake. He said he talked to you. I assume you want to discuss the details of the conversation."

Kassie nodded. "Yes. Some of the families made preparations for memorials next week. Shadow's family scheduled his on Saturday and Taco's will take place Sunday, late afternoon. I want to attend both. I called Julio Hernandez with the FBI. We need security and I don't want to take Emma with me. I want her to stay at the cabin. Matthew, I won't lie. I know you and Jameson take turns watching the cabin. You can't keep this up. Michael has a pediatric practice and can't be here all the time. It's bad enough he's driving back here at all hours to stay with us."

"We'll figure it out. I can reach out to some ex-military

friends for help. What about Julio? Can he loan us a few men?" Matthew asked.

Sighing, Kassie admitted her fears. "Julio's positive he rooted out all the dirty agents. Roger or James blackmailed two good men by holding their families hostage, allowing Roger time to get me out of the hospital. I don't want to take any chances with Em. Julio will personally fly in to watch over Em this weekend. It's still a short-term solution." She whispered, concerned Emma might overhear despite her distraction with her art. Little ears always seemed to hear things they weren't supposed to.

Matthew sat back in the chair and took a sip of water. "Chase spared no expense in the alarm system here. After the slip up of Rachel using the old code and showing up unannounced, we've since changed the code and the locks. We need to secure the entire mountain. Especially while you have the construction crews on the other side. We've background checked the employees and verify daily as they come in. I have a couple of guys who specialize in security. I'll give them a call and see what they suggest."

Kassie's nose scrunched as she thought of Chase's ex and her unexpected visit to the cabin. Kassie discovered Rachel naked in Chase's bed. Kicking her out butt naked was the highlight of her day until Jake and her godparents, Maddie and Joe, delivered the news about Chase and the team.

"Michael, will you and Jameson be available to go with me? Julio and Matthew can watch over Emma. I'll pay you for your time. I placed a call to Saint's family to see when they plan to have his memorial. I haven't heard back. Leo, left me instructions and his family isn't to be contacted." Kassie took a sip of tea to disguise the break in her voice at imagining the men who became her family over the last year as gone forever. To her, they seemed invincible.

Keeping Kassie

"I'll go with you. These men saved my life too and I want to pay my respects. You aren't paying me to watch over you. I'll always be here for you and Emma." Michael took her hand and gave it a squeeze.

Kassie drew her hand away. She watched as the men exchanged another silent communication with each other.

"Kass, when will you have Chase's memorial? Jake mentioned he talked to you about it," Matthew spoke up.

Kassie endeavored to keep her voice from wavering. She wanted the men to take her seriously and not someone struggling with accepting the inevitable. "I'm not having a service for Chase until I see some proof. I know you think I'm refusing to face facts. If a slim chance presented itself, Leo and the men would've taken it. After all, they're a highly trained SEAL team."

Changing the subject to keep the three serious men from lecturing her further, Kassie suggested, "Why don't we have some dinner? I have meatloaf in the oven with mashed potatoes and green beans. I'll have Joe reserve the company jet for us on Friday night. Taco's from San Diego. His wish consisted of a sunset ceremony at the beach and a going away party. Leave it to Taco to request tacos from a food truck at his funeral."

The men chuckled.

Calling Emma down for dinner, they listened to the almost five-year-old talk about her preschool class with Melody. Kassie watched as Emma animatedly described her classroom and teacher to the men. A pang hit her heart when she realized the life she envisioned as a family with Chase and her having dinner and listening to Emma talk about her day, might never come true. She swallowed down the lump in her throat as she got up from the table to busy herself in the kitchen, disguising her emotions from her friends. Despite her efforts, the observant men noticed.

When Emma finished her meal, Michael offered to give her a bath and read her a story. Matthew picked up the plates from the table and Jameson started securing the cabin for the night.

Jameson insisted on continuing his watch from outside and Kassie sent a thermos of coffee and a few snacks with him. He nodded in thanks as he closed the door.

Kassie tucked Em into bed and cracked the door. Going back downstairs, she joined Michael and Matthew in the living room. Matthew sat in the overstuffed chair by the fireplace, while Michael took a seat on the couch. Kassie sat on the opposite end.

"What do you know about Shadow's funeral?" Michael asked quietly.

Kassie's nose scrunched as she remembered the stark funeral invitation she received. She called his family twice only to be informed they didn't wish to speak with her personally, but they looked forward to seeing her at the funeral if she decided to attend.

"I don't know. It seems like it will be ostentatious. I can't picture Shadow wanting a formal funeral. He preferred to blend into the background and at the last second, surprise you. He's the kind of guy to pop up out of a coffin and yell, *'just kidding!'* I can't imagine him wanting a formal ceremony."

The men chuckled and agreed.

"I dislike how fast this is accepted. I feel they rushed this process and not much time has passed since the crash." Kassie sighed as she rubbed her tired eyes.

Matthew leaned forward with his elbows propped on his knees. "I know you don't want to hear it. Sometimes bad things happen to good people. You need to accept what's happened."

Kassie bit her tongue to keep from throwing Matthew's advice back into his face after the last few months. His cool professional persona didn't hide the hurt he faced when Kassie set boundaries on their friendship.

Matthew continued, "I know personally how difficult it is holding on to hope only to find out it was all for nothing. I think you've lost enough and putting off the inevitable won't help you or your little girl upstairs."

Michael's brows furrowed at how Kassie would take Matthew's advice. He watched them like a ping pong game.

"You didn't let go, Matthew. You searched for my sister for three years only to discover me. It must mean something when not a single team member was located. Maybe they don't have the means to get back to us, held captive, or hurt." Kassie threw out every possibility that crossed her mind. "I have to have more information other than they crashed into the ocean." Kassie met Matthew's eyes, daring him to challenge her.

"I think you need to get some rest. How about I take the first shift in here and Matthew, you go get some sleep. Both of you need some down time." Michael suggested gently as he helped Kassie from the sofa and gave her a gentle push toward her bedroom.

Kassie glanced back toward Matthew before closing the door a little harder than usual. She refused to relent. The discussion was far from over.

CHAPTER THREE

Kassie made her way to her bedroom from the bathroom plugging in strategically placed nightlights around the room. After her kidnapping, she avoided sleeping in complete darkness until she returned to Chase and the mountain. Since Chase left on a mission as a favor with Leo, she resorted back to using them. Claire Meyers, her therapist, assured her it amounted to a normal stress response and to give herself time.

Turning on the lamp on the nightstand, Kassie sat cross-legged on the bed and leaned against the pillows. Placing the packets next to her, she pulled Leo's out of the group. He was like a brother to her. On the front of the envelope, he wrote in bold black letters. *Do not contact family.* Breaking the seal, Kassie dumped the contents of the packet on the bed. One envelope contained her name, and the other surprised her when it fell onto the blanket and the label read, Catherine Mitchel. Obviously, Leo and Catherine's past needed peace. Setting it aside, she opened her envelope.

Dear PITA,

First, I want to apologize for my mistake of ordering Chase to sleep with you as part of the mission when you hesitated to cooperate. I've experienced the military life for years and I sometimes forget how emotions come into play. I ask your forgiveness for failing to remember what it means to be in love with someone.

A long time ago, Catherine, or as I call her, Kit Kat, and I knew the feeling. I made a stupid mistake and a bad judgement call. I let my pride get the best of me and I lost her. Her family became mine. Carol Reese took me in when my own kin refused to feed or clothe me. She gave me a home, much like you. Catherine's dad, Henry, treated me like a son. His encouragement provided the catalyst for me to enter the Navy and become a SEAL. I'll always be grateful to them.

If you're reading this, I didn't make it back home. Spread my ashes on Serenity Mountain and know I'm at peace. All my demons are buried and at rest. Please watch over Kit Kat. Ash, her husband, and one of my men, died due to my mistakes. As SEALS, we promise to take care of the widows of our fallen brothers. My trust provides security for Kit Kat and her *family. It's the least I can do. Please deliver the enclosed letter to her.*

I will always feel honored to have watched over you and Ladybug. You've become a little sister to me. You know, the kind who pesters you to death and makes you want to pull your hair out. LOL. Thank you for reminding me family means everything. PITA, I love you, even if you did shoot me in the ass.

Leo

KASSIE CHOKED BACK the sob and let out a laugh as she read the end of Leo's letter. She vaguely wondered about the story between Catherine and Leo. Both remained closed mouthed on what occurred between them. Grabbing her list, Kassie scribbled a note to go see Catherine the next day. Catherine and her mom, Carol settled into Serenity with Catherine's daughter, Melody, a few weeks before the news of the helicopter crash. Kassie knew Catherine grieved over the loss of her friend. Now with the additional information, she knew how much Leo meant to Catherine.

Scooping up the rest of the packets and placing them on her nightstand, Kassie decided to open Shadow's envelope later. The emotional letters overwhelmed her as she tried to reject the idea of the team as gone forever.

Kassie closed her eyes and pulled Chase's pillow up to her nose. Inhaling his scent of the mountain, she spoke aloud, "I don't know how, but I will find you. I promise. I refuse to give up and will continue to believe in you. I love you, Chase."

Keeping Kassie

Closing her eyes, she prayed no matter what, he knew she waited for him to come home.

CHAPTER FOUR

Chase tipped the canteen back and took a sip of water. He'd kill for a cup of hot coffee to help him stay awake. The hot and sticky days sucked, but the nights cooled and allowed a break from the heat. Taking out the last bit of clean gauze in his pack, he changed the dressing on his arm. He preferred to hold on to their supply of antibiotics. He might need it for the rest of the team.

With his head bandaged, Leo lay on the ground nursing a cut on his leg. Next to him, Taco suffered a broken leg, Chase suspected a concussion, and several cuts. A large gash marred Shadow's chest and still oozed blood. Saint sported a goose egg on his forehead and a long jagged cut down his side. The new corpsman Leo recently hired, and the pilot died on impact.

While they lost two in the helo crash, the team had rescued two men on their mission. One was thin and gaunt, his beard and hair hung down in thin stands and every bone in his body stuck out. Loose skin replaced strong muscles. Mottled bruises old and new covered his body. Faded scars showed what the man endured, and he struggled to stand on his own.

Though severely beaten, the other man wasn't as thin as his partner, and he maintained his muscles. Chase wasn't sure what his story was as his swollen face prevented him from talking.

Neither man spoke since the team rescued them from the village. It reminded Chase of the hovel he and Michael spent time in while held in captivity and he knew firsthand the torture and brutality these men suffered.

Hooking up another IV to the skinny man, he went to the next injured and offered water. Luckily, he discovered in the far back of the cave, a small steady steam coming off the rocks. With the heat of the day, the stream kept them hydrated and allowed them to clean wounds. After making a contraption to catch more of the water, Chase collected enough to keep them going for a little longer. Food remained their biggest issue. They rationed the MRE's, giving a little more to the skinny man at regular intervals to get his calorie intake up.

As he lay down, his thoughts drifted to Kassie. He closed his eyes and conjured her image. Her long red wavy curls, her deep blue eyes, the smattering of freckles along her nose and her smile. Worried she had probably heard about the helicopter crash by now, his thoughts dwelled on how she took the news. The last few months proved traumatizing for Kassie after the kidnapping by Roger Chapman, Stanton's right-hand man. He prayed she continued with her counseling.

Emma came to mind. He smiled as he thought of his little Ladybug. Thinking of his girls made him even more determined to figure out how the hell he would get him and his team home.

Saint leaned against the cave entrance covered with rocks and brush. Leo insisted on taking his turn, but one of the men conveniently woke to relieve him earlier than planned. He refused to admit his injuries intensified more than he let on. Shadow snuck down the mountain and stole some clothes. Blending in with the villagers, he managed to grab some bread, and overheard the rumor everyone on the helo perished on impact of the crash. Now they needed to figure out how to get out of the area with the two additional men, and Taco wasn't in any position to be moved.

After several discussions, they decided to lay low and let the men gain some strength before attempting to go to the village to steal a vehicle. Chase listened as the team strategized their plans. They knew what they needed to do. His job consisted of keeping them all alive for it to happen.

His mind drifted back to Kassie.

Don't give up, Princess. I'm coming home to you.

CHAPTER FIVE

Kassie volunteered to drop Emma and Melody off at preschool. Standing in front of Catherine's rental home, Kassie rang the doorbell and waited. Carol Reese opened the door and watched as Matthew helped Melody into the car.

"Carol, I need to talk to Catherine. May I come back after I drop the girls off?"

Carol swiped her eyes. "I'm sorry, Catherine's not up to company, Kass."

Kassie gently squeezed the older woman's arm in a comforting manner. "It's important. Please tell her I need to speak with her. I'll be back after I drop off these two hooligans." Kassie indicated the two girls chattering away to each other in the back seat.

Carol nodded her head and closed the door.

Stopping by Bryanna's Bakery, she grabbed a basket of muffins. When she got to the register, Bryanna added some fresh scones. Her eyes damp as she looked at Kassie.

"I slipped some chocolate chip cookies in there for the

girls. I can't imagine how devastated you must be. If you need anything, please don't hesitate to call me."

"Thank you. We haven't lost hope yet. I appreciate your support." Kassie turned to walk away but stopped. "Chase and I were thrilled to see this big old building get some love and attention. I'm happy to see the bakery succeeding. The cute tables add to the warmth of this place." Kassie looked around at all the changes Bryanna masterminded since purchasing the building. "You know, I'm working on the hospital and the community cabins on the mountain. I think we need to sit down and discuss you providing some daily treats when we open."

Bryanna beamed her appreciation. "You let me know when you're ready and I'll be there."

Kassie gave Bryanna a hug, said her goodbyes, and walked out of the bakery. Matthew fell into step beside her. "Are we headed back to the house?"

"No. I want to see Catherine again. I've barely talked to her since we got word of the crash and Carol's picking Melody up in the afternoons from the preschool." Kassie held on to the goodies as Matthew wove through the town.

"Maybe she's having a hard time dealing with the men's death. The team originally started with her husband," Matthew offered.

Kassie bit her lip. "Matthew, I want to ask you something. You know people. Can you call in a favor? I can't take someone's word Chase died with no evidence. On the slim chance they survived, I have to believe he'd find his way back to me. Please don't say you think I need to accept it and move on. You out of all people know you can't rest until you know for sure."

Matthew pulled into Catherine's driveway. Shutting the SUV off, he turned and faced Kassie. "I'm sorry, Kass. I

Keeping Kassie

already reached out. You need to understand, they crashed in the sea. Even if they survived the crash, the temperature of the ocean alone…it's not looking promising."

Kassie absorbed the news. "It doesn't mean the rest of the team didn't get out." She gripped the basket. "They might be waiting for help. We can't let them down."

Matthew swiped a hand over his scruff as he glanced in her direction. With a sigh, he reluctantly told her, "Kassie, I don't want to see you hurting anymore. I think you need to be prepared. Have you talked with Claire?"

"Yes. I've talked to Claire." She knew they worried over her mental health, especially since a traumatic recovery took an undetermined amount of time. Claire helped her sort out her feelings, and she continued seeing her on a weekly basis. "I'm talking to Catherine and her mom. Then I'm crossing the street and getting my hair cut at Samantha's Salon."

Matthew escorted her to the door. Carol led them inside. Once Matthew secured the home, he took a seat in the kitchen to let the women have their visit.

Catherine made her way downstairs and Kassie threw her arms around her friend. "Cat, I'm worried about you. Come sit down next to me."

Taking time to get her friend comfortable, she handed her a plate as Carol returned from the kitchen with a pot of coffee and a teapot. Handing a muffin to Catherine, Kassie commanded, "Eat. You need it."

Catherine placed the dish on the table. "I'll eat something in a bit. What did you need?"

Kassie studied her friend. She saw her pale face, yet her cheeks held a dark red hue. Tears had ravaged her eyes making them red and puffy. Cat gathered her red hair into a messy bun and her clothes appeared to have been slept in for several days.

"I want to talk to you about Leo. Before the team left, they filled out packets and left them with Jake. Leo asked me to give this to you." Reaching into her purse, she pulled out a letter and a key chain.

Catherine pulled the letter to her chest. Carol immediately put the cup down and joined the two women on the couch. They clung to Catherine giving her support as she burst into tears.

"Cat, why didn't you tell me about you and Leo?" Kassie asked her friend.

Catherine shook her head, "It happened a long time ago."

When Catherine gained control over her emotions, she took a sip of the tea and set the cup on the table. "I'm sorry Kassie. How are you and Em holding up?"

"We're fine. I've explained to Emma about the helicopter crash and we're looking for the team. She prays every night we find them." Kassie plucked a scone from the basket.

Catherine stared at her friend. "Are you serious?"

Kassie met her friend's eyes. "What do you mean?"

Catherine let out a half huff, half laugh. "Are you kidding me? You're fine? I don't think it's healthy for you to mislead Emma in believing Chase will return." Her voice held an incredulous tone. "I hope you've continued seeing Claire."

Kassie immediately bristled. "Yes, I've kept my appointments with Claire. Can't you believe, for a moment, there's a small possibility they survived? Hardly any time has passed since we got the news. Agent Rhodes hasn't heard anything else. As farfetched as it may seem, the team consists of the best of the best."

Catherine stared at Kassie in disbelief. "I know it's hard for you to hear, especially after everything you went through, but Chase died, Kassie. He's never coming back! You'll keep Emma's hopes up and then it will hurt her even more." Catherine said vehemently.

Feeling uncomfortable, Kassie rose from the couch and indicated to Matthew it was passed time to leave. "I'm not willing to accept they disappeared into thin air. They're a SEAL team. They have survival skills and extensive training in water. Emma knows we're looking for him. She doesn't need to be told anything until we know for sure..."

"They're gone Kassie! Becoming a Navy SEAL doesn't give you special powers or something. Yeah, they have abs you can lick for days, but it doesn't give them immortality. You need to face it. You can't run, you have to stay and mourn like the rest of us!" Catherine nearly shouted at Kassie. Tears fell from both women's faces as they glowered at one another.

"I think we need to be leaving Kassie." Matthew gently took her arm and led her to the door.

With one last view of her friend, Kassie walked out the door.

CHAPTER SIX

Walking across the street, Kassie accepted the tissue Matthew handed her. She blew her nose and swiped under her eyes. Walking into Samantha's spa relaxed her. The comforting scents filled her nose as she thought about the first time Chase sent her to Samantha for a complete spa day. Samantha gifted her a piece of herself back with that makeover and they became fast friends.

Samantha walked into the lobby, gave Kassie a hug, and handed her a cup of tea. "I'm finishing up a client."

Accepting the drink and sniffing it to find it laced with bourbon, Kassie swirled the fluid in the glass. At nine thirty in the morning, her best friend handed her an alcoholic beverage. She must look worse than she thought. The morning evolved to crap. Kassie tipped the cup back and took a healthy swig.

She sat on the velvet couch and surveyed the room. The waiting area drew the clients in with comfortable furniture and relaxing scents. Today, hints of lavender and citrus filled the room. Thinking back to her confrontation with Catherine, Kassie downed the cup of bourbon laced tea, and played with the handle while she waited for Samantha.

Kassie remembered the day Chase dropped her off, and he returned to pick her up in the same lobby where she sat. His gaze never left her and made Kassie feel exactly like a princess. Shy and leery of his motives at the time, Kassie placed barriers between them, yet Chase broke down every single one.

Samantha came around the corner. "I'm all set. Let's go." She grabbed Kassie's hand and took her into the back room and sat her in the stylist chair. Feeling Kassie's hair, she frowned and went about the room gathering bottles, sprays and jars. When she finished, she directed Kassie to the washbowl.

Kassie leaned back and let Samantha scrub away her troubled mind.

"Are we talking about it?" Samantha rinsed the shampoo out of her hair and added a hair mask.

"Am I wrong? I know the reality of finding them alive decreases with each day that passes. I'm not trying to avoid it. Everyone seems to accept they're gone. We received the news and two weeks later, I'm already heading to funerals. I feel it's too soon to throw the towel in and go on with my life."

Kassie peered at her friend's face as Samantha finger combed the moisturizing solution through her hair. Samantha's mouth settled in a frown. Her eyebrows furrowed as she concentrated on combing through the mass.

"It's not wrong, Sweetie. I experienced this when I lost Liam. It was the hardest thing I've ever done. Only a boot and a bloody hand came home to us." Samantha turned away from Kassie and wiped her face with a fresh towel.

A small sniffle escaped as she tried to gather herself. "A

grenade went off. One of the team members witnessed him standing in the vicinity of where it exploded. When they got there, the scene was bloody and body parts...you get the picture."

Kassie held Samantha's hand. "I'm sorry. I didn't mean to dredge up something so painful. As horrible as it was, you had witnesses to verify Liam died. Lost at sea doesn't make sense to me. I need more."

"I loved Liam more than life itself. I see him in his son. LJ has his mannerisms and the same color of hair and eyes. When Liam's parents ask if LJ can stay with them, I always agree. It's like having a piece of him with us. It took me a long time to accept it. Choices didn't exist, Kassie. I needed to raise LJ and get on with life. Liam may be gone, but I'm still here and responsible with the task of raising his son and keeping the memory of his father alive."

Kassie swallowed the lump in her throat. Mourning the loss of her and Chase's baby now stung deeper. The hospital now represented her and Chase's child. She'd do everything to ensure it became the most sought out facility in the US.

Samantha jolted her out of her daydreaming. "Are you up to staying for lunch?"

Kassie shook her head. "No, I need to talk to Maddie and Joe. Joe has taken over the hospital construction, and I want to get an update from him on the progress. Maddie's hovering. I'll weigh a ton at the rate she keeps baking cookies and beignets."

Samantha laughed. "I saw her and Bryanna Thompson talking a couple of days ago. Maybe she'll start working with Bryanna."

"I think she's recruiting Bryanna to provide a break station for the construction crews. I asked Joe to schedule them around the clock. We have crews starting on the transition cabin subdivision while another works on the hospital." Kassie waited for Samantha to wrap her hair in a towel before she progressed to the stylist chair. Taking out her pen and notebook, she started making a note while Samantha cleaned out her sink and grabbed her scissors.

"I know the importance of what the hospital represents, but why so fast?" Samantha questioned as she waved her scissors in the air at Kassie, indicating she needed to uncross her legs before she started to trim her hair.

"I don't know. I have this urge pushing me to get it done. The electricians wired the inside of the hospital, and three cabins are on the verge of completion. We'll finish those then move on to the next three for a total of twelve. Plus, I guess it keeps me busy." Kassie stated quietly.

Samantha wrapped her arms around Kassie's front, "Promise me something."

"What?" Kassie met Samantha's gaze in the mirror in front of her.

"If you haven't heard anything in two months, I want you to let Jake have a memorial for Chase."

Kassie started to refuse when Samantha raised her hand.

"Hear me out. I understand your need to cling to hope right now. Jake needs closure. The town needs to say their goodbyes to the man they helped raise. When you've exhausted all means trying to find him and you're ready to let go, you can do it in your own way, with no one the wiser. Will you think about it?"

"I know Jake feels horrible at losing Chase. Your request isn't unreasonable. They don't need to know of my search for Chase and the team."

"Exactly. You can't put a time limit on grief. You have to

get through it a minute at a time, an hour, and then a day. When you're ready to say goodbye, you'll know."

"You don't think they made it, do you?" Kassie asked.

Samantha put down the scissors and leaned against the counter in front of Kassie. "No. I don't. Maybe it's because I've gone through this, I refuse to tell you how to handle it. My job is to support you as a friend. I'm here, regardless of what you find."

"Chase told me no matter what happened, I needed to remember he'd walk through hell to get back to me and Em. I have to believe in him."

Samantha smiled softly and patted her shoulder. "Then I pray they're all safe and headed back home to us."

CHAPTER SEVEN

Leo paced the cave. With food supplies low, Shadow snuck off to the village. They needed some medical supplies. Without a medical facility, Chase hoped he aligned and splinted the bone in Taco's leg properly. The two rescued men slept peacefully.

"Doc, give me a SITREP. Do you think we can make it down to the village in the middle of the night? Saint and I can carry him." He pointed to the emaciated man lying at his feet.

"Glue holds Saint's side together. The strain of helping carry someone might split it open. Taco will need two to carry him and a lot of morphine. I've got a limited supply. Our other rescued guy should be able to walk on his own. I'll carry the other man." Chase wiped his forehead with the back of his hand. "I need to check your head wound."

"Later, Doc. I may need to search for Shadow." Leo glanced at the entrance of the cave.

"I'll go," Chase offered. He knew Leo continued to suffer from migraines and nausea from the concussion.

"No. I need you here to keep these two alive. I don't know

what we'd have done without you. With so many of us injured, having you here is a Godsend, thank you. You've proven yourself to be inventive in dire situations," Leo motioned to the splint on Taco and the contraption catching water.

"I think after the last few months and all of you taking care of my girl, we're even. If one of us hurts, all of us do. I'm honored to be part of this team." Chase briskly dismissed Leo's comments.

"Are you worried about Kassie? I regret asking you to come when you and Kassie finally got your heads out of your asses," Leo stated.

Chase chuckled, "I won't lie. I'm worried this might push her over the edge. I pray she holds on until we get home."

"Kassie's stronger than we give her credit for. How many twenty-one-year-olds do you know who can outrun the mafia with a chronically ill kid? Then survive a kidnapping. Kassie may be twenty-four now, but she has the maturity of a forty-year-old. Do you think she'll consider medical school?" Leo walked to the entrance of the cave where Saint stood guard, spoke with him and then headed back to Chase.

"I'm leaving it up to her. If she wants to go to school, we'll figure it out. If she's happy, I'm happy," Chase grinned.

"Good for you." Leo seemed to stare right through Chase.

A movement at the entrance caught their attention as Shadow appeared.

Both men rushed forward as Shadow stumbled. A sack fell from his hand as they approached. His other hand clutched his side. On instinct, Chase motioned for Leo to hold Shadow steady. As Chase moved Shadow's hand, he slumped in Chase's arms while blood ran down his side.

Chase slowly lowered him to the floor with Leo's help and began separating the material to see how bad the wound was.

Chase and Leo exchanged a knowing glance, words didn't need to be spoken.

CHAPTER EIGHT

Matthew gripped her arm as he guided her to the back seat. Lines around his mouth and his constant vigilance jerked Kassie from relaxed to on guard.

"What's wrong, Matthew?" Kassie questioned as he got into the SUV and pulled out of the driveway and headed toward the preschool.

"It's not time to pick up Em. She has an hour left." The hackles on her neck rose. Matthew's jaw ticked as he concentrated on their surroundings. He drove faster than usual. His actions reminded her of how the team behaved when she and Em were in danger.

"Something's wrong. I need to know, tell me." A pit formed in her stomach as she waited for him to respond.

"Don't get worked up. Jameson called. He said to get to the school. I don't have time to get Michael here and I can't leave you at Samantha's unguarded." Matthew's voice clipped out the words.

On high alert, Kassie counted the seconds until they

pulled up to the preschool. Jameson carried Emma to the SUV. One arm held Emma while the other lingered on his weapon as he scanned their surroundings. Kassie buckled Em into her car seat while tossing her backpack next to her.

Jameson nodded to Matthew before running to his vehicle. In tandem, Matthew and Jameson pulled onto the street. Kassie distracted Em by asking her about her day.

"We saw butterflies. I saw six different colors and then we painted our favorite one!" Emma grabbed her bag and began to pull out her drawing.

"Shit. Hold on!" Matthew exclaimed.

Kassie covered Emma with her body as a truck slammed into the side of their SUV. Matthew pressed the gas and plowed through without stopping.

"Mama!" Emma cried.

"It's okay, Ladybug. Matthew's getting us out of here." Kassie tried to reassure her despite her own fears blossoming.

Kassie heard the distinct sounds of gunshots.

"Take Em out and get on the floor." Matthew ordered as he swerved back and forth to evade those firing on them.

Following Matthew's command, Kassie unbuckled Em and pulled her tight into her body. She hung on for dear life as Matthew jerked the car to the side while speeding down the country road. Jameson's voice came over the Bluetooth.

"They're coming up fast, I'll try a pit maneuver. Michael's on his way down." Jameson's deadly calm voice bellied the seriousness of the situation.

The SUV fishtailed as Matthew turned onto the access road leading to the cabin. More shots pinged against the SUV. The driver's side mirror shattered making Matthew flinch. The back window burst into shards. Kassie gasped as the foam from the backseat exploded. The car seat rocked as bullets clipped the top.

"Kass, when I say, you grab Em and go. Run into the woods. Don't go toward the cabin. They'll expect you to go there. Head back into town. Get to Jake or Joe! Keep your eyes open!" Matthew issued orders to her in quick succession, Kassie didn't have time to think. Emma cried as the vehicle swerved around a curve and Kassie's arms tightened about her. Matthew slammed on his brakes. Two dark vehicles blocked the road.

"Stay down but shift to the passenger side," Matthew directed.

Kassie pulled Emma toward the side Matthew instructed and shielded her with her body.

Matthew started to back down when more vehicles sped up to the rear.

"Oh God, Matthew." Raggedly, Kassie cried.

"Get out of the vehicle with your hands in the air. We want the kid." A man yelled.

Kassie held tighter to Em. The only way they would take her daughter was if they pried her from Kassie's dead arms!

"Not gonna happen. Did Stanton send you?" Matthew called out.

"I have a message for the woman and instructions to bring the kid." The man yelled again, "Get out of the vehicle!"

"Kassie, they can't see the backseat passenger side of the car. When I say run, slip out the door and don't look back." Matthew ordered.

"Matthew." In an instant she knew Matthew planned to sacrifice himself to give her and Emma a chance to escape.

"What's the message?" Matthew yelled back. He slipped a gun into her hand. "Safety's off, point and shoot like Chase

Keeping Kassie

taught you. Don't stop. Don't turn back." His eyes met hers, he smiled a sad smile and his chin lifted.

Kassie shoved the gun into her waistband and put her hand on the door handle waiting for Matthew's signal.

"I'm supposed to tell her... James only asks once," The man yelled.

Metal crunching forced Kassie to peer out from the back seat. A tractor bulldozed the cars blocking their way to the cabin. Men scattered in the chaos. She ducked back when the clunk of the bullets hit the bulldozer.

Matthew maneuvered the SUV to the side of the road and jumped out. Running around the back and to the passenger side, he threw the door open and pulled Kassie out of the vehicle. Grabbing Em, Matthew pushed her into Kassie's arms as he yelled, "*Go!*"

Kassie ran as fast as her legs could carry her. Branches stung her face as she tucked Em's head to her shoulder and held tight.

"Keep your head down, Em." Kassie breathlessly instructed as she zigzagged between the trees.

"Mama, I'm scared." Emma cried.

"It's okay, baby. We'll make it to Jake, and he'll help us." The sound of people running through the woods and the sound of gunfire got louder. Knowing holding Em and trying to protect her presented a problem, Kassie searched for a place to hide.

Spying a tree with low branches, Kassie adjusted the gun for quick access and swiftly lifted Emma high enough to grab the branches. "Climb as high as you can sweetie," she pushed Em higher.

"Emma. You know how Shadow taught you to play hide and seek? We need to play it now. No matter what you hear, you stay here until I come get you, or Matthew, Jameson or

Michael. You need to be quiet, like Shadow taught you. Do you have your phone? Turn it on silent like Taco showed you." Kassie swallowed hard. "If the sun starts to set and I'm not back, you call Joe. Only come down for Jake or Joe. They'll find you, but you have to be really quiet. Can you be a big girl, and do as I say?"

Emma's wide blue eyes stared down at her mama. "I know how to play Shadow's game. I'll be quiet."

"You can't see me, but I won't be far away. Don't call out for me." Kassie waited until Emma climbed high enough in the tree the foliage camouflaged her. Giving her a reassuring smile, she whispered, "I love you, Emma. More than chocolate ice cream." Kassie pressed her fingers to her lips as a final reminder for Em to stay silent before she walked over her footprints, making it appear as if they ran away from the trees.

Moving to the opposite side of the woods, she braced herself behind a tree. She still saw the limb where Emma sat, and anyone getting close to her daughter. Her hands shook, as she took a couple of ragged breaths. Time seemed to stand still. Kassie closed her eyes and focused on Chase's instructions on how to shoot. She hadn't picked up a gun since she killed Roger. Chase expressed concern over it causing a trigger for her and wanted Kassie to continue counseling before they resumed practicing. Kassie listened intently to the sounds in the woods to determine the men's location. Biting her bottom lip, she steeled herself to do whatever it took to protect her child.

They drew closer. Kassie's pulse beat faster. She heard her heartbeat in her ears. Her eyes frantically searched out the sound as she waited for them to enter the clearing. Checking the gun again, she bided her time. The first man entered the clearing. Molding herself to the tree, Kassie

Keeping Kassie

watched as he scanned the area, turned and said something to someone coming through the trees. Kassie aimed the weapon.

A woman with red hair stepped out, turned in her direction, and a wide smile appeared on her face.

"Hello, Kassie."

CHAPTER NINE

Shadow's fever grew higher. The stab wound wasn't deep, but it was now infected. Chase did his best to clean the wound but had no antiseptic. Rummaging through the sack, they discovered Shadow managed to grab clean linen, rice, lamb, dates, naan bread, and an assortment of vegetables. A few articles of clothing and two women's burqas cushioned the food. On the bottom lay two sets of keys.

The last three days Chase tended his injured. Shadow's wound resisted the antibiotics. Daily, the morphine supply dropped. With Shadow's new injury, it left them in a precarious situation with team members helping the injured and no one capable of guarding their six. Time also became a worrying factor. Leo stated anyone searching for them stopped after the first week, due to time of the year and where they crashed.

"Doc, what if we rigged something to drag Taco?" Leo assessed the two men they had rescued. "He can walk, and I can carry the other."

Chase considered the possibility. "Taco will be in pain

Keeping Kassie

either way. If he's dragged, he'll feel every bump and rock down. It'll be faster than letting him walk but leave a trail unless we have someone coming from behind. With all the injuries, it will be slow moving. I can carry the other guy. You're more effective with a gun in your hand."

"We need to bug out in two days. Saint scouted the village. They're preparing for a party. Possibly a wedding. As small as this village is, most will attend, providing us an excellent cover. We can use the women's burqas to cover these two." Leo gestured toward the rescued men and grabbed the canteen with fresh water and took a swig.

"Ready or not, I think we need to go for it. Shadow needs more than I've got here. At some point he'll worsen if we can't get his infection under control." Nodding to the two rescues, he added, "They need immediate attention. I've done all I can here."

Leo nodded, "Get some sleep and I'll cover the night shift."

"I can cover it. Why don't you get some rest and settle the migraine eating you?" Chase watched as Leo's eyes widened, surprised his tactics at masking the pounding headache failed.

"No. You've cared for all of us plus stood for guard duty. You're one step away from falling over and we need ya, Doc. I can't sleep at night. It's easier for me to take the shift."

Not bothering to argue with Leo, Chase went to check on all the men before bedding down. The worst of the two men gained more lucidity over the last couple of days. He mimed asking for water yet still struggled with speaking. The other separated himself from the group and moved further back into the cave. He allowed Chase to examine him and help with getting nutrients but often preferred to be left alone. Chase let him be.

With Saint's water replenished, Chase lay down on the ground. He closed his eyes and let his mind float to the mountain. Still summer, the flowers in bloom, he pictured Kassie curled up in the reading nook in their room with Em, reading a book. The mere thought of his girls brought a smile to his face. Worry for his godfather, Jake, hit him in his gut. Jake considered him a son and news of his demise wouldn't go well.

Drifting off to sleep. Chase's mind wandered to Kassie and the night he proposed. When he pulled the blankets back, the fire next to them made her red hair gleam in the firelight. The contrast of the long darker tresses against her creamy white skin in the moonlight made her appear angelic.

"*I love you, Chase Winters.*" She whispered as he made love to her. Her hand stroked the stubble along his jaw.

Then the dream veered, and Kassie lay next to him as she cupped his face in her hands.

Come home, Chase, I need you. We need you. I'm scared...

Chase sat straight up off the floor. Sweat covered him. His hands clenched. The dream felt real. Running his hand through his hair, he pulled himself together. Whispering into the night, *"I'm coming home, Princess. Don't lose faith."*

Getting up, Chase checked on the men and went outside the cave to relive himself before taking over for Leo. Leo gave him a nod as Chase took the weapon and stood guard.

Leo appeared haggard, but he imagined they all did at this point. Watching the sun rise, Chase prayed, "I'm coming home, Princess. I'm coming home to you."

CHAPTER TEN

Kassie stared at the redheaded woman in front of her. She appeared eerily familiar. The woman smiled as Kassie kept her gun trained on the man.

"*Milaya*, I know you find this amusing, but there's nothing humorous about a nervous woman protecting her child with a weapon aimed at me. So, unless you want to take me home in a body bag, please explain why you're here." The man insisted with a Russian accent. He swiped his hand through the hair on top of his head slowly to ensure Kassie knew he didn't intend to make any sudden moves.

The woman stepped forward, "Come, Luv, you know me! Do you intend on greeting the people who sent your team in to save you as if you don't know them?"

Kassie licked her lips as she studied the woman. A memory flashed from the back of her mind.

She was lying on the cold dirt floor after Roger beat her. She felt the loss of her child and decided to give up. She was talking to someone when the woman in front of her leaned over her. "Hang on, Kassie, help is coming. I'm sorry, Lass. I know you're hurting, and I've sent Ivan to get something to help with the pain. I've dispatched my man to fetch the team of men looking for you and they're on their way. Don't give up. I've been where you are, I know the pain. The next time I see you, we'll both be free."

"Next time I see you, we'll both be free." Kassie repeated the last words the woman said to her before the man gave her something for pain.

"See, Ivan, she has no intention of shooting you." The woman took a step forward. Kassie yanked the gun in her direction.

"*Milaya,*" The blond man growled out the endearment.

"Luv, come. Your man needs tending. Only a tiny bit in the shoulder. It took three of my men to hold him while I located you. Very protective, that one. My man reported your other guard has an arm wound. The one who plowed through the vehicles with the tractor has a nasty cut on his head," the woman beckoned.

Kassie stood in indecision. She wasn't leaving these woods without Em. If she chose wrong, Kassie jeopardized the safety of herself and Em.

"I'm not going anywhere. Tell James Stanton, he's not taking my daughter." Her mama bear found its way to the surface.

A sad expression appeared on the woman's face. "Kassie, don't you remember me? I'm your friend. Hurting Emma is the furthest thing from my mind. I'm sorry about your sister. I stayed in Ireland longer than planned. I rushed back when I heard the news, Luv. You disappeared."

"You came back for me?" Kassie put the dots together. This woman mistook her for her twin.

"Of course, I came back. I made a promise to you. I'd never leave you or your daughter to James. I'm sorry we

Keeping Kassie

didn't save your sister." True regret showed in the woman's face. "I'm here now. James is hiding out like a snake in waiting. He's trying to get Emma before he disappears. I came as soon as you left for the mountain to protect you. We've been watching from afar. Your men added extra security on the mountain, and my men infiltrated your crews building the hospital to keep eyes on everyone."

"After the accident with Roger, I have trouble with names," Kassie hedged. The memory of the woman now in the forefront of her mind.

Cocking her head, the woman studied Kassie for a moment. "I'm Victoria Stanton, and this is my husband, Ivan."

Kassie's mouth opened of its own accord and shut again. "You died in a car accident."

Victoria laughed, unruffled as Kassie pointed a gun toward her husband. "I see that despicable man must have hit your head a few times too many. James Stanton *thinks* I died in the car accident. We'll let him believe it for a little longer. Now, will you allow Ivan to remove your child from the tree and carry her back? I'll even let you carry the weapon and hold it on him the entire way."

"*Milaya!*" The man protested emphatically.

"Luv, she won't shoot you. She's afraid, but we'll jog her memory a bit and she'll apologize to you for thinking of you in the same league as James." The woman rolled her eyes at Kassie. If the situation wasn't so dire, she might have laughed.

Without peering at her daughter, Kassie called out. "Emma, can you climb down on your own, sweetie?"

"Yes, Mama," the sweet voice yelled down the tree.

Victoria shaded her eyes as she watched the little girl climb down like a monkey from a tree. When she neared the bottom, Kassie held the gun on Ivan as she extended her other arm out to Emma as she dropped down from the last limb and ran toward Kassie.

"You walk ahead of us, Victoria. Ivan in front of you. If you've hurt my friends, I'll drop you like a sack of potatoes. Do you understand?" Kassie's voice hardened.

Ivan frowned at Victoria. She smiled at him.

"Ivan, go ahead. Hello, Emma. My name's Victoria. I'm a friend of your mama's. I've waited a long time to meet you. When we get to the cabin, I have some lovely treats for you." Victoria followed Ivan out of the clearing. Kassie maintained enough distance between them, any attempt Victoria made to grab the gun would prove futile. Instructing Emma to grab onto her shirt, she concentrated on holding the gun.

"My mama says I'm not supposed to talk to strangers. Can I talk to her, Mama?" Emma asked as she clung to Kassie's shirt.

"You may talk to her as long as I'm around," Kassie answered. She watched as Victoria turned her face slightly and frowned at her words. Until she knew more about this woman, she wasn't trusting her not to snatch her daughter any more than James.

"My mama says guns aren't toys. I'm not supposed to touch one if I see it. Dr. Chase taught her how to use it cause she's a grown-up. He says even big people have to learn to respect it before they have one. It's being sponsible." Emma chatted as they walked.

"Responsible, Em." Kassie automatically replied. Victoria giggled and kept walking forward.

"Dr. Chase sounds like a very smart man. I like him," Victoria stated.

"I love him. My mama loves him too. He got lost in a big

Keeping Kassie

ocean and now we got to find him," Emma sadly volunteered.

"I shall add him to my prayers. Kassie, you must be devastated," Victoria sympathized.

"My mama's not *devested*, she says don't give up hope. Love is worth fighting for." Emma's nose scrunched as she observed the woman in front of them.

Kassie sighed. They approached the road. Kassie corrected her daughter. "It's devastated Em. Not devested. Let's play the quiet game until we see Uncle Matthew."

"Then can I talk to Victoria? She said she brought me treats." Emma wanted permission from her mama.

"Let's find Uncle Matthew and Jameson then we'll see." Kassie scanned their surroundings. "Ok, stop. Ivan, go first and tell Matthew to come to me. Victoria will stay here until you return."

Ivan began to shake his head. A growl emanated from his throat as he glared at Victoria.

"Go on, Luv. She won't hurt me. Stop acting like such a big baby. Kassie, which one do you call Matthew?"

Kassie locked eyes with Ivan. She noted his displeasure at walking away without the woman. Determined, she refused to walk into an ambush. "The tall black-haired man with the cowboy hat. Go get him and bring him to me. If I see anyone else, I won't hesitate." She gestured toward Victoria.

Ivan's eyes narrowed and he shot an angry glance in Victoria's direction. He walked off mumbling something under his breath about Victoria's behind might be as red as her hair when this was finished.

A few minutes later a relieved Matthew ran in her direction. "Home is where my heart is!" he shouted.

To ensure Emma wasn't ever lured to leave with anyone

else, Kassie taught her the phrase. The secret greeting helped Emma determine her safety person in case of an emergency. Matthew and Jameson practiced it with her daily. Matthew shouted the code to let Kassie know he wasn't forced into luring her into a false security. Letting out the breath she unconsciously held, she lowered the gun.

"Uncle Matthew! Uncle Michael!" Emma yelled. Michael ran right behind Matthew. Seeing the girls safe and sound, Michael patted Matthew's shoulder as they jogged up to the group.

Hands clenched, Matthew's red face showed his aggravation as he glared at Ivan and Victoria. He scooped up Em. Oblivious to the fact blood soaked his arm and blood ran down Michael's temple. Ivan stood in front of Victoria.

"Don't make me regret saving you," Ivan gritted out as Matthew and Michael neared.

"Kass, you and Em holding up, okay?" Matthew's eyes ran down her body searching for any injuries and then to Emma.

"You've got an owie!" Emma exclaimed. Matthew shifted Em away from the blood.

"I'm fine, Ladybug. Uncle Michael bumped his head on the tractor, and I got some on me. Don't touch it. I don't want to ruin your pretty outfit." He shot an angry glance toward Ivan and Victoria.

"Kass?" Matthew questioned. "They saved us, I don't know who they are, but she says you know her?"

"She sent Chase and the team to save me. Let me introduce you to Victoria Stanton." Kassie watched as Matthew and Michael took in the news.

"You're supposed to be dead. Stanton killed you along with his competition years ago," Matthew stated.

"That's what they keep telling me. What can I say? I'm

Keeping Kassie

very much alive. Ivan, have the men take care of the mess. Your vehicles are beyond repair. Why don't you ride up to the cabin with us? We can chat over a cup of tea." Victoria walked toward a large black vehicle.

Kassie plucked Em from Matthew and held her head close to neck. "Close your eyes, Emma. Don't open them until I tell you. I mean it," her Mama Bear voice came out and Emma immediately complied.

Kassie saw the bodies and blood all over the road. She wished to avoid the images before her too. Kassie tried to feel bad for the men lying on the ground, but they tried to take her child and she felt no sympathy.

"Are you sure about this?" Matthew held her arm and whispered in Kassie's ear. Michael flanked her on the other side.

"She knows me like you did, Matthew," Kassie whispered and glanced down at Emma to convey the message Victoria confused her with her sister.

Cars filled the driveway. Joe and Maddie stood on the porch with Jake.

Maddie walked down the stairs and immediately took Emma by the hand and hugged Kassie tightly. "We've been so worried. All these men."

"It's ok, Maddie. I know her. She sent the team to save me," Kassie added to allay Maddie's fears.

Joe hugged Kassie and led her into the house. Jake followed as they entered. Kassie went about putting hot water on the stove for tea. All the men dispersed except for Kassie's team, her family, and Ivan stood with Victoria. Maddie brought out a platter of goodies and placed them at the long kitchen table. When the tea steeped, she placed it on the table with assorted drinks for the men.

Victoria spoke first, "I know we have a lot to discuss.

Some of it may not be quite appropriate for children. Emma, come here, Luv. Let me have a good peek at you."

After a nod from her mother, Emma walked up and met Victoria's gaze with one of her own. "You look kinda like my mama."

"I do. And you resemble your mama and me." Victoria reached out and took a stray curl from Emma's shoulder and stroked it lovingly. A sad smile appeared as she took the child in.

Seeing Emma and Victoria side by side, Kassie surmised if one didn't know better, Emma easily passed for Victoria's grandchild.

"Dr. Chase says my mama is the most beautiful woman in the world!"

Chuckling, Victoria agreed, "Dr. Chase reminds me of another man." Ivan smiled down at Victoria and the couple shared a silent conversation. A man came in with a bag and dropped it next to Victoria as she took a seat at the table.

"Emma, I got this for you. I understand you love to paint and draw. Maybe you could make a picture for me while I speak with your mama?" Victoria waited until Emma pulled out the art supplies which were a child's dream come true.

"I can draw butterflies. I make them at school!" Emma exclaimed as Maddie took her hand and the bag.

Maddie glowered at Victoria as she took Em's hand and led her up the stairs.

"I'm sorry, Victoria. Maddie's very protective. We've recently reunited, and she isn't letting us out of her sight," Kassie tried to explain Maddie's odd behavior. Rollo came to stand by Kassie's side and her hand ran through his fur.

"I believe you get some of your strength from her. She's protecting her family and there's no need to apologize."

Victoria smiled as her eyes never left the older woman and Kassie's daughter until they turned into Em's bedroom.

CHAPTER ELEVEN

Leaving as soon as the sun set, the team made their way out of the cave. When Shadow scouted the village, he determined which two vehicles to steal to carry them all. With no means of communication, each group would be on their own.

"From what I can determine, I think we crashed in the Caspian and we're in Iran. We need to get across the border to Turkey where we can find help. I don't want to take any chances in villages. We'll need gas. So, we'll grab what we can and go as far as possible. Keep an eye out for a phone. Shadow will need meds before we cross the border. We'll have to skirt around patrols and unfriendlies in the area." Leo assigned their tasks.

When they finally made it to the outskirts of the village, they left the injured men hidden in the rocky outcropping near the edge while the others grabbed supplies, food and extra gas.

The wedding began. Between the music and the celebration, Chase grabbed food from the tables. Saint started the

Keeping Kassie

truck and headed back to the injured men. Leo grabbed the other vehicle while Chase searched for medication and clean linens. When they found what they needed, they loaded the half-starved man in the car with Chase and Leo and the other in the truck with Saint, Shadow and Taco.

"Leo let me drive. You'll fall asleep at the wheel." Chase's aggravation bubbled to the surface at Leo's insistence at driving the entire time.

"Listen Doc, I need you to focus on keeping us alive. I know what I'm doing," Leo sleepily replied.

"Last time I checked, I knew how to drive. What good is it for me to be a doctor if you fall asleep at the wheel with a head wound and kill us all? Get your head out of your ass. Your nose keeps bleeding, you have a migraine and I'm following Saint," Chase groused.

"Damn it. What if something goes wrong? I have to get you back to PITA!" Leo replied agitated.

Chase let out a laugh. "Let's see, Leo, how well this is going. First, we crash into the ocean, then we hide in a cave for three weeks with literally the packs on our backs, no communication devices, rescued two men on the brink of death, every one of us are injured in some way, and you won't let me drive in case something goes wrong?"

A silence rang in the car. Then a chuckle from the backseat came from the scrawny half-starved man.

Leo let out a laugh. "I guess this isn't a luxury vacation. I'm sorry, Doc. I'm not trying to be an ass. I feel responsible for asking you to come shadow the new corpsman. You and PITA just got engaged."

"Why in the hell do you call my girl that ridiculous name?" Chase bantered to keep Leo awake and talking. Taking back roads, they bounced through the rutted rural areas with a small truck and a car. Taco probably felt every bump. They looked like a bunch of traveling clowns in tiny cars with all their bulk.

"I can't call her Princess. That's your name for her. She's like a little sister. Then she shot me. You know. So, she is a pain in the ass. AKA PITA," Leo reasoned.

A chuckle from the backseat surprised Chase. The man pulled himself up to a sitting position. His strength gradually improved from Chase's care, yet he was still as weak as a newborn babe, "She shot your sorry ass?"

Leo rubbed his jaw, "Welcome back, brother. Damn glad to see yours."

"A woman shot you in the ass?" the man's weak voice came out raspy. Chase handed him the jug of water.

Leo indicated Chase with a nod of his head. "I don't know if you remember this guy, but we saved him and his friend on one of our last missions together. Chase, you probably don't recognize this scrawny ass. I'd like you to meet Liam "Whiskey" O'Neil."

"Shit, Leo." Chase glanced in the backseat and back to Leo. "Then who's the man in the truck with Saint and Taco?"

The deafening silence in the car didn't bode well. Leo finally responded. "It's Ash, Catherine's husband."

Stunned, Chase stared ahead. "Why didn't you tell me?"

"I wasn't sure what we'd find. I positively confirmed one of the prisoners was this asshole. I hoped Olaf, Catherine's brother, was the other."

"Is there any chance Olaf made it?" Chase asked quietly. Leo hadn't shared the story of what occurred between him and Catherine. Chase bet Olaf was the reason why they were there.

Keeping Kassie

"No. Olaf didn't make it. I saw him get hit. I don't remember anything else but rounding the corner and seeing him get shot and then the explosion. I woke up with some man over me who didn't speak English, treating my wounds."

Whiskey adjusted himself in the worn backseat. Chase knew he lacked any padding to sit comfortably. He'd attempt to grab something soft for him to sit on when they stopped.

"It's good to see you again, Whiskey. I never got to thank you for saving me," Chase replied.

Whiskey grew quiet for a moment. "It sounds like we're even now."

"I guess we'll have to wait to see if Ash can tell us what happened. His jaw's still pretty swollen," Leo stated.

"Good luck. I didn't know he even existed in the same camp," Whiskey sounded confused. "I gave up on you even coming back to find me."

"I never stopped searching. It's been a shit show. We'll get some answers when we get stateside, and you recuperate," Leo reassured him.

"Leo, where's my Sunshine and my boy? Has she moved on?" Whiskey lay back down across the seat.

"She's never forgotten you, brother. Your son's a miniature of you. I didn't tell her I found you," Leo replied.

Chase knew Leo didn't finish what he started to say. He wasn't sure what he would find.

"Good. I don't want her to see me like this," Whiskey's sad voice drifted off as he went back to sleep.

"What about Catherine, Leo? Don't tell me there isn't anything going on between the two of you. Where does Ash fit into this?" Chase's voice lowered to keep from disturbing Whiskey.

Leo frowned. "Ash is home. There's nothing more to discuss. Catherine will have her husband back."

Chase knew Leo lied. Leo clenched the wheel when he said the other man's name. Chase surmised Leo planned to bring Catherine's brother back to her. He tabled the discussion for later. Right now, they needed to figure out how to get all of them home.

CHAPTER TWELVE

Kassie peeked in on Emma, double checked the alarm, the windows, and the doors. The day had turned into a long one and she craved a hot shower and her bed. Michael stayed in the guest room on the lower level and Kassie insisted Matthew stay upstairs in order to tend to his wound in the morning. Jameson walked the perimeter, preferring to stay outside.

Walking to her bedroom, Kassie stopped, startled by a soft knock at the door. Jameson blocked the doorway as Victoria waited for permission to enter.

"Didn't want to wake you." Jameson muttered, giving Victoria the stink eye.

The men held reservations concerning the newest development of Victoria Stanton. To be honest, Kassie wasn't sure either. To give her credit, the woman saved her life.

"I'm sorry to disturb you. I wanted to talk to you alone for a moment if I may?" Victoria's eyebrow arched at Jameson's arm. He refused to budge and gave Kassie a slightly negative shake of his head.

Rolling her eyes, Kassie opened the door and pointedly

addressed Jameson. "Matthew and Michael can guard me. I won't be long."

Victoria agreed, "I promise to be done within an hour. You can pat me down if you like. Ivan won't like it, but I'm perfectly fine if it makes you feel better." The sassy woman turned to blow a kiss to her husband leaning against a tree in front of the house.

"It's not necessary, Victoria. Come in." Kassie allowed Victoria through the entrance and gestured to the couch. "Can I offer you something to drink?"

"No, Luv. I know you're probably exhausted but I need to clear the air with you, and I didn't want an audience earlier. I take it your godparents and the men don't know everything that has transpired between the two of us?" Victoria took a seat in the chair next to the fireplace while Kassie sat on the couch.

"I'm not sure what you mean?" Kassie feared Victoria was ready to call her bluff. Curiosity about what Victoria knew prompted her to act as her sister.

"I feel like you're dreadfully distant. I understand how upset you must be. I was absent when your sister died. I thought I controlled all the moving pieces. The one thing I didn't count on was Roger. The spineless bastard always skulked around James and then Phillip. I let you down." Victoria's regret filled eyes focused on Kassie.

"I'm sorry, Victoria. The incident with Roger has caused some of my memory to be fuzzy. I remember you from the tunnel and Ivan giving me something for the pain. I knew I was dying." Kassie relived the memory in her head as she spoke.

"Yes, I sent the team for you immediately. I promised I'd see this through, but I worried for you, Luv." Victoria sympathized.

Keeping Kassie

"It wasn't your fault Roger stole money and blamed me for it going missing," Kassie offered.

Victoria stiffened. "Roger tortured you because he thought you stole ten million dollars?"

"Yes, he assumed I took the banking codes he gave Phillip. He alleged I hid the money. I tried explaining to him if I took the money, I would've taken Em and disappeared. He refused to listen and nearly beat me to death. Wait, I didn't tell you how much…"

Victoria blanched at her words, appearing sick. Shaking her head back and forth, tears pooled in her eyes. "I'm sorry, Luv."

Confused at the stark reaction from Victoria, Kassie leaned in and held her hand. "Are you all right?"

Victoria stood, took a seat next to Kassie on the couch, and gripped her hand. "I've a confession, Luv. I stole the ten million dollars. Your memory must be hazy. You gave me the banking numbers. I've slowly removed the money from James's accounts for a long time. Phillip wanted control and his father refused to give up the reins. I refused to allow Phillip access to those funds. He trafficked women and children. I've taken enough now, James is getting desperate. All his connections will want payment and he won't have it. Then we will begin the next phase of our revenge."

Kassie felt the blood rushing through her veins. The pounding in her head grew louder. Her pulse raced as black dots appeared before her eyes. Kassie controlled her breathing to deter the panic attack which threatened. "Revenge. My sister died all for revenge?" she whispered.

Victoria took in Kassie's features and frowned. "We talked about this, Kassie. You agreed."

Kassie stood up and walked to the window before turning to face Victoria. Her eyes threatened to spill tears, but she angrily blinked them away. "No. I didn't agree to anything. I'm not Kassie. I'm Kaitlyn." She clenched her fists and ranted furiously at the woman on the couch, "Because you and my sister wanted your revenge, I lost my child. I can't have children. James was going to jail. Why didn't you let them be punished for their crimes? My sister died because Roger wanted the money. Emma is..." Kassie faltered. She already said too much.

Victoria stood and slowly walked to Kassie. Placing her arms around her, Victoria held her close. "I apologize, this must come as a shock." She led Kassie back to the couch.

"Let's start at the beginning. I met your sister after Emma was born. I lived in Ireland when she and Phillip married. Phillip was unable to have children and at first, I believed she pulled one over on my son. Thus, interfering with my plans." A chuckle escaped her. "I confronted her and demanded she leave, mainly for her own protection. She adamantly refused. I ...threatened her. She wasn't concerned for her life. She begged for yours and Emma's."

Kassie leaned back on the couch tucking her feet under her and waited for Victoria to continue.

"She told me James raped her...your parent's accident, and him threatening you and Emma. We agreed on a plan. She supplied me with certain information, and I provided her with evidence against James and Phillip. The FBI found the evidence on the flash drive hidden in Emma's doll. When I assumed you died, I planted damning paperwork and the location of the USB. The day your godfather was shot, I knew James put a hit on you. So, I countered. Emma wasn't in danger. I sent a message to James, if he killed you, I'd hurt Emma."

Victoria hastened to assure Kassie, "I never will hurt a hair

Keeping Kassie

on Em's head. James thinks I'm dead and someone in the cartel called the hit. Which is exactly what I wanted him to think. Now, he's desperate. He's trying to go underground and take his daughter with him. I never meant for any of this to happen. Kassie protected you. Phillip beat her until she agreed to push you to accept Roger's proposal. He became incensed when you called off the wedding because you found Roger cheating. Now, tell me, how did you switch places with your sister?"

Kassie blew out a breath and told her what happened the day her sister died and how she ended up in the tunnel where Victoria found her.

They cried together as Victoria told her of her life with James.

"So now you go by Kassie to protect Emma. You lost yourself because of me and your sister. I can't make up for the past, Luv. But I'll do my best to do right by you and Emma. You've been caught in the crossfire between James and me. I think he picked your sister because we resemble each other." Victoria attempted to comfort Kassie, "Tell me, Luv, this is all the bad. What can I do to help you find the good."

Kassie sat quietly. Drawing her knees to her chest, she placed her chin on top. "You can't bring my sister back. I've accepted what I know about my twin. I'm not ready to forgive her yet. I do have two requests."

Victoria smoothed Kassie's hair back from her face. "If it's within my power, I'll do it."

"First, Chase and the team's helicopter crashed into the sea. The military concluded their search. I need to know one way or another. Do you have contacts who can help us?" Kassie asked.

"I'll talk to Ivan. He has family in Russia. I'm sure he can order a search." Victoria gripped Kassie's hand. "What is it, Luv? What else?"

"I'm fully aware James might have succeeded in taking Emma today. Matthew, Michael, and Jameson have sacrificed working extra shifts along with Jake and Joe to keep us safe. I want you to teach me how to protect myself and Em. One day, James will make another move to grab us. I refuse to wait for someone else to save me. I'd die before I let him have her, but I need to learn how to protect us. I never want to feel helpless again."

Victoria smiled at Kassie. "I think your sister and James underestimated you. I'll see you first thing in the morning. We shall begin. You've had your life yanked away from you and that is the bad. Now I'll help you get it back and that is the good."

Without Chase and the team there, she didn't feel safe. James continued to be a threat. Determined, Kassie vowed to learn whatever she needed to in order to protect Em.

"After I fulfill your requests, I'll be traveling with Ivan. From time to time, I'd like to visit little Emma. I desire to have a relationship with her and you. James took my ability to have children away by pushing me down a flight of stairs. I won't replace the relationships with the women you have in your life. Your sister and I grew close because she lived my nightmare and I desperately wanted to help her. I've watched you for months. You're a fighter."

"If you succeed in finding the team for me and helping me learn how to protect myself and Em, I'll consider it," Kassie replied.

"I'll see you in the morning. And Kassie? I'll make it so you'll never have to worry about James ever again. I want your promise when the time comes, you'll let me handle

James. I know how apt you are for keeping promises and I plan to hold you to it."

Kassie nodded her head. "You have my word."

Victoria stood to let herself out. "Ivan and I will have the men broken into teams and they can help with security until James skulks out of hiding. It'll give your men a break." She scanned the room and strategically placed nightlights. "Is Emma scared of the dark and requires this many nightlights?"

Kassie felt the heat rise to her face. She shook her head. "No. Since the kidnapping, I can't sleep without the nightlights unless Chase stays with me." Kassie refused to meet Victoria's eyes as she confessed such a silly fear.

Victoria's hands cupped her face, pulled Kassie toward her, and placed a sweet kiss on her head. "When Ivan first rescued me, I struggled believing I was safe. I slept with a knife under my pillow for the first six months. Don't be ashamed. When I'm done with you, you'll never fear the dark again."

CHAPTER THIRTEEN

Chase rubbed the dirt and sand out of his eyes. There was no water to spare. With Shadow's fever spiking, Chase needed to find a medical facility or a doctor. On the outskirts of Turkey after outrunning some unfriendlies, they abandoned the vehicles. Shadow, Taco, Whiskey, and Ash desperately needed medical care. He really wanted Leo to slow down but he knew Leo's stubbornness. Leo took the responsibility of his men seriously.

When Chase announced he needed to go into town, Leo pitched a fit. Still suffering from headaches and nausea, he wasn't in a position to fight. While still on his feet, Saint didn't know enough about medications to choose the correct ones. Chase needed to be the one to go. Saint stayed on watch.

They required other necessities, such as another way out of town, and preferably a phone. Recon of the area helped them learn about a small clinic in the middle of the town. Chase planned on waiting until the end of the day to try to bribe the doctor with what little cash they carried between them. Hopefully, the US dollar didn't put them at more risk.

Keeping Kassie

Saint followed him to the edge of the small camp. With the rocky overhang, Liam, Ash and Taco rested in the shade. Leo sat in the middle trying to keep Shadow's fever down. Chase watched as Leo's gaze flitted from Ash to Whiskey as if he attempted to work something out in his head.

"Here's the gun. Take it with you. Double back a few times before coming back to camp," Saint instructed. "Are you sure you can't tell me the names of the medications and I can get it?"

"The team needs you here." Chase took the gun and left the camp.

Chase watched as the clinic's patients dwindled until the last one left. Walking brusquely across the street, he opened the door, shut and locked it. A small man with glasses and a colorful robe turned to stare at him. His eyes grew wide as he realized Chase wasn't from the village.

Chase held his hand up. "I'm not here to hurt you. I need medication." He gestured toward the medicine cabinet with the gun.

The man held his hands up and slowly walked toward the cabinet. Unlocking the door, he stepped aside allowing Chase to see what medications he stored. Chase motioned for a sack and pulled some bottles from the shelves. Not wanting to leave the man without anything, Chase took only what he desperately needed while keeping one eye on him.

"Do you have bandages? Fluids?" Chase asked, knowing the man most likely didn't speak English. Motioning for him to have a seat, Chase rummaged through the drawers. He found some clean linen, and something smelling like antiseptic.

Reaching into his pocket, Chase pulled the remaining cash they carried. "This is all I have. I'll place it here and leave. I won't hurt you," He tried using a soothing tone. "Now if I can only find food and water."

"There's a well out back. You searched for strong antibiotics. Your friend must be badly hurt, yes?" the man asked.

Surprised he spoke English, Chase answered. "I won't hurt you. I need food, medicine, and a phone if you have one."

The man shook his head. "We have *polis* patrolling area. They search for men in two vehicles. Said they looted the last town."

Chase jaw clenched. "I assure you we didn't loot anything. The *polis* lie."

The older man chuckled. "We have, as you say, good *polis*, bad *polis*. They're hunting for you. I don't have a car, but next week a medical van will come to the area with my supplies." He picked up the money and handed it back to Chase. "This money will do me no good. When you get home, you send me payment in our money. I'll give you the address of my niece who lives in a bigger city and it won't raise questions."

"My friend can't wait until next week. I need these things now. Give me the address and I'll be sure to send you payment."

"Bring your friend to the clinic. I live in the house next door. I'll hide you and I can provide care. I'm a doctor." The man pointed to his chest. "My name is Ahmet."

"Thanks, I'm a doctor too. I don't want you to get in any trouble I need to get food and a phone." Chase assessed the room taking inventory of any useful items.

"The phones here. We don't get ...rec.." Ahmet struggled with the word.

"Reception?" Chase finished.

"Yes. The medical van will have a better phone. He can

Keeping Kassie

be trusted if you pay a fee. Wait till it's dark, then come to the back of my house. I have food and can buy more. I live alone. My wife died. Leopards live around here. If you shoot, you'll surely be found and outnumbered."

"Ahmet. It's more than me and my friend," Chase answered. "It can cause trouble for you. I'll take back what I can."

Ahmet shook his head. "You come to house. If you come in two cars there are many of you. Yes? You will not forget Ahmet? I want to come to US to be a citizen. Can you help me and my niece? It requires funds and your government's permission. It's worth the risk. Don't forget payment to pay the medical van driver. He has six children. How many of you?"

Chase hesitated and weighed the options. What if it was a set up? Whiskey couldn't hold on in some primitive jail with "bad polis" as Ahmet called them. The men needed real care and food to revive so they could escape.

Ahmet paced the floor. "Go get your men as soon as it's dark. I'll go to get more food and I'll take the sack." He held his hand out for the sack Chase filled.

Chase's hand gripped the bag tighter. If he handed over the meds, Shadow and Whiskey might die.

Ahmet lowered his hand. "The rebels killed my wife. They said she stole items. We have no need to steal. Her family lives here, and I stayed for her to be close to them. The *polis* wanted medicine and for me to work only for them. I sent my niece to a big city to avoid her getting hurt. She's young. I want her to go to school and have a good life. Not experience poverty and war."

Chase stood in indecision. They hadn't met any friendlies. They barely escaped the two groups hunting them.

"I take bag to my home." Walking across the room,

Ahmet pulled out a sack of plums, nuts, and pumpkin seeds. He set the food on a cloth and began to tie it. Taking a bottle of the antibiotics out of Chase's bag, he made a show of placing it inside the cloth as a goodwill gesture. Motioning Chase to follow, he found a jug with a cork. Going into the back of the house, he drew water from a well as Chase stood in the doorway to keep out of sight.

"Take this with you. I need to hurry to get what you need. I feed many who come to my clinic. It won't alarm anyone. You stay quiet in my house while I work during the day. Then leave when the medical van comes. We have a deal, yes?" Ahmet waited until Chase nodded his head.

"I can ensure the funds get to you for our safe return to the US. I can find people to help you, but I can't guarantee the government will allow you in. I can only promise to do my best."

Ahmet handed him the jug. "Stay toward the back of the town. I hope no one noticed you coming through the front door."

"I made sure before I came in," Chase assured the man.

"The *polis* have eyes in the village," Ahmet warned.

Chase walked out the back and waited until Ahmet left through the front. Chase followed him to the other side of the town. Watching him from across the road, Ahmet bartered for vegetables and rice. Returning to his home, Chase waited to see if anyone showed up asking questions. Somehow, he felt the team finally caught a break. The transportation and phone meant medical care, food, and one more day closer until he returned home to Kassie. A couple of hours passed, and no one came in or out of Ahmet's home. Chase slowly made his way back to camp to talk to the team.

CHAPTER FOURTEEN

Kassie lay on the bed thinking she'd die. Every single muscle and tendon in her body hurt. Her exercise clothes clung to her, drenched in sweat. Victoria showed up in Kassie's bedroom at five in the morning the next day. Dragging Kassie out of bed, into workout clothes, she handed her a bottle of water and started barking orders like a drill sergeant.

"Ah, ah, ah..." Victoria stopped Kassie's groaning. "You agreed to do as I say. You want to be strong; I'll make you strong. Stop whining. Ivan has already made calls and working on finding out what happened to your men. Now get up and let's go," Victoria commanded.

Of course, Matthew researched everything on Victoria Stanton and Ivan. He didn't find much, but he knew enough to know about the mafia families. Bringing his concerns to Kassie, she confronted Victoria.

"Why didn't you tell me you and Ivan headed not one, but two mafia families! You asked me to trust you. Victoria, I can't have my child surrounded by mafia!"

Victoria regarded the beautiful view of the mountain.

"Our family's businesses legitimatized as soon as Ivan found me. I admit some of our dealings with James remain in somewhat of a gray area. I kept it from you because I didn't want your opinion swayed before you got to know us. Yes, my men do certain... jobs, I won't lie to you. It's out of necessity in our world. If you want us to leave, you have every right. Regardless, I'll still have a team of men on you and Emma to ensure you're safe."

Kassie relented for the time being. Since Em attending school without a contingent of bodyguards wasn't an option, she decided to keep Em at the cabin with Maddie and Joe. Matthew, Jameson and Michael moved in with them. Victoria and Ivan stayed in Chase's parents' cabin.

Kassie wasn't sure where the other men stayed. They seemed to melt into the surrounding area. She rarely saw them. Matthew and Jameson seemed to know the location of each man. Matthew stayed on alert, but Kassie realized the extra men lessoned his stress on watching her family.

Ivan discussed security with him, and they held meetings every morning. She knew Matthew outwardly pretended to accept the arrangement, but she bet he held off giving Ivan a rundown of everything. In truth, Kassie trusted Victoria, but after the last few months, she wasn't taking anything for granted.

Today, she planned to attend Taco and Shadow's funerals. Jake and Michael waited in town so they could fly together. Victoria accompanied her, while Ivan, Julio, and Matthew guarded Em and her family.

Maddie walked into the bedroom. Her mouth formed a thin line as she observed Kassie on the bed.

"I don't understand why you're doing this, Sugar. I'm surprised at you! This woman waltzes in here and takes over. You gave Ivan permission to teach Emma how to defend herself. Have you seen what he's teaching her? He's instructing her to hit men in the ...well, I'm not even saying it! I can imagine the notes coming home from school! Don't let me get started on you! These early morning sessions and learning how to fight." Maddie shook her head. "What in the world has gotten into you? Joe can hire more security..."

Kassie sighed. Maddie wasn't happy about Victoria. "When Stanton's men nearly got us, I felt utterly defenseless. Matthew and Jameson did everything possible, and it still wasn't enough. If Victoria's men hadn't shown up when they did, I'd be dead, and Em would've disappeared with James forever."

Maddie's eyes narrowed. "Have you talked to Claire? Carol says you and Catherine got into a fight last week. You haven't talked to her since. I don't understand what's going on in your head." Maddie shook her head again.

"I'll tell you what's going on. I miss Chase. I can't go on with my life wondering if he's waiting for me to find him this whole time. Catherine took the military's word for it. Everyone gave up without a fight. I need to know the truth. I know you love me, but it's my business what Claire and I talk about. I'm tired of being asked if I've made every decision based on what Claire advises."

Maddie pursed her lips in disapproval. Sighing, she pulled out the black skirt and jacket Kassie planned to wear to Shadow's funeral. "What did you decide on for Taco's memorial?"

"I'll wear the dark blue sundress with the navy sunhat. I can pack my own clothes, Maddie," Kassie answered irritably.

Maddie angrily sat down on the bed. "Look at you! You can barely move! That woman will be the death of you. You're still recuperating from your leg healing."

Kassie closed her eyes. "I know you don't understand this. Please let me do this my way."

Maddie sighed and took a deep breath. "Fine. When you get back, we'll sit down with Jake and have a talk. He is mighty upset."

Kassie sat up. "I'm sorry Jake's having a difficult time. Chase told me not to give up. He never gave up on me." Eyeing the diamond and sapphire band on her left hand, she continued. "I choose to trust in my love for Chase. If something shows up proving he's gone, then I'll accept it." Kassie hoped Maddie understood.

"We're worried about you. You've handled a ton of *gris-gris* lately and I don't want you to get hurt again." Maddie swept Kassie's bangs to the side to meet her eyes.

Kassie smiled. "I'm blessed to have you and Joe here. I can't even think about not having you in my life, again. You know, I love you, right?"

Maddie squeezed Kassie to her side. "We love you. I might not completely agree with how you're coping with things, but I'm extremely proud of you, Sugar. I hope you know I only want the best for you."

Kassie kissed Maddie's cheek. "I do know. You and Mama provided such good examples of how to fight for family and love. You might not agree, but you taught me to do whatever I need for my family. You didn't give up on me and Emma."

Maddie's eyes widened as she understood what Kassie tried to say. She nodded her head. "No. We never gave up." Squeezing Kassie's hand, Maddie rose from the bed. "You better get a move on. The men are waiting. Don't worry about Em while you're gone, she's exactly like her mama." With a wink she slipped out of the bedroom and left Kassie to pack.

CHAPTER FIFTEEN

Laying Whiskey on the soft blankets that Ahmet laid on the floor of his bedroom, Chase set to work. True to his word, Ahmet readied medical supplies as well as food simmering in pots. A tray of cheese, nuts, figs and olives graced the table with pots of tea and water.

Buckets were filled with fresh water so they could bathe. Fresh bars of homemade soap made with olive oil sat next to towels in the kitchen. Ahmet worked on Shadow while Chase made Whiskey comfortable. Ash sat against a wall and watched as the two men worked on the most severely injured men on the team. Leo kept watch while Saint washed up. Then they switched places. Chase moved to Taco while Ahmet made a poultice for Ash's jaw.

"What's eating you, Leo?" Chase asked as he handed him a bowl of the flavorful soup and placed a kabob of lamb meat on a plate with some of the fruit and vegetables.

"I'm in disbelief at our luck in finding Ahmet. Food, fresh water for bathing, antibiotics, and we need to wait five more days to get a ride home. Almost too good to be true."

"I watched Ahmet. He did everything I'd do with Shadow. He knows what he's doing. I regret not having a phone available. I want to hear Kassie's voice right about now."

Leo frowned. "Hopefully soon." His attention focused on Ash. Ahmet offered him soup. Ash barely touched it. They hadn't eaten any real food in two days and the man's refusal to eat concerned him.

"Come on brother. What's bugging you?" Chase pushed.

"Does it seem odd to you they stayed in the same camp and neither knew about the other? You saw the camp. Whiskey was brutally beaten and burned. What about hearing him scream? There's no way with the injuries sustained, he stayed quiet. Ash maintained muscle tone and although his jaw hurts like a bitch and he's lost weight, what about the rest of him?" Leo continued to regard his teammate.

"Maybe they used Whiskey against Ash, and he doesn't want to admit he might have done or not done something they asked. You know those fuckers play mind games. They'll need extensive medical care and therapy when we get home."

"They'll have everything they need. Let's get them home." Leo growled.

"I'll get Taco cleaned up, help Ash and then get Shadow comfortable." Chase stuffed the olives in his mouth savoring the flavor.

"I'll help Ash. You check out the other two. Saint said you already checked his wound. Get some sleep Doc, I'm on watch tonight, Saint will be on watch tomorrow. You're assigned to care for these guys. Keep an eye on the other doc."

Chase grabbed a container of water and headed to where Whiskey lay. The poor man struggled a quarter of the way to Ahmet's dwelling before his legs gave out. Chase easily carried him. Now with soup in his stomach, Chase wiped away some of the grime to ascertain if anything else needed to be addressed. Then Chase encouraged Whiskey to eat a bit more while he gave Shadow something for pain and examined his wound himself.

※

TWO DAYS LATER, Shadow's fever broke, much to the relief of the team. Whiskey sat for longer jaunts and Ash began chewing most of the rice and soft foods. Leo and Saint refused to let Chase take rotation in guarding the house. It wasn't large, and they moved silently through the rooms. Chase got up through the night with Whiskey and Shadow. Leo insisted Chase rest throughout the day until he caught a good night's sleep. Although things proceeded adequately, they all needed to stay on alert until the medical van showed.

True to his word, Ahmet went to the clinic in the morning leaving the men with a breakfast of eggs with vegetables and strong tea. They snacked on fruits and vegetables while dinner consisted of rice with vegetables and meat.

Chase grabbed a bed roll and laid next to Shadow, who had fallen into a healing sleep. Chase wanted to be close if his fever spiked again. Settling down, he closed his eyes and his thoughts drifted to Kassie. Was she coping with his disappearance? He imagined the pain she must have felt when he texted her and never showed up. Recalling her fear of the dark, he became apprehensive, wondering if she was sleeping. He prayed he wouldn't find her broken again. His girl fought her way back from hell. As if trying to send her a message through mental telepathy, he called out to her. *Don't give up, Princess, I'm coming home to you.*

CHAPTER SIXTEEN

Jake barely greeted Kassie as she entered the plane, sat at the table, and buckled up. Sensing Kassie wanted to be alone, Victoria and Michael took seats at the front of the plane.

Opening Shadow's packet, Kassie dumped the contents on the table. Pulling out the letter addressed to her, she opened it and began reading.

Kassie,

I'll keep this short and sweet. Get ready for the shit show known as my pretentious family. They'll probably send out invitations for my funeral. They didn't give two shits about me or my service to this country. Do me a favor. Please don't let them send me away like some buttoned up stiff with a stick up his ass.

Let me go the way I want. I can picture

their shocked faces and I laugh. I'm gonna need it where I'm going.

My second request. Please make sure Avie Rahimi receives my insurance money. She has a little boy. I don't know where she's at since we saved her on a mission, but I'm sure you'll find her. Tell her I'm sorry I didn't reach out to her, I felt it was for the best. I've regretted my choice since the day I let her get on the plane alone and scared.

You've become my family. I love you and Ladybug. Thank you for showing me what a real family resembles. I left you a letter to read at my funeral. Read all of it. Remember, it's me talking, not you. Let me have my final say.

Shadow.

Jake made his way down the aisle and sat across from Kassie. She eyed him wearily. Having a feeling she knew what he wanted to discuss, she straightened and put the contents of Shadow's packet together. Ignoring Jake for the moment, she took out her notepad and wrote Shadow's request to find Avie. Scribbling a sidenote to talk to Mathew. He busied himself on trying to find a former patient of hers, José, before the news about the crash came. Hopefully with Victoria's men helping, Matthew's time would be freed up to track down José and now Avie.

Keeping Kassie

"I have got to talk to you, Kassie," Jake coldly regarded her.

Kassie smiled sadly, "I know. Dealing with Chase's disappearance must be excruciating for you. He was like a son. I hope you know I'm not trying to make this harder."

Jake didn't respond to her peace offering. "When we return, I want to have the memorial for Chase."

"I'm sorry, Jake. I intend to wait until the team's ceremonies are done first. This weekend, I'll be attending Shadow's and Taco's and next weekend, I'm heading to Alabama for Saint's. When I return, we can plan the service," Kassie hoped he heard the sincerity in her voice.

"I'll plan the memorial. There's no need for you to bother yourself, I can handle it myself. I'll be doing it when we get home."

Kassie immediately bristled. She loved the man who sat across from her with defiance in his eyes, but his demands didn't sit well with her. She was Chase's fiancée! "Jake, I'm asking you to reschedule. I'm not ready. I'm willing to discuss it with you. I know you need closure."

"I know you and my godson experienced something which only comes around once in a lifetime. I encountered the same with my Bonnie for thirty years and there isn't anyone who can replace her. You must move on. Chase would be thrilled to see how much work you poured in on the hospital and the cabins. You'll turn it into something special. The town and I will be having his memorial and whether you attend is up to you." Jake slid out of his seat and went back to his original one.

Kassie's narrow gaze never left him. She never wanted to shake a man to his senses as much as she did Jake. With her attention focused on Jake, she didn't realize Victoria slid into the seat right next to her.

"This is a lesson, Luv. Take all the anger you have and swallow it down. Never show your hand. Keep a poker face. He's hurting. He's trying to strike out, although not intentionally. I want you to relax your face and breathe through your nose. Think about the beautiful mountain you live on. Dream of Chase and all the things worth fighting for."

"He's not even trying to have hope. Catherine hasn't called or brought Melody up to play. I know they have every reason to believe I'm not dealing with it. I struggled after the team saved me. I *need* to know. Why is that so hard to understand?"

"Grief comes in many forms. We all deal with it differently. Look at me." Victoria waited until Kassie's blue eyes met hers. "I'm living proof of Ivan's love. For all he knew, James killed me the day he took me. He didn't give up. Think on that, Luv."

Laying her head on the window she closed her eyes and drifted off. She dreamed of the night Chase proposed. Chase kept the nightmares at bay while she recovered and attended therapy with Claire. Even knowing having children together might prove impossible, his faith in her was undeterred. When she peered into his eyes, she marveled at his love and acceptance of who she was.

A tear rolled down her cheek as she dreamt of lying in the empty bed, worried if he sustained an injury, experienced cold, or hunger. The dream shifted to sunset on the mountain. She and Chase loved spending their favorite time together cuddled in the reading nook in their bedroom. Chase's voice echoed in her head. *Don't give up, Princess. I'm coming home to you.*

She jolted awake as the plane landed. His voice sounded tired and raspy, but she recognized him. Kassie knew

Keeping Kassie

without a doubt, Chase continued to fight his way back home to her.

CHAPTER SEVENTEEN

It had to be the longest week of Chase's life. Two more days to go, and the men felt like climbing the walls. The waiting was the hardest part even when everything went well. With food and water, Whiskey grew stronger, but remained critical. Shadow improved daily. Taco's leg continued to hurt. Even braced, his leg couldn't bear weight. Ahmet stuck to his promise and helped them.

The team sat in a circle in Ahmet's bedroom and began discussing their plans. Ahmet assured them the medical van contained enough room for all of them. Making a list of their most essential needs, water, food, and medication, they discussed the possibilities of what might go wrong. Shadow intended to wear traditional Turkish garb and ride up front with the driver. One, to be sure the driver stayed on the up and up. Ahmet vouched for him, but they preferred to keep their guard up. Two, it allowed him to warn them of potential issues.

Ash and Whiskey carried no weapons. The rest of the team retained their KA-BARS and managed to hold on to two guns with a limited amount of ammunition.

Keeping Kassie

Leo recovered from his migraines gradually, Saint and Chase recuperated with the food, water, and rest. While well enough to fight, Saint planned to cover Shadow if needed.

Leo met the eyes of each man on the team. "I know this seems easy, but we need to stay vigilant. No slacking on the homestretch. I'm not thrilled bringing another unknown in the picture and we still have a long way to go. At the first opportunity, we need to get to a phone."

A crash next door from the clinic drew three of the men to their feet. Muffled arguing ensued and they heard furniture breaking.

Leo indicated Saint stay with the injured as Chase and him investigated the commotion. Going through the back door of the clinic, they saw two men holding a knife to Ahmet's throat. With no idea what they said, Chase noticed the fear in Ahmet's eyes. Grabbing a huge pottery jar, he hurled it at the head of the man holding the knife. The stunned man slowly took a step back as Chase advanced. Leo already grappled the other man down on the floor. Chase slammed his fist into the guy's face making him drop the knife. Ahmet handed them rope to tie the men up.

"Ahmet, who are these men? What did they say to you?"

"They know you're here. Someone has seen you. You need to leave immediately. They sent a man to get *polis*. Hurry, my friends. I'll keep them here as long as I can."

Leo exchanged a silent communication with Chase. If they left Ahmet, he'd be dead before they even left the country.

"Ahmet, you can't stay. They'll kill you and possibly go after your niece. We need to leave immediately. Grab what you need."

Ahmet ran around the room adding supplies in a sack.

Opening the cabinet, he shoved as many meds as possible into the bag.

"Ahmet, we don't have time, we need to go," Chase urged.

"Not for us. Medication can be traded. I'd rather take it than leave it for them. We may need it for food," Ahmet explained. Going through the back to his house, he grabbed a few blankets and wrapped up the remaining food from breakfast. "I'm ready."

Ash, Saint, and Whiskey stood ready to fight. Whiskey held a hard stance, and his eyes held a determined glare, despite the fact he was too weak to fight a kitten. Chase walked over to pick him up.

"No, I can walk a bit. When I get tired, you can carry me, but let's bug out." Whiskey headed for the door.

Saint grabbed Taco and the team followed Ahmet out the back. Leading them down a rocky path, Ahmet carried the bags. This allowed the men to be ready to fight if they ran into trouble.

Chase's thoughts flashed to Kassie. He didn't know what would happen, yet his determination pushed him forward. He'd fight like hell for his brothers, and for himself, but most importantly, for the love of his life.

CHAPTER EIGHTEEN

The church overflowed with people coming to pay their respects for the fallen hero. When Kassie and her friends arrived, a family representative showed them to seats in the back of the church. An older woman impeccably dressed in black with a matching hat and widow's veil stood next to a somber man in a black suit. A woman with long blonde hair in a body-hugging suit and a black hat stood next to a man who Kassie recognized as Shadow's older brother.

As Kassie scanned the room, Shadow's letter came to mind. Toward the front senators, congressman, and young men dressed in uniform surrounded the family. An empty black coffin with a huge arrangement of red, white and blue flowers adorned the top.

The service began with the priest. When he finished, one of the congressmen stood up and began reading telegrams from other political leaders. Kassie's hands clenched the in-memoriam pamphlet tightly. None of this pertained to Shadow! What about the people who knew him? Who came to bear witness to the fact the world lost a wonderful man? Yes, Shadow sacrificed for his country. He also taught her daughter how to hide in plain sight. He colored butterflies with Emma. Shadow sat quietly for hours with Kassie watching old movies as she struggled to regain control over her life. He brought her candy bars in rehab and stood outside her door within her sight to ensure she knew she was never alone. Shadow made mouthwatering enchiladas and rice. Who intended to speak to the gathering about the man she loved as a brother? Surveying the crowd, who seemed bored to tears, Kassie made a decision. Opening her purse, she pulled out the letter Shadow instructed her to read. Shadow entrusted her to not let this be his goodbye.

Standing up and making her way to the end of the aisle. A large man put his arm out to stop her when Michael pulled back his jacket to show his weapon and raised his brow at the man and the arm he placed across Kassie. The man hastily backed out of the way. Kassie's heels clacked on the polished floor echoing through the church. The congressman at the podium stopped talking as she approached and indicated for him to sit. Confused, the man glimpsed at the older woman for direction. She stiffly nodded. Her mouth firmed as she angrily shot daggers at the young woman. Stepping up to the podium, Kassie began to speak.

"My name is Kassie Stanton."

The hushed murmurs grew louder at the recognition of her name. Kassie waited until the church fell silent again. "Shadow was my friend. His commitment to his country was a great honor. He became a Navy SEAL. I got to know Shadow when he protected my daughter and I for months and saved my life. It's an honor to call him part of my family. We love him very much. Upon his funeral, Shadow asked me to read the following letter."

> Dear Congressmen, Senators and my family:
> Thank you for coming to the show. Since it's my party, I feel it's only fair I get to have a say in how I go out of this world. My family never cared about me unless it was to brag about some shiny medal I earned while I risked my life. To you, I leave them all. Kassie will deliver them when she retrieves my belongings. To my brother and my ex-fiancée Crystal, may you always have each other. I think that's enough misery for both of you.

Kassie's face felt warm. But she wouldn't let the man who silently sat next to her lending his strength and support when she had none, leave this world without his final say.

> To the rest of you, I most likely don't know you. I apologize profusely for making you sit through this. For the few friends I have left, I reserved the bar across the street from the church. Henry will close the bar to the public on the day of my memorial. So, march over there and give me a proper goodbye. Drink in my honor and tell everyone what a wonderful

man I am. I may be dead, but I still like a good story.

The woman reading this, and my teammates became the family everyone deserves. I only hope one day all of you experience the loyalty and love that I've received. To Kassie, I hope you and Chase have a wonderful life together with Em.

Kassie's voice began to falter.

I let the woman I love go and regretted it ever since. Let this be a reminder to all of you. Life is too short. Don't go to funerals of people you barely know. Go live your life with the people you love and be happy.
In the meantime, I bid you farewell from below.
--Shadow

Michael helped Kassie down. Jake stood at the door. Victoria discreetly slipped out to avoid any cameras as Kassie exited. As Kassie walked down the middle aisle, the crowd began to talk, and she heard the snapping of pictures. No wonder Shadow wrote the note. The people held no connection, no remorse for such a special man. It all boiled down to perception. Jake opened the door and fell in step to her left as Michael

Keeping Kassie

took up the right. Kassie didn't see Victoria but knew she remained close.

Walking into the establishment across the street. An elderly man in his eighties, glanced up. A row of shot glasses lined the bar and he poured the alcohol going down the line. Kassie and the men took seats at the end of the bar and watched as people slowly began to file in. Michael rubbed his hand up and down Kassie's back in a soothing manner, finally letting his hand rest on her shoulder. The hushed crowd collected their shots and waited for Kassie to speak.

When everyone collected their glasses, Kassie raised hers high. "To my friend and my protector. Wherever you are, know you aren't forgotten, we love you and someday we shall meet again." Glasses were raised and everyone downed their shot. A few people used their phones to record Kassie, but she refused to hide in the shadows. To everyone else, Kassie's salute echoed of someone saying goodbye, but to those close to her, her speech held a double meaning.

Jake slammed his shot glass on the bar and walked out as the older woman in black angrily stomped in. Her cold grey eyes shot fire at Kassie. "You can't do this! My son deserves honor and respect! Not some eulogy at a trashy bar! You aren't welcome here, Kassie Stanton. We don't want your kind here," she sneered.

Victoria stood in the back of the bar. A scarf now covered her head and glasses shaded her face. She caught Kassie's eye as the bar suddenly went silent. Nodding her head, Victoria raised her chin and sent Kassie a message.

Kassie took in the crowded room. "I'm here to honor your son. Shadow may have done all the things those fancy telegrams said, but at the end of the day, he loved, laughed, and lived. He was more than a man honoring his duty to this country."

Michael stepped next to Kassie, "To the man who saved my life. He carried me through the desert and literally threw me in a helicopter. When I left the hospital, I saw him on the tarmac. I saluted him and the team. He was already on his way to save another. That was the kind of man he was." Another toast rang throughout the bar.

The older woman, her son, and the blonde stood silently as one after another, people recalled Kassie's friend. Some told funny stories; others offered insights or advice the quiet man who rarely spoke passed on as he sat in the back and quietly observed. Shadow rarely garnered attention, but he remained seen.

Shadow's brother walked to the bar and picked up a shot. "To my baby brother. I wish I had told you when I had the chance how much I admired you. I wish I knew you like the people in this bar."

Shadow's parents made their way to Kassie. His mother dabbed her eyes with a laced handkerchief. Kassie steeled herself as the woman grew closer. The woman's eyes filled with tears.

"You truly knew my son. Somewhere along the way, I lost sight of my son. I never knew him for the man he was."

Kassie wrapped her arms around her and gave her a hug. "He knew exactly what you intended to do and in his own way, he made it right. Maybe he reminded you of who he was and I'm sure you made him happy by coming in here today."

Shadow's father nodded his head in a slight acknowledgement as he guided the woman by the shoulder and moved her through the crowd. Kassie stayed until the last guest left. She, then, turned to Henry.

"I need to settle Shadow's tab."

Henry shook his head and laughed. "Shadow paid for it

long ago. The day he enlisted, Shadow took me aside and said, Henry if something happens to me, I want you to march over to the church and read this letter." Henry pulled an envelope from the cash register. "I mustered the courage to do it today and walked in as you made your way up the aisle. Shadow made sure to plan ahead, and he sent me 50.00 every week for two years with a note. It read, don't go cheap Henry. He sure was an enigma. His family lived for money, and he walked away one day and joined the Navy."

Kassie placed her hand over the bartender's and gave it a light squeeze. "Thank you for doing this."

Kassie rose from her seat and her friends made their way out of the bar and headed to Taco's funeral.

❄

THE GROUP BOARDED the plane and headed to San Diego. Kassie went to the restroom and changed out of her funeral outfit and into jeans. The others followed suit. Once again, Kassie pulled out a yellow packet. Kassie found the letter addressed to her and various members of Taco's family.

> Dear Kass,
> I want to thank you for making Chase the happiest man on earth. I've never encountered love, but if I ever do, I'd want it to be exactly like what you and Chase share. I don't have any huge requests. I wish you and your family all the happiness in the world. First, I want you to pay off my parent's house with

my insurance money. Second, ensure the team never gives up on Ragu. My teammate, Ragu, disappeared after our failed mission. I know what they said he did. My heart says he didn't cause the mistakes he was accused of. He needs us. Our team never recovered after the loss of Olaf, Whiskey and Ash. We can't help them, but we can still clear Ragu and give him back his dignity.

Don't cry for me, wherever I'm at, I'm watching the sunset, eating tacos, and waiting for the next wave to hit. Give Ladybug a hug for me and remember to eat tacos on Tuesdays for me.

Love,
Taco

Shaking her head, she put everything back in the packet and gathered everything she needed as they landed. Jake didn't speak to her. In fact, he seemed distraught and angry. When everyone deboarded the plane, Jake hung back as they got into the vehicles.

"You go on ahead. I think I'll catch a flight back to Seattle." Kassie started toward Jake when Victoria took her arm and gently shook her head.

"Of course, Jake. It's your decision. I'll meet you back at home." Kassie wasn't happy. She wanted Chase's godfather to remain part of their lives. She hoped to ease the tension between them and conduct a civil conversation concerning

Keeping Kassie

Chase's service.

Victoria pulled an arm around her shoulder. "He needs time, Luv. He isn't mad at you. He's angry at life."

Kassie nodded and slipped into the car.

❄

Arriving at the beach the next evening, Kassie saw why Taco specified a party. The setting reminded her of him. Taco was always cool, calm, and relaxed, regardless of the situation. Immediately, Taco's family greeted her. They wore swimsuits, and strategically placed pictures of Taco were everywhere. Balloons and chairs created an aisle. The beach soon filled with more guests than seating allowed. No one complained as they stood in the back whispering and talking amongst the others.

Music began and Taco's parents held a wreath full of flowers and walked down the aisle. When they got to the water's edge, they turned and faced the crowd.

"Our son was an amazing individual. He loved nature, the ocean, his family, and everyone standing here today. He enjoyed serving his country and we know whatever operation he joined in, he helped someone. Our son carried a kind and caring soul. We thank you for coming to celebrate him. We love you, Taco." His parents waded into the ocean and through the waves until they got a big enough wave to carry the flowers into the sea. The sun settled on the water as the couple made their way to the beach. Two people handed them towels. Everyone sat in silence as the music played, reflecting on memories of their beloved friend and family member. A screen showing pictures of Taco growing up played in the background while his parents changed.

Kassie swiped the tears from her eyes. This showed what

love was all about. The thought she might have to do this for Chase shook her to her very core. She didn't want to say goodbye. They didn't get the chance to start their life. It wasn't fair. She discovered life threw punches when you least expected it with her sister. Now, it seemed as if all the insecurities and hurt bubbled to the surface. She lamented all the wasted time she questioned Chase's motives and his love.

Taco's parents came out of the covered tent, freshly dressed. His mom's eyes pooled tears as she accepted the condolences of people coming to pay their respects. As Kassie neared, Taco's mother gathered her in her arms and held her tightly.

"I've heard so much about you and your lovely daughter. Thank you for coming. I know you're going through your own grief. It means the world to us." The woman smiled at Kassie and swiped away a tear.

Kassie nodded, unable to speak. Rounding the corner of the tent to compose herself, she pulled a tissue from her purse. Michael started to follow, and she waived him away. She needed a moment alone. The pain in her chest as she pondered how to say goodbye to Chase if they didn't hear any news soon, broke her heart.

Watching the ocean, Kassie spied a man standing in the distance. His black hair was tied into a ponytail, and he sported a beard. He didn't seem homeless... maybe unkept. He fell to his knees and held his face in his hands. Kassie knew exactly how he felt. Although he held himself apart from the crowd, he grieved the loss of Taco.

Grabbing a bottled water, Kassie walked down to where the distraught man knelt. Michael and Victoria followed.

A few steps away from the man, Michael grabbed her arm. "Kass, I know him. He helped rescue me with the team.

Keeping Kassie

I think his name was Ragu." Michael continued to view the man.

"Why wasn't he with Leo and the team?" Kassie asked confused.

Michael leaned in. "I'm not really at liberty to say. The team suspects he was wrongly accused of something and dishonorably discharged."

"Oh no. Yet he still came to the memorial." Kassie whispered. She wondered about the mistake Taco mentioned in his letter and decided to speak with Matthew about the best way to gather the official records and talk to Ragu.

"Why didn't he come to Shadow's?" Michael wondered out loud.

Kassie rolled her eyes, "He probably didn't get the embossed invitation."

Slowly approaching him, Kassie called out from behind him. "Hello, my name is Kassie. My friend recognizes you. Are you Ragu?"

The man jumped to his feet. "I'm not here to cause any trouble. I wanted to pay my respects." He began to back up.

Michael approached him. "No man, you aren't causing anything. I'm the doctor you saved a long time ago. It's good to see you, Ragu."

Michael held his hand out and Ragu swiped his hand on his shorts before he shook it.

"I haven't kept in touch with the team. I found out about Taco purely by accident. What happened?" Ragu asked Michael.

Michael stepped forward. "The helo went down while they completed a mission. The official report says they are presumed dead."

"So, the rest of the team? They're all gone?" Ragu asked distressed.

"As far as we know. Yes," Michael quietly told him.

Ragu turned away from them. The anguish in his posture called out to Kassie. Wrapping her arms around him, she held onto him and cried. She felt the bones in the skinny man and a hint of alcohol. Given the situation, maybe he felt the need to over imbibe? When he got control of himself, he smiled down at her. "Thank you, it's been a long time since I've gotten a hug. You know me, but I haven't met you."

"I'm Kassie Stanton. You saved my fiancé, Chase Winters. Why don't you come up with us and join the party?"

Ragu shook his head. "No, thank you. I'm not someone they care to see. I don't want to add to their stress. Do you know when the other funerals are?"

"Saint's is next week. Leo will have a memorial on Serenity Mountain. He didn't want a service. It will be family; you're welcome to join us." Kassie rubbed his arm and gave it a gentle squeeze.

"Thank you. If I give you my phone number, will you send me the information?" Ragu pulled out an old beaten phone. His hands shook as he handed it to Kassie.

Smiling, Kassie took the phone and added her number and texted herself, to obtain his. "If you have any issues with getting to the services or need a ride, will you let me know?" She doubted the distraught man would appreciate her questioning him during Taco's memorial and she lacked the military knowledge to discern what mistakes occurred during a mission. When she returned to Serenity, she'd ask Matthew for help and continue communicating with Ragu.

Ragu nodded. "Thank you. I better be going. I appreciate you telling me."

The food trucks arrived, and chairs covered the beach as some people danced, others sat and ate tacos. A bon fire lit the beach and people roasted marshmallows and reminisced about Taco. Kassie walked through the crowd, listening to stories of her friend.

Finally, she made her goodbyes to Taco's parents, assuring them she'd keep in touch. Kassie wanted to go home.

They boarded the flight and Kassie excused herself and headed to the bathroom. Sliding down the wall she cried. Sliding her knees to her chest, she muffled her sobs with her knees.

Please Chase, come home to me. I need you...

CHAPTER NINETEEN

The team skirted the cities and Ahmet ventured into the villages to barter for food when needed. Shadow followed since he excelled at slipping in unseen. The dry and rocky terrain added to the difficulty of the injured men to walk for extended periods of time. Leo halted the group to make camp for the evening.

Chase helped Whiskey to sit up and eat. The swelling in Ash's jaw reduced, but he made no effort to talk. Chase observed him for signs of PTSD and did his best to give him only soft food when possible. After some convincing, Leo went to rest. He had paced nonstop and transfixed on Ash and Whiskey when they were occupied elsewhere. Leo took personal responsibility for everything the team endured. If Chase guessed, he blamed himself for Whiskey and Ash too. In truth, Leo drove him crazy.

Chase stood as he heard the call indicating Ahmet and Shadow had reentered the camp.

Shadow threw a bag on the ground and headed to wake Leo and the rest of the team.

Ahmet stood wringing his hands and waited until the men circled around Taco to include him in the discussion.

"Ahmet heard something in the village," Shadow announced.

Almost as one, the team turned their gazes on the poor man. "There's talk in the village. Men offered a huge reward for an American group. When I went to barter, they asked if I learned anything about the American men on my journey."

Leo's brows furrowed. "I don't think this can be the group from Ahmet's home. We lost them days ago."

"Do you think it could be allies?" Chase asked.

Saint and Leo shook their heads. "We crashed in the Caspian. They gave us four maybe five days tops. Then we were presumed dead or missing. Our allies stopped searching a long time ago. Let's take inventory of what we have and bug out."

Chase dug in the bag for a pain pill. "I'll take Whiskey. We haven't stopped long enough for him to rest,"

Leo nodded. "Ash, you and Ahmet help Taco. Shadow, can you carry the supplies? I'll take the front, Saint you cover the back."

The team went into action. Within minutes they cleaned the camp.

※

JUST BEFORE THE sun went down, Leo spotted a cave. Checking to make sure there weren't any critters inside, he declared it clear and helped get Whiskey and Taco settled.

Leo built a fire and Ahmet made rice and vegetables. As soon as he finished, they doused the flames. The men ate in silence. Leo and Chase took first watch and Saint and Shadow volunteered to take the second. They sat on the edge of the cave. When the men finally fell asleep, Leo spoke to Chase.

"What do you think PITA's doing right about now?" Leo's worried voice wasn't one Chase wanted to hear.

"I don't know. I'm worried this might be too stressful. I hope she's talking to Claire. I know Jake will be there for her, not counting Joe and Maddie."

Leo sat quietly as he pondered the darkness. "I thought I was saving Olaf," Leo admitted quietly. "I hoped to erase some of the hurt I caused her."

Chase knew Leo referred to Catherine. "I'm sure that after all this time, Catherine has moved on. She may not want to be married anymore."

Chase barely saw the outline of his friend rubbing his jaw. "No. When I told her Ash died, she went into shock. It about killed her. She'll blame me for not rescuing her husband sooner."

"You don't know how she'll react," Chase disagreed.

"I've known her a long time," Leo grunted.

"Leo. Talk to her. Don't make assumptions. Kassie and I almost lost one another because we didn't communicate. Give her a chance to decide what she wants to do," Chase attempted to convince his friend.

"It's not the same. She's never forgiven me for her brother. We fought before I left. It seems we can't get it right. Sometimes, things aren't meant to be."

"Bullshit. How many times did you tell me to get my head out of my ass with Kassie? You pushed me to talk to her. You don't know what she'll think or feel about a man who reappears in her life three years later. What about Samantha?"

Leo stood. "Samantha and Whiskey loved each other.

She's never gotten over his death. She'll welcome him with open arms."

"I don't want her to see me like this. I'm weak and probably have a million different parasites feeding off me. I don't want you to take me back. I need time to heal." Whiskey stood next to Leo.

"You're supposed to be resting. You barely made it today even with Chase carrying you." Leo's voice went from friend to boss mode instantly.

"I wanted to talk to you. We don't know who's trying to track us down, but if it comes down to it, leave me. I'll only slow you down," Whiskey wheezed out the words to give them an out.

"You know that's not happening, brother. I've searched for you for over a year, when I first got an indication you might still be alive," Leo's voice turned deadly.

"We can't pretend I don't have multiple issues. I don't want Sunshine to see me like this. I refuse to traumatize my kid the first time I meet him," Whiskey argued.

"Damn it, Whiskey. I'd rather die than leave you again. It's not happening. If you slow us down, then we all go down together. We aren't splitting up like last time. We're sticking together. Now get some damn sleep or I'll ride your ass all day tomorrow if you decide to be a whiny bitch," Leo vehemently whispered.

Whiskey turned toward the cave and laid back down.

"I don't know what happened on your last mission. Don't let the past dictate how you handle this. Get your head clear." Chase left Leo to his thoughts as he walked the perimeter.

CHAPTER TWENTY

Joe met the plane as it landed, and Kassie bounced off the stairs and into his arms for a hug.

"Welcome home, Little Bit."

"Thank you, Joe. Where's Em? I looked forward to hugging her."

"Plans changed. Melody and Catherine stopped by, and the girls started playing. Maddie and Catherine made tea, I volunteered to come get you."

"I'm glad you did. It's good to be home." Kassie started walking toward the cars surrounded by Victoria's men. "And Matthew?"

"He's with Em. Jameson offered to drive. How did everything go?" Joe opened the door and let Kassie slide into the back seat, and he climbed in.

"Shadow's funeral started like a nightmare. Shadow made sure to correct it in his own way." Kassie described the happenings from the memorial.

"Shadow knew to count on you, Little Bit. And Taco?" Joe listened intently. His hand never left Kassie's.

Keeping Kassie

"Oh, his family said goodbye in such a wonderful way. You felt all the love. He was truly blessed." She leaned her head on the older man's shoulder. "I'm grateful Em and I found our way back to you and Maddie. I don't know what I would've done without you. I know you want me to accept Chase is gone. If I must, I'm glad I have the two of you here to lean on." Kassie squeezed Joe's hand.

"We're always here, Little Bit. We love you. I'm mad at all the years we've lost, but we can only make up the time and can't dwell on the past." Joe kissed the top of her head.

"The moment I saw you and Maddie at the pizzeria, all those empty years disappeared. I'm living for today and all the tomorrows. Do you think once I've spent some time with Em, we can go see the hospital and cabin progress?" Kassie asked.

"Absolutely. Don't you want to rest up a bit?" Joe asked. "Maddie made you lunch and she's making jambalaya for dinner. Take some time to relax."

"I'm fine Joe. Victoria kept her word and I'm feeling stronger every day. I have an appointment with Claire in the morning and I want to start making a list of supplies we need for the cabins."

"You remind me of your mother. Nathan and Abigail would be so proud of you." Joe leaned down and kissed the top of her head.

"I hope so," Kassie whispered. "I hope John Winters approves of everything we're doing to the hospital. I can't explain it, I need to have it done. Maybe it's because it will give me a part of Chase. All his dreams are coming true. I miss him." Chase's dad, John Winters, had planted the seed of his dream in his son. They planned to accomplish the goal together but his dad passed away from a heart attack.

"I know you do, Little Bit. I wish we could take this pain away from you," Joe sadly whispered.

"I'd do it all over again. I never experienced this kind of love before, but after having a tiny taste of it, I know how blessed I am to have it in my life," Kassie admitted as they pulled into the driveway.

Maddie pulled Kassie into a hug as soon as Kassie walked into the door. "Welcome home, Sugar."

"Thank you, Maddie. Do I smell fresh cookies?" Kassie kissed the older woman's cheek.

"Right out of the oven exactly how you like them. Catherine and Miss Melody came to pay us a visit. The girls went upstairs. I'll fetch Em."

A squeal from the top of the stairs and the patter of two sets of feet sounded as the girls came running down the stairs. Emma ran straight to Kassie and wrapped her arms around her. Kasie pulled Melody into the embrace.

"Oh, I've missed you. Did you draw me any special pictures?" Kassie excitedly asked while keeping an arm around each girl.

"Yes, Mama. I'll go get them!" Emma headed to the stairs as Melody began to follow.

"Melody, we need to get going. Grab your shoes and your doll," Catherine called out to her daughter.

"Hello Catherine." Kassie greeted her friend who rose from the kitchen table and started packing up her things. "Please don't go. We haven't had a chance to visit."

Catherine ignored Kassie's request as she grabbed her purse. "I dropped off Emma's classwork, I thought she'd enjoy the art projects."

"Cat, let's discuss what happened before I left..." Kassie began.

"There's nothing to discuss. I know you've gone

through a ton of stuff, Kassie. Yet I have to say something even if other people think it's best you live in this dream world of yours. You, out of all people, know bad things happen to good people. I won't have Emma telling Melody love conquers all. Wishing away all the bad things isn't healthy for you or Em. It's been weeks, Kassie, and the longer you wait, the harder it will be on your little girl and you. I love you, but I don't want to watch you self-destruct again."

Melody bounded down the stairs and slipped her shoes on while Catherine waited at the door. Kassie didn't say a word as she watched her friend leave. When the door closed, Kassie went in search of Em.

Pushing open the door, Kassie surveyed the room. Chase painted the room pink for Em regardless of the fact Kassie tried everything to push him away. He kept his faith she'd return. Why was it terrible she put her faith in him to return this time? Sighing, Kassie walked to the other side of the bed to find Emma sitting on the floor sniffling and holding on to her favorite doll Molly. Rollo curled up by her side.

She sat next to Emma and gave Rollo a scratch behind his ears.

"Hey Ladybug, what's the matter?" Kassie asked softly. "Melody will be back to play soon."

Emma turned her big blue eyes to Kassie. Tears tracked down her face and she hiccupped as she threw her arms around Kassie's neck.

"Whatever it is, sweetie, we'll figure it out. Tell me what's wrong," Kassie soothed Emma as she ran her hand up and down her child's back.

"Melody said..." Emma hiccupped. "Melody said Dr. Chase isn't coming home. He's in heaven like her daddy and your sister."

Kassie pulled her closer and let her own tears fall. She held Emma and spoke soothing words until Emma calmed.

Pulling Emma away in order to observe her face, Kassie explained to Em. "You know I told you the helicopter Dr. Chase and the team rode in went into the big ocean?"

Emma nodded her head and wiped her eyes.

"Well, when the rescue team got there, Uncle Leo, Uncle Taco, Uncle Shadow, Uncle Saint and Chase weren't there. The ocean is very cold, and most people can't swim in the ocean for very long. But Uncle Leo's team has special training. They know how to do things most people can't. We don't know if they're lost or in heaven. The most important thing to remember is how much we love them and they're right here." Kassie pointed to Emma's chest. "They will always be with us until we can see them again."

Emma laid her head on Kassie's shoulder. A few minutes later, the child's breathing evened and Kassie knew she was sleeping. Careful not to wake her, she eased from the floor and placed her on the bed. Covering her with a light throw, she eased out of the room with Rollo at her side.

Maddie met her at the bottom of the stairs. "Is everything all right?" Her forehead wrinkled in worry as she glanced in the direction of Emma's room.

"Melody told Emma that Chase went to heaven." Kassie sat at the kitchen table and picked at the chicken salad stuffed into a tomato Maddie made for her.

Maddie grabbed a towel and began to dry the dishes. "Sugar, maybe you need to think about having Chase's service. It might give both of you some closure."

Kassie placed the fork on the plate. "I don't think I'm hungry. Em fell asleep. I need to go out for a bit. Can you keep an eye on her?"

Maddie dried her hands on the dish towel. "Of course, Sugar..."

"I don't want to talk about this right now. Please Maddie." Kassie walked out the front door and headed to the barn. She knew exactly where she wanted to go. Saddling Scarlett as Bear taught her, she led her out of the barn and closed the door. Turning the horse along the path of the lake, she headed to where she knew she'd find Chase.

Tying Scarlett to the tree, she made her way to the place where Chase proposed. The fire ring stood untouched since the night he made love to her beside it. She closed her eyes and remembered the firelight flickering around them. Chase's hand softly brushing and stroking her body as he held her close. The taste of whiskey on his tongue as he licked her lips. He smelled like the mountain.

Standing on the edge where they watched the sunset, she called out, "I'm not giving up! Do you hear me, Chase Winters? I need you! Come home to me!" She plopped down on the ground and cried. For once, Serenity Mountain didn't offer her the solace she needed the most. Only one man could do that, and he was missing...

CHAPTER TWENTY-ONE

Leo swiped the sweat from his forehead. The team continued to be tracked. Saint and Shadow doubled back while the rest kept moving forward. Between the injured and Ahmet, Leo shouldered the burden of keeping them moving. It didn't help their coms disappeared into the ocean. Chase felt the tension radiate off Leo.

The sun started to set, and Leo pushed the group on until they found a little rocky overhang.

"Doc and Ahmet, help get Whiskey and Ash settled. We still have water, fruit, and nuts, we aren't lighting a fire." He raised his nose in the air. "They've made camp, I can smell the smoke. If I can smell them, they can smell us." Leo surveyed what little of the area the low light revealed.

An hour later a signal rang out indicating Saint and Shadow approached their camp. Shadow slid down the wall of the overhang and Chase handed him the water first. He still needed rest regardless of what he wanted the others to believe.

"SITREP?" Leo asked as he handed Saint the other canteen.

"You won't believe it. It's Russians," Saint reported.

"Russians?" Leo repeated. "What the hell? Why would they be hunting us?"

Saint sat down next to Shadow. "We didn't make out much. They're determined to find us. Shadow and I have a plan. They aren't making a secret out of their location. The men are about as quiet as a herd of elephants. They don't even have guns at the ready. If they intended on using us as hostages, they have to know a SEAL team has skills to take them down easily."

Leo digested everything Saint said. "The problem lies in our numbers. Whiskey and Ash can't help, Ahmet, no offense, we can't count on."

"I can help." Chase volunteered. "What do I need to do?"

"Stand down Doc, you aren't going anywhere."

"Leo. You need to lead the team. Shadow isn't strong enough to fight off an attack. Chase remains the better option. It's better than trying to outrun them. We still have a long way to go," Saint reasoned.

"No. Damn it. Doc needs to be here to patch those assholes. We can't afford to lose him," Leo bit back.

"Leo." Shadow eased up from the wall and joined the group except for Whiskey and Ash. "Can I have a word?"

Leo walked to the edge of the camp and the two of them carried on a hushed and angry argument. Finally, Leo relented.

Coming back to the group, Leo gruffly replied, "Saint and Doc will sneak into camp and see if they can nab one of them. We need to find out why they're hunting us and if they've alerted anyone else to our presence."

Chase gathered what he needed. Making sure his KA-BAR stayed within reach. They didn't want to use a gun if they could avoid it. An American team found in this territory provided an excellent excuse for other groups to join in on the search to fill their pockets.

Saint led the way back to the camp. It proved easy with the fire going and the sound of the men talking. Saint motioned for Chase to get comfortable. They needed to wait for the group to settle down for the night.

Three hours later, two men sat in front of the fire. Saint inched closer to the camp with Chase directly behind.

"From the sounds of it, they didn't stop drinking vodka. Let's wait it out and see if one goes for a piss. We can snatch and grab. Circle around to the opposite side of the camp as me. If the one on the right goes, you grab him. I'll grab the one on the left." Saint instructed quietly.

Chase made his way to the opposite side. Thankfully, Leo insisted he and Michael train like a SEAL. He learned a few things in the Navy, but he remained typically in a hospital, not sneaking around in a desert in the middle of the night.

Just as Saint predicted, the man on the left got up, and disappeared behind the tents. The right one stood and headed toward the other end of the tent. Chase hastened his way behind the man and choked him. The man was nearly unconscious when Chase heard the click of a gun.

"Ah Comrade, I think it's best if you let my friend go," The Russian man lazily replied.

Chase spun the man in front of him. The knife held to the man's neck. "Put the weapon down or I'll cut your friend," Chase demanded. Shit, the last thing he needed was to be captured.

The man slightly hesitated, "You are American. Yes?"

"Drop the weapon," Chase instructed forcefully.

The man stepped forward. Holding a cigarette in his mouth, Chase saw the orange ash light up as the man

Keeping Kassie

studied him. The campfire gave off enough light he saw the Russian's silhouette.

"American?" The man repeated.

Chase held the knife closer to the man's neck. Taking a step back, he refused to let the man get closer.

"Gregor, end this foolishness." The man ordered.

Chase felt the air behind him change as someone from behind hit him in the ribs, knocking him sideways. He released the prisoner he held. Chase ducked the next swing and gripped the knife as he swiped the man in the arm. The man advanced with the cigarette still in his mouth.

"American?" He half demanded, half questioned.

Chase's jaw firmed and he summoned up the last of his energy. He refused to allow anything to keep him from getting home to Kassie. He circled the man ready to fight.

"Why are you following me?" Chase inquired through gritted teeth.

The man slowly relaxed his stance as Gregor got to his feet. Both men laughed. Chase refused to let it distract him.

The man took one last drag on his cigarette before dropping it to the ground and grinding it into the dirt.

"We are searching for American men. A doctor and a team of military." The man eyed Chase. "You have a team with you? I have a message from Ivan and Victoria. We intend no harm."

"You've got the wrong person. I don't know an Ivan or Victoria," Chase insisted.

Gregor shook his head and said something in Russian to the other man. He in turn pointed the gun at Chase and then said something to Gregor.

Gregor ran his hand through his hair. "You know Kassie Stanton? His English came out thick but the hair on the back of Chase's neck stood up when he heard Kassie's name mentioned.

"What about Kassie?" his voice hardened as he barked the question.

Gregor smiled and nodded. "Kassie?" He pointed to the tent in the middle of the camp.

Confused Chase stayed in place. What happened to Saint?

"Where is your team? Are you the only one alive?" The other man questioned Chase. Gregor seemed more relaxed and kept pointing toward the middle tent and talking fast in Russian.

Quick as a flash, Saint grabbed the man with the gun from behind. Gregor started yelling, waking up the entire camp. Men came running from all the directions as the gun went off.

CHAPTER TWENTY-TWO

Victoria swung the knife again, barely missing Kassie. Not waiting for her to recover, she struck out again, slicing a thin line across Kassie's forearm.

"Ow! That hurt! I thought we were practicing! Not going for blood," Kassie complained.

"Do you think Stanton's men will let you rest?" Victoria's eyebrows went up as she watched Kassie shake her arm and ready herself for the next attack.

Kassie narrowed her eyes and concentrated as Victoria taught her. Be aware of your surroundings. The last three weeks Victoria and Ivan got her up at the crack of dawn. Except for Shadow's and Taco's memorials, they practiced daily. Sometimes three times a day. Kassie felt the changes in her body. Muscles she didn't know existed, strengthened, and tightened. She developed definition in her thighs and stomach, and her arms were stronger.

Flying out in the morning for Saint's home in Alabama, she planned to finish the exercise with Victoria, then she steeled herself to talk to Catherine. She needed her friend, and something more was going on other than Kassie's refusal to accept the disappearance of the team. Victoria struck her again.

"Damn it!" Kassie hissed.

"Stop daydreaming or I'll really give you something to cry about," Victoria chastised.

Focusing on Victoria, she held her stance. A movement to the right made her swerve and punch out. Ivan coughed as he held his stomach. His face lit into a smile. Victoria smirked. "Very good. You remembered to use all your senses. Now go shower, eat some breakfast with your family."

"Ivan, did I hurt you?" Kassie worried as she moved toward him.

"Pshhh, it mimicked a mosquito hitting me. Go eat, Little One."

Kassie chuckled, clearly delighted she got him. "It's Little Bit. Joe and Maddie call me Little Bit."

Ivan smiled. "Hurry back, Little Bit. I'll practice with Emma this afternoon after her nap. Then tonight, you and I will practice again."

Kassie made her way around the lake and her steps lightened as she skipped up to the front porch. Maddie made eggs, bacon and homemade biscuits. She turned around and saw Kassie's arm.

"Good gracious! She cut you!" Maddie's eyes sparked fire as she grabbed Kassie's arm and held it under the kitchen sink.

"It's a scratch, I'm fine," Kassie explained.

Maddie clucked around her like a mother hen. Wrapping her arm in paper towels. Her eyes rounded when she saw blood seeping on her shoulder. Her back shot straight and she glared at Kassie with disapproval in her eyes.

Keeping Kassie

"I swear, Sugar. I don't understand you! Why are you doing this? Joe already told you; we can hire security. Matthew has the whole mountain rigged with all kinds of things. No one can hurt you." Exasperated, Maddie threw up her hands and grabbed an oven mitt to pull out the biscuits. Once she finished with the food, Kassie tugged her to the nearest kitchen chair and sat her down.

"I know you and Joe don't understand. For nine days I stayed in a deep dark tunnel freezing and scared out of my mind. I worried Roger would get Emma. James Stanton attacked us on our own turf, and we weren't prepared. Matthew almost died. Emma nearly disappeared forever and I lacked the knowledge and skills to protect us, Maddie." Kassie pleaded with her godmother.

Joe walked out of the office and placed his arm around Kassie. Maddie's eyes locked onto Kassie and back at the cut on her arm and shoulder.

"Little Bit, we can't say we approve of the methods, but if it makes you feel safer, we'll support it. We're concerned, that's all," Joe conceded.

Kassie squeezed Maddie's hand. "I know. James Stanton doesn't play fair. We've lost enough. I won't let him take Em or anyone else I love. You waited three years for me and never stopped searching. Would you have stopped if someone asked you?"

Maddie's chin went up and her steely grey eyes met Kassie's. "Sugar, I'm sorry. You went through something we can't even imagine. Maybe I'll ask Victoria to show me and Joe some moves. We're family, we fight together." Kassie hugged both of her godparents.

"Where's Em? I'm starved!" Kassie asked.

"She's making her bed and will be right down. Go ahead

and eat while it's hot. Then you need a shower!" Everyone chuckled at Maddie's announcement.

Kassie piled her plate full of eggs, two pieces of bacon and two biscuits. One good thing about working out... her appetite came back with a vengeance. Seeing the butter on the table, she remembered Chase watching her as she debated to ask for the condiment. He patiently waited for her to be strong. Now it was her turn to practice perseverance. She resolved herself to do whatever it took, for him.

❋

Maddie and Carol drove off with two bodyguards, leaving Kassie alone with Catherine. Kassie knocked on the door and waited.

"Mama did you forget your key again?" A disheveled Catherine answered the door. Upon seeing Kassie standing there, she huffed out a breath and stuck her nose up in the air.

"Can I come in?" Kassie asked through gritted teeth. They were best friends, not mortal enemies.

"It's not a good time." Catherine started to shut the door when Kassie stuck her foot in and pushed the door wide.

"I think it is. You don't seem to mind when I tell you it's not a good time. Remember when you moved me completely out of my apartment?"

Kassie pushed her way through the doorway.

"It was for your own good," Catherine argued.

"What bug's up your butt, Cat? Seriously? I'm supposed to fall apart because you deem it's appropriate. What the hell? We're best friends. You haven't showered in days. Your hair resembles a bird's nest. You've obviously been crying."

Keeping Kassie

Kassie crossed her arms waiting for Catherine to say something.

"Leave me alone, Kassie," Catherine's voice held no emotion as she demanded she leave.

"No. Something's wrong, and I wrapped myself up in everything to keep myself busy. I wasn't paying attention to you. You insisted Leo help me when I was struggling. You begged me to trust you. Now you need to trust me. I want to know what I'm missing," Kassie cut to the chase.

A single tear ran down Catherine's cheek. "I can't talk about it."

"Why? If you can't tell your best friend, who can you tell? I can call Claire," Kassie offered.

Catherine shook her head as Kassie grabbed her hand and dragged her to the couch. Grabbing a wad of tissues from the tissue box, Kassie thrust them at Catherine.

"Out with it then. I love you. You helped me. What's going on?" Kassie persisted.

"I messed up. Now it's too late," Catherine cried.

"What happened?" Kassie rubbed her friend's shoulder before pulling her in for a hug as Catherine went through a crying jag.

"It's Leo. We got into a fight before the team left. I can't seem to control my emotions around him. The past keeps repeating itself. Only this time, he's not coming back." Catherine wiped her eyes and blew her nose.

"Oh honey, I'm sorry. I'm sure Leo knows you didn't mean it. I mean I swore at him, called him all kinds of vile things trying to get him to leave. He smirked like...like... you know... one of those men who oozes testosterone and dares you to do something knowing damn well he'll do exactly as he pleases. Freaking cocky peacock!"

Catherine chuckled behind the tissues. "I'm sorry Kassie. I took it out on you."

"Why, Cat? I don't understand how you supported me when Leo told you I was running from the FBI and accused of murder, yet you can't support me now. I'm not delusional. I'm fully aware Chase may be gone. I also know he's with the best team out there and I can't take some government official's word saying he's gone."

"Kassie, I've gone through this before. Sometimes people don't come home. You went through this horrible experience and this whole town is grieving the loss of Chase and his friends. Yet, you're determined he's out there. I feel like a traitor. I don't want to believe the worst. I want to have the same faith as you," Catherine confessed as she met Kassie's eyes.

Kassie stared at her best friend. It suddenly dawned on her. "I know you care about the team. I do too. I love Chase with everything I have. I think you have feelings for Leo, and it scares you to believe there's a slim chance."

Catherine's eyes widened and a faint blush crept into her cheeks. She started to deny it.

"It's written all over your face, Cat. Admit it. You have feelings for Leo. I'm sure this crash has drudged up feelings you'd rather forget. Love is worth fighting for. I saw the way Leo salivated over you when you weren't aware. Leo's committed to getting back here as much as Chase if I am coming even close to the truth between the two of you."

"Come on, Kassie. Do you honestly believe the entire team escaped a helicopter crash?" Catherine's voice sounded desperate, almost pleading.

Kassie cupped her hands on both sides of Catherine's face. "Yes. I do," she whispered to her friend.

Keeping Kassie

Catherine's arms clung to Kassie's neck as she clung to her. "I'm sorry. I'm a total ass."

"No. We support each other. Now go change and take a brush through that squirrel's nest. We'll grab Samantha, and head over to Bryanna's for some yummy treats. I need to talk to her anyway."

With another squeeze, Catherine let go of her friend and headed to the stairs. "Give me a half an hour!" she called and raced upstairs.

CHAPTER TWENTY-THREE

Chase woke up to Saint leaning over him in sheer panic.

"Oh, thank God, Doc. I thought I got you shot!" Saint ran his hand over his scruff.

Chase felt his arm. "I did get shot! Why the hell does my head hurt?"

Gregor leaned over and placed a cold wet cloth on his head.

"When you got shot you took a step back and fell. You hit a rock on the way down," Saint explained.

"How long ago?" Chase asked.

"About forty-five minutes. Good news...these assholes aren't attempting to kill us. You won't believe it. Do you think you can walk? We gotta make it back to camp." Saint helped Chase sit up. Nausea rolled in the pit of his stomach, but he held it off by breathing in through his nose and out his mouth.

A tall blond man with a high and tight cut came in through the tent. "Ah your friend finally woke. Drink this."

Keeping Kassie

He thrust a cup of something at Chase. "vodka helps with everything."

Chase glanced at Saint and chugged down the shot. Funnily enough his stomach seemed to settle.

"What the hell's going on?" Chase grimaced as his head pounded and Saint tightened the bandage on his wound.

"I'm Liev. This is Gregor and you met Aleski earlier. Ivan Rostova ordered us to find you."

Chase grimaced through the pain as he placed a hand to his head and side eyed Saint. "Who in the hell is Ivan Rostova?"

Saint shrugged. "Can you bring me some more bandages? Then I'll get my friend up and we can get to the others."

The men yelled orders and nodded at Chase and Saint before leaving the room.

"Ivan Rostova leads one of the biggest mob families." Saint whispered before anyone else came in. "He said Victoria Stanton is with Kassie. They're protecting her and Emma. He doesn't know a ton. Ivan sent them to search for us and bring us back. They heard about Ahmet's place and decided on a hunch to head this way."

"The freaking mafia is guarding my girl! Last time I checked, the mafia were still the bad guys!" Chase's voice rose and promptly went back to a whisper as his head refused to cooperate.

"Shhh. From what I can remember from reading. Ivan Rostova legitimized all his businesses. You don't want to mess with him, and he keeps other families in their places. He lets them do what they want in their territories, but he doesn't allow for mercy if they breach his domain. I don't know how this all pieces together. They're here to get us home, back to Serenity Mountain."

Chase didn't miss the light in Saint's eyes as he said it. They were all tired, sick, and injured. Serenity Mountain sounded like heaven to his ears.

By the time the men came in, Chase stood with a bit of help from Saint and insisted they leave at once to return to the others.

The Russian men packed up the camp and doused the fire in a matter of minutes. The group headed to where the team waited. Chase succumbed to the grin sliding across his face. If Kassie sent these men, via Victoria, she remembered her promise not to give up. He felt the pride for his woman build up in his chest. Kassie held out hope for him. Sophia Winters, his mom, wished for someone of Kassie's qualities as Chase's wife. He couldn't help but think how happy his parents would be knowing Kassie was at his side.

Saint entered the camp area first. Going directly to Leo, Saint explained what they had learned. A few minutes later Chase led the group of men into the camp. Aleski ordered watches, and before the team blinked, the Russians set up camp, made them a meal, and passed around vodka like water. Shadow slipped out of camp to scout the area.

Liev approached Chase as Leo patched Chase's arm and checked the knot on the back of his head. "Doc, ya gotta stop hitting your head. You already gave yourself one concussion not long ago when you wrestled the tree branch."

"What about you?" Chase gritted his teeth. Leo wasn't known for his patience or nursing skills.

"Stop whining, it's a scratch. I skinned knees worse than this." Leo prodded. Chase knew Leo still suffered from migraines occasionally and guessed the leader didn't want his weakness known.

"Liev, explain this to me again. How is Victoria Stanton

Keeping Kassie

alive, and why did Ivan send you to locate us?" Leo questioned.

Liev poked the fire. The two leaders faced off. Leo trying to get all the facts and Liev determined to prove he didn't answer to Leo.

"Ivan Rostova ordered us to find you, your bodies, or something even if it required us to swim in the fucking ocean. We picked up your trail after your altercation with the village bullies. I see you brought a pet with you. Liev jerked his head in Ahmet's direction.

"Leave him alone. He's with us," Leo demanded.

"I'm wondering how you plan to get him into the US?" Leiv gave the fire a few more cursory pokes with the stick.

"We're attempting to get him to his niece since our original plan failed. We ran into a few unfriendlies out here. It's taken us longer than expected," Leo explained.

"We have orders to escort you to the nearest country which can get you home. We can take you back to Russia and get you on the next flight home. Your comrades display many injuries. It will slow us down. But we can provide security, we have food and numbers," Liev assured Leo.

"Do you have a phone?" Chase asked.

"Yes, I have a sat phone. I have orders to only let you speak to Ivan. He'll instruct me from there," Liev wasn't budging.

"Fine. Let's go make the call. Doc, you want to come with since Kassie is somehow involved?"

The men went to the tent and Liev spoke Russian, sized up Leo, and laughed. Chase figured they all appeared pretty pathetic at this point. They survived the helo crash in the ocean by some miracle. Hid out in a cave, found Ahmet, ran from unfriendlies and any one of the team members fantasized for a nice steak dinner instead of lamb. Beggers couldn't be choosers and it kept them alive.

"This is Leo." Leo spoke on the phone. He listened while he stroked his chin. Nodding his head now and then. "What about Kassie and Emma?"

Chase moved closer to the phone to try to hear what this man told Leo. His heart pounded in his chest at the worried tone in his voice.

"How many men? What about my men? I see. The family?" Leo interrogated the man on the other end of the line.

"Can we speak with Kassie? I see." He shook his head negatively at Chase and held up one finger to indicate he needed to wait.

"Leave Matthew on security. He's good. Ok, I'll check in tomorrow." Leo hung up the phone.

Turning to Chase, he frowned. "May I use your tent for a few moments?" Leo addressed Liev, who didn't bother to reply as he walked out.

"Stanton tried to snatch Emma. Victoria Stanton pretended to be dead. She's the one who sent us the information on where to find Kassie in the tunnel. They stopped the kidnapping. Matthew kept Kassie and Emma safe as they surrounded them. Ivan's men came in from behind. He said Matthew pulled Kassie and Emma out of the car while Michael distracted Stanton's men. Victoria and Ivan found them after they disposed of the assholes." Leo gave him a condensed version.

"I need to get home, Leo. The bastard can't have my girls." Chase felt the rage build up in him.

"Listen to me. Ivan has teams circling the mountain. Matthew set up some electronic security system from the top of the mountain all the way to the bottom. Some of Ivan's team integrated with the construction workers. A squirrel can't fart on the mountain without someone knowing about it," Leo tried to talk down the now stressed Chase.

"She and Emma are defenseless. We need to get back there." Chase raked his hand through his hair. How could he protect them when they were stuck halfway around the world? This mission wasn't supposed to last this long.

Leo winced as he delivered the bad news. "Jake gave our packets to Kassie. She's headed to Alabama with Victoria and a contingent of men. Maddie and Joe kept Emma at the cabin. Matthew stayed with her."

"Kassie's off the mountain? Damn it!" Chase stopped. "She thinks we're dead."

"Ivan said Kassie and Emma are holding up fine. She asked Victoria to search for us. We'll get more details. Ivan says he isn't informing them of finding us. He's hoping it will make Stanton crawl out of his hiding place. He assures me Victoria has them secured. They've even switched planes at the last minute, no one knows where they leave or come back from," Leo offered.

Chase didn't like it. His fists clenched as he thought of Stanton going after Kassie and his Ladybug, his jaw ticked. "Do we trust them enough to care for our family?"

Leo nodded. "I don't trust anyone but our team. Ivan's getting Matthew and will call us back. Then we'll go from there."

❄

LIEV GAVE the men the tent and left the phone. "Keep conversations to a minimum and we leave at daylight."

An hour later, the phone rang. Leo answered. "Leo"

Chase heard Matthew talking.

"Chase is here with me now." Leo handed over the phone.

"Doc," Chase answered gruffly, steeling himself for whatever Matthew Cartwright said.

"Don't worry about Kassie. Listen, we have things covered here. The girls will be ecstatic to learn you're safe. Get home and don't get your ass killed," Matthew Cartwright ordered.

"Don't tell her yet." Chase swallowed the lump in his throat. "Anything can happen between now and us getting back. I texted her before we left telling her I was coming home and then the helo crashed. I don't want to get her hopes up."

"Understood. If she ever finds out about this conversation. You're taking the blame," Matthew bantered.

"Take care of my girls 'till I get home and thank you for protecting them from Stanton." Chase gratefully replied. The click on the line let him know Matthew hung up.

"Leo, what's the SITREP?"

Leo slapped Chase on the shoulder. "Let's get the team. We need to get Ahmet's niece. Ivan will keep them in Russia until they can get them to the United States legally. They have lawyers and will have a safe place to stay. It's on the way to Russia, we won't lose any time."

"What are we waiting for then? Let's go home." Chase sighed.

"I couldn't agree more" Leo slapped him on the back. "Let's go tell the team."

CHAPTER TWENTY-FOUR

A bone-tired Kassie sighed as the plane took off. Between the training with Victoria, spending time with Em, and making changes for two cabins to be wheelchair accessible and ordering everything for the three completed cabins, she lacked even a moment to herself. Now heading to Saint's memorial, she needed to go through his packet. While an honor, the last wishes of these men drained her emotionally. How could she say goodbye to Chase's team members but not Chase? She struggled to keep her faith but as the days moved on, she felt it waver. Kassie headed to the table with the envelope. Resting her head on the back of the seat, she closed her eyes and prayed she was doing right by all of them.

Slipping the contents on the table, she found copies of his life insurance, a letter to his mother and one to her. The same list all the team members filled out with instructions on their home, belongings, and personal items. Thinking of Saint brought a smile to her face. His deep southern drawl and warm brown eyes always comforted her.

Sliding her finger along the seal, she opened his letter.

Dear Kassie,

It's been such a pleasure to meet you and little Em. I'd like to thank you for showing me love can find a way through anything.

You'll meet my mama, and I can guarantee she's gonna offer you a piece of pecan pie and a glass of sweet tea when you walk in the door. Don't bother to turn it down, she won't hear of it.

I'm putting you in charge of my life insurance money. I have two brothers, one died in a car accident, and one lives near mama. If he knows she has the insurance money, there's no other way to say it, he'll bleed her dry.

My mama worked hard to raise three boys when her husband left her. She's worked all her life and has nothing to show for it. She gave up everything to make a life for us. Please make sure this money helps her to retire and to do what she loves. She loves to bake and cook. Tell her to keep making those delicious pies for me. There's enough there to pay off the house and if she needs anything, she can come to you. You have a good head on your shoulders, and y'all will get along just fine.

I got my nickname from her. She addressed all my letters when I enlisted to my darling Saint. Man, did I get ribbed for that. But *those boys didn't complain none when she included tins of homemade pecan bars and treats for us. Make sure she knows I love her and I'm doing this so she can enjoy her life. Tell her it's time.*

Thank you, Miss Kassie. May God bless you and Ladybug.
Saint

KASSIE SWIPED her eyes as she put away the documents. She set them to the side as Victoria slid into the seat opposite her at the table.

"You're tired, Luv. You need a nap." Victoria suggested as she watched Kassie dab her eyes.

"Maybe I wouldn't be exhausted if I wasn't woken up at three this morning with a knife to my throat." Still cranky, Kassie felt pissed from the morning surprise.

"You asked me to help you learn to defend yourself." Victoria's eyebrow arched as she challenged her.

Kassie huffed. "Honestly, I live in a cabin which is locked up like Fort Knox. Matthew, Michael, and Jameson stay with us, and your entourage of men. I don't think a snake could slither into the cabin without one of you knowing."

"Kassie," Victoria reprimanded gently. "Will you or Emma always be on Serenity Mountain? Will you never go on trips, shopping, school field trips?"

"No." Kassie groused. "I wasn't expecting to be woken up with a knife to my throat. Especially when I'm headed to Saint's service."

"Do you think Stanton's men will care if it's a holiday, or

a vacation if they go after you?" Victoria prodded, trying to get Kassie to see her side of things.

"You've made your point. I have a problem with knives at my throat. It hits too close to home." Kassie softly admitted.

"Ah. Luv, let me tell you something. You can be afraid of all these things because I know how scary they are. Or you stand up to the bully who terrified you of all those things," Victoria advised.

Kassie squinted out the window at the billowy clouds. "I'm not as strong as you are, Victoria." She turned her attention back to the woman when Victoria didn't respond.

"You are, Luv. You kept a promise to your sister when you didn't know who James Stanton was. Do you realize he's killed cartel members for more territory? These ruthless men who create evil in this world, don't take security lightly. They see and know everything about an opponent before entering a room. You, my darling, so innocent and naïve of the world, bested James Stanton for three years. You shot Roger Chapman after he tortured you nearly to death. You even held me and Ivan up and protected Emma. You don't give yourself any credit," Victoria outlined why she disagreed with Kassie.

"Ha!" Kassie loudly exclaimed causing everyone on the plane to turn. She narrowed her eyes. "You and I both know after all this training you've done with me, you purposely didn't take the gun."

Victoria giggled. "You looked utterly ridiculous. Your stance was completely off. Is that how your American Army man taught you? You let Ivan get too far ahead. You even took the time to correct your daughter, while holding us at gunpoint."

"It's not funny." Kassie tried to contain her composure but thinking back to the day Victoria saved them made her laugh. Ivan and Victoria worked with her on balance, weapons, and gaining strength emotionally, mentally, and physically. "Chase isn't an Army man, he's a Navy doctor."

Victoria shook her head, "Same difference. Why do you have to always complicate things?"

Kassie snickered. "In America, the branches of the military matter greatly to the people who serve. They believe their branch of the military is better than the others. Victoria, you're an American. How do you not know this?"

Victoria assessed the people on the plane and leaned over the table as if to tell her a big secret. "I never needed the military. I have my own army." She smiled broadly at Kassie.

Kassie face palmed herself. "Sometimes you make me forget who I'm talking to. If you explained to me a year ago that I'd be in love with the most wonderful man, live in a cabin with my family close, and work with two heads of a mafia family, I would've laughed in your face."

"I give you my word once we're done. James Stanton and his enemies will never whisper your name or Em's again. You can live happily on your mountain."

Kassie dropped her chin and lowered her voice. "Now I need to find Chase." Agony echoed in her voice as she spoke.

"I once thought my love died. He searched for me for years. He refused to believe I was dead and buried. He didn't give up. He kept his faith. Sometimes that's all we have. Don't give up easily. Until you find the answer you seek, one way or another, remain strong."

Kassie smiled warily and shifted in her seat. With each passing day it got harder to believe Chase would make it home.

CHAPTER TWENTY-FIVE

The rain pelted the team as they deboarded the plane and helped get the injured into the vehicles lined up waiting for them. Chase breathed a sigh of relief. The team reunited Ahmet with his niece and flew to Russia with them and Ivan's men.

Liev ordered three doctors to be ready as the vehicles pulled into a large, gated estate. Exhaustion dragged their feet as Ahmet and his niece followed a servant to their rooms. In a separate wing, men carried Taco and Ash for x-rays. A doctor attended to Shadow's wound by giving him pain meds and IV antibiotics. Other medical personnel treated Saint's and Chase's wounds. A doctor examined Whiskey in a separate room for PTSD and aided him in taking his first shower in three long years. After seeing his men cared for, Leo finally consented to be examined. Chase's guess at a concussion proved correct.

Taco, Ash, Whiskey and Shadow stayed in the medical suite, while the others went to their rooms. A phone sat on the bedside table tempting Chase to call Kassie. Their mission took six weeks and then they strived to get home for a little over two months. Chase longed to hear her voice. The fact they weren't on home soil kept him from reaching out for the connection to Kassie. Anything could go wrong. He needed to see her and hold her in his arms, feeling her body pressed next to his. A knock on the door distracted him from the temptation.

Leo walked into Chase's room. A bottle of vodka in one hand and two glasses in the other. Setting the libation on the table, Leo sat and raised an eyebrow in question to Chase as he poured a liberal amount in each glass. Chase nodded and took a seat.

Raising his glass, Leo toasted, "To going home."

Chase raised his glass and downed the strong drink. Letting the warmth fill his gut, Chase regarded his friend. Knowing they all needed showers, shaves, and a full night's rest, the fact Leo sat in his room meant he needed to talk.

After the third shot. Chase put his hand over his glass. Leo poured another drink and set the bottle aside.

"I don't know what to do. Whiskey doesn't remember shit. Ash's face reminds me of a meat grinder, and he's lost weight, but he hasn't said a word. I've caught him leering at me when he didn't think I was paying attention." Leo sipped on the vodka. His head fell back against the chair.

"I'm sorry you didn't find Olaf. I'm sure you're disappointed. Will you tell me what you're thinking or do I have to guess?" Chase waited for Leo to settle his thoughts.

"When I took Emma and went into hiding," Leo paused. "I thought I got through to Kit Kat—Catherine. Then when the kidnapping occurred, and we stayed in Corpus Christie, a switch seemed to flip. When I sent her home with Melody, she backed off and became cold toward me again. Any progress made on the run completely disappeared into thin air." Leo swirled the liquid as his finger traced along the edge of the glass.

"I assumed we could take back the future my mistake deprived us of. Now Ash is alive. I don't know if I can watch them together. It crushed her, the day I informed her Ash died. I won't deny her the chance to have her family back. I owe it to my teammate to take a step back and let him claim his woman. This was my fault. Damn it. It hurts like hell." Leo took the last swig of his drink as he rubbed his chest.

"Don't you think Catherine has a say? Why don't you wait until we all get home and see how the dust settles? Who can say Catherine hasn't changed? Three years changed Catherine and Ash. It's a damn long time and feelings change," Chase offered.

Leo turned his watery blood shot eyes toward his friend. "Would your feelings go away if you stayed separated from Kassie?"

Chase remained silent. His love for Kassie was never-ending.

"That's what I thought," Leo stated. He rested his elbows on his knees. "I dated her for three years. I asked her to be my wife. I fucked up on the mission, she refused to forgive me, and we broke up. Two months later she married Ash and announced they were expecting a baby. They were inseparable. It killed me to see his hands on her. But I stuck it out because I screwed it all up. Kit Kat never forgave me. Ash stepped in and she found the love of her life. Now I sit in purgatory watching them together again."

Chase gripped Leo's shoulder, "Don't jump the gun. You don't know what will happen when you get back. You don't know what Whiskey and Ash have experienced. Catherine's made a new life for her family. You hounded me about Kassie. I think you need to get stateside and discuss it with her. Don't make assumptions. Lay your cards on the table. Kassie and I shared the same mistakes. I didn't communicate with her. She assumed I'd let her go because she can't have kids after what that asshole put her through. You know I'd go through hell for her. Ladybug is already mine. We have a family and if we decide on more, they don't need to have my blood running through their veins to be mine."

Leo ran his hand through his overgrown beard. "I need to talk to Ash and figure out what happened. He disappeared from another team. Reliable sources told me he died. How did he end up in the same camp as Whiskey and neither of them knowing?"

"No. What you need is to take a hot shower, shave and get some sleep. Once we've all gotten some rest, then you can talk to him. Did you need to contact Agent Rhodes?"

"Yeah. I wrestled all day trying to figure out how to tell her we were saved by the mafia. I debated whether I should get us to a base and then contact her. The last thing we need is to come under the scrutiny of the government for having contacts with the Russian mob."

Chase nodded his agreement. He wanted to get the full story from Kassie before making any judgements. After all, he was grateful the team received assistance and good medical care from the professional staff.

"Go shit, shower and shave, Leo. We survived hell and won. I'll check on our men. There's no need for you to rush back. You need to rest the rock you consider your brain. I mean it," Chase ordered.

"Saint is already showered and sleeping, he said if you can cover the men for a few hours, he'll relieve you," Leo stated.

"Sounds good. Leo. Don't do anything stupid. Get stateside and wait until you can think clearer before making any decisions." Chase warned.

"I hear you. I'll head back." Leo stood and made his way to the door. "Thanks for saving our asses out there." The door closed behind him.

Chase headed to the bathroom and went through the toiletries on the sink. He stared at his reflection in the mirror. His blood shot eyes, the scraggly beard and weathered skin made him appear rough and haggard. His thoughts returned to Kassie. He ached to call her and let her know he survived. Matthew gave his word Kassie held up better than they gave her credit for. The discord between the two men, because of Kassie, eased. Chase owed Matthew a debt of gratitude for protecting his girls when he couldn't. Chase didn't want his first conversation with Kassie to be over the phone. He wanted to smell the lavender shampoo in her hair as he ran his fingers through the wavy tresses, to kiss those full lips and taste her. The eyes in the mirror sparked back to life. Even his soul knew where he belonged. He needed to get back to the mountain, to his home and his love.

CHAPTER TWENTY-SIX

Saint's family held his memorial in an old wooden church in the middle of the country outside of Montgomery, Alabama. Fields of cotton and soybeans surrounded the area. Everyone in the small community showed up to support Edie Johnson, Saint's mother. Kassie and her friends settled in the back. When the service finished, Mrs. Johnson rose from the well-worn pew and took the picture of Saint in uniform from the easel and hugged it to her chest as she made her way down the aisle.

At the sight of Kassie, the woman stopped and took Kassie's hand in hers. "Thank you for coming. Please stay and join us for dinner. The church ladies have been cookin' up a storm."

Kassie smiled "We'll join you."

As one of the last to leave the church, the mourners in front of her surprised Kassie as they began unpacking their cars and trucks. Men pulled out tables and chairs while the women covered them with sheets. They worked together setting up everything. A group of men on the side of the church tended to big vats of boiling cooking grease and other men pulled large coolers from the beds of their trucks. Kassie's friends scattered and each lent a helping hand. An older woman put Kassie in charge of silverware and plates. Victoria oversaw setting up the children's table. Victoria's men helped with the large coolers. Gallon jugs of sweet tea, lemonade and water lined one table. Another surface held pecan, apple, cherry, and blackberry pies, and cookies. Red velvet, chocolate fudge, and mandarin orange cakes cut into slices, lay under a mosquito net. Big bowls appeared on the long table. A typical southern menu sat before them. Collard greens, fresh corn, cornbread, blackeyed-peas, baked beans, fried okra, and a selection of salads graced the table family style. A loud whistle pierced the air. Two young men started bringing over metal trays filled with fried catfish, fried chicken and hush puppies. Women collected the children to sit at their assigned table as another group helped the elderly get seated and served. Saint's mom sat at the head of the long community banquet. Smiling, she motioned for Kassie and her friends to join them to her right while her son sat on her left.

The preacher quieted the crowd down. "Lord, we ask you to bless this food we've prepared in honor of Carter "Saint" Johnson. May God bless his soul. We ask you to watch over his kin and friends during their grief. Carter was a good man and an amazing son. We thank you for the time to cherish him and the opportunity to reap the blessings he brought to this community."

A chorus of amens followed. Dishes passed along the table and stories of Saint echoed in the fresh country air. Laughter, tears, and hugs filled the day.

As people drifted off, Kassie and the others helped clean up. Saying goodbye to the last of the guests, Mrs. Johnson approached Kassie.

Keeping Kassie

"Come sit with me, child." She took Kassie's hand and led her to a couple of chairs. "Raymond!" she shouted. "Bring us a glass of sweet tea and a piece of pecan pie."

Kassie cracked a smile. Saint guessed correctly about the pecan pie and sweet tea.

"Mrs. Johnson, it's a pleasure to meet you. Saint holds a special place in my heart. He saved me and my daughter, and I wanted to pay my respects."

"Saint sent pictures of you and your lovely child. He talked about how proud he felt to serve on the team and helpin' y'all. I'm grateful you made it."

"Mrs. Johnson, I know today was tiring. Saint left instructions with me to carry out and I wondered if we could speak privately at your home?" Kassie asked gently.

"Of course. The church ladies have baked enough casseroles for a month, and we have enough leftovers for supper. Why don't you pop in at about six? We can freshen up and take a bit of a rest. Please call me Edie, child. I feel like we're family."

❋

AT PRECISELY SIX. Kassie knocked on the door to Saint's boyhood home. A younger version of Saint answered the door.

"Are you the lady who has Saint's stuff?" He didn't waste any time getting to the point.

Kassie's shoulder's straightened and she set her eyes on the young man before her. "I'm here to speak privately with Ms. Johnson," She steely replied to the rude greeting.

"Mama, Mrs. Stanton's here," he called upstairs.

Showing Kassie and Michael to the living room to have a seat, Saint's brother sat across from them.

CASSIE COLTON

"You know my mama's pretty torn up about Saint. His funeral cost a fortune and I don't know how she's gonna make ends meet this month. Saint sent her a monthly check. Do you know if he left her any life insurance money? She's getting older and I'm kinda worried about her staying alone. I think she'd do better in a retirement home with her friends. It costs money. Something she doesn't have enough of."

Kassie gripped her purse, narrowed her eyes, and clamped her mouth shut to keep from telling him what she considered Edie's problem was. A glance at Michael confirmed he was on the same page. His fist balled up in his cupped hand and like the rest of the team, his jaw ticked, the only indication Michael was attempting to control himself.

Edie came down the stairs. A smile lit up her face at seeing Kassie and Michael. Her eyebrows knitted into a stern warning as her eyes settled on her son. "Miss Kassie, this is my youngest son, Theo."

Kassie stiffly nodded her head.

"Theo, go get some sweet tea for our guests, and I already got food warming in the oven." Edie turned to her son, who didn't budge from his chair.

"I wanted to hear what Mrs. Stanton has to say, Mama. Saint wanted me to take care of you if anything happened. I have a right to be here," Theo stated.

Kassie barely tolerated the smug face Theo made in her direction.

"We could use some sweet tea, Miss Edie. Michael told me how parched he was. We aren't used to the humidity here." Kassie backed up the older woman.

Edie gave Theo the "mom look". "Theo, our guests

requested some tea," Edie smiled sweetly yet her voice held a warning to her son.

Theo jerked up from the chair and stomped into the kitchen. Michael and Kassie made small talk until Theo returned and loudly set four glasses of tea on the table. He began to take a seat when Kassie interrupted him.

"I'm sorry Theo. Saint left me with some very personal instructions for your mother," Kassie explained.

Theo waited for his mother to insist upon him staying. When she sat back in her chair and clasped her hands together as if she had all the time in the world, Theo got the message. His invitation to stay wasn't forthcoming.

A sly smile appeared. "Whatever you say to her, she'll be repeating to me when y'all leave. I found you on the computer when we got home. How much money you gonna give mama?" By the way Theo smiled, Kassie knew exactly what he had discovered.

Edie's flabbergasted body rose from the chair. "Theo Johnson! You'll not disrespect me or my guests in my own house!"

Theo leered like a hungry wolf. Without a doubt he saw the naked pictures of Kassie as soon as he did the internet search. She should be used to this, but it still rankled.

"Theo, you're right. I'm here to tell your mother Saint decided to pay off her home. Any other needs your mother has, will be handled through a trust. From time to time, the trust will make welfare checks to make sure all funds go directly to Ms. Edie's care and well-being."

Theo's chest puffed out. His hands clenched into fists. "What did Saint leave me?"

"Saint left you some sage advice. He said stop mooching off your mother and get a job," Michael blandly stated.

Kassie's hand flew to cover her mouth to disguise the

laughter that threatened as Theo stomped out the front door, clearly mad and embarrassed.

"I'm so...sorry, Ms. Edie I meant no disrespect," Michael apologized.

Silence echoed uncomfortably around the room until Edie Johnson started to giggle. The giggle grew to laughter as she slapped Michael on the knee.

"It's been too long since a man entered this house and Theo needed to be put down a peg. No need to apologize, he may be the youngest but there ain't any sense in that poor boy's head. Saint promised to come visit me after he returned. I hoped he'd help with Theo and well...come on to the kitchen while I get us some food. Then we'll sit and you can tell me what my baby did. Ain't no mother been so blessed than I was when my Saint came into this world." Edie brought them into the sunny yellow kitchen. A small wooden table sat in front of a big bay window, and something smelled amazing coming from the oven. Edie motioned for them to take a seat as she served supper.

Kassie sat back in the chair, completely stuffed. Edie Johnson baked one mean pecan pie. Between the pie and tea, she debated how fast someone entered into a sugar coma. People in the south took their tea seriously.

"Edie, Saint left a packet with instructions. I wasn't lying when I said he has enough money to pay off your home and he's left you a letter. I'm supposed to tell you it's time to enjoy yourself. You've worked hard and it's time. He put me in charge of the rest of the funds. Is there anything you need?" She put her head down struggling on how to break the news to Edie that Saint feared Theo would take advantage of her.

Edie pulled tissues from her pockets and blew her nose. Another dabbed her tears. "So, I don't get any money?"

Keeping Kassie

Kassie hastened to assure Edie her son left her well provided for, "Yes, you have money. Saint wanted to make sure it went to you. No one else."

Edie Johnson bit her lip. "No one else?"

"I'm sorry, Edie. Saint left clear instructions. I can use the money for you and not your son," Kassie informed her.

The older woman debated for a moment as she dabbed at her eyes. "If I have a need, I can ask you?"

"Yes," Kassie reassured her.

"I asked Saint to come home some months ago. He promised to return after he completed a job watching over you and your family. I urged him to come as soon as possible. It was important."

Kassie held Edie's hand. "Do you need help? Your son protected me. I'm the reason he didn't return home. I'll do my best to help you."

Edie let out a deep sigh. "It's not me that needs helpin'. I recently discovered I might be a grandmother."

"Oh, you must be thrilled. When is the baby due?" Kassie asked.

"Well, that's what I needed to talk to Saint about. I reckon I'm gonna need some help with this and I can't count on Theo. You see, Saint married Clarissa a long time ago."

"Saint was married!" Kassie exclaimed. "I didn't know!"

"No, honey. He divorced Clarissa ages ago. They married right outta high school. They seemed happy together and about six years ago Clarissa was involved in a terrible car accident. Saint came home and tended to her until he needed to return. He enlisted in the Navy to ensure their future. Unfortunately, Clarissa got hooked on pain medication and by the time Saint came home again, she sought stronger drugs. He placed her into a rehab, and she tried to stay clean the first six months."

Kassie sensed that Edie's story didn't end in a favorable outcome. As a nurse, she treated drug addicts and knew the struggle they faced daily. Kassie allowed Edie to tell her story without interrupting or asking questions.

"Saint asked me to let her live here. He made sure to call or write when he deployed. The next time he came home, Clarissa seemed good. Then she started skipping Sunday dinners, not attending church, and missing meetings. She didn't come home until late at night or sometimes not at all. I expressed my concerns to my son."

Michael sighed. He knew what was coming.

"When he came home, they fought like cats and dogs. She accused him of moving her here so I could report back to him. He only wanted her to have a support system. She left the next day. He located her and spent his month at home caring for her. Things settled down but she refused to move back here. Saint set her up in her own apartment. She refused to answer my calls or the door if I tried to check on her. Then Saint went on a mission and came back badly injured. He stayed in the hospital for a long time. When he finally made it back home, she went missing again. Clarissa cashed his checks for rent, but never paid the landlord. He kicked her out three months after Saint moved her in. She sold everything they owned. Saint spent weeks on the streets searching for her. He brought her back home and admitted her for drug addiction again. Clarissa made it three months. Then one day, Saint got a call from Leo, and he flew out to Seattle. He came home ready for a fresh start. I saw the hope in his eyes. He prayed it would help Clarissa. That night she disappeared again. Saint hired a private investigator to find her. Saint begged her to go with him. She wouldn't hear a word of it. He divorced her six months later."

Keeping Kassie

"It must've devastated, Saint." Kassie commented. She wished she could put her arms around Saint and give him one more hug.

"It did. She told him his injuries made him half a man. Clarissa said some mighty ugly things and he'd been nothing but good to her. About six months ago, I drove to Montgomery for a doctor's appointment. I saw her on the street and hardly recognized her. I tried to convince her to come home with me. She asked for money. When I refused, she brought out a little girl and told me I wasn't refusing her but my granddaughter. To be honest, Clarissa lied a ton. One look at the child and I emptied my purse out right then and there. I called Saint and asked him to come home. Since the accident, I hired the same investigator, and he says she's living in a run-down old warehouse in downtown Montgomery."

"Where is she?" Kassie wasted no time taking her dishes to the sink and clearing the kitchen. Michael helped knowing Kassie refused to let Saint's child suffer under those conditions.

"Honey, you can't go down there. Montgomery has some unsavory areas. They'd eat up a little bitty thing like you."

"I won't be going alone. Do you want custody of her if I bring her to you?" Kassie already made a mental list of lawyers Joe kept on retainer, a rehab center Clarissa could enter, and she texted Victoria.

"That's why I needed Saint. I can't take her. I have some medical problems and my age plays a huge factor. The state would never award custody to me. Theo would be the only one who could take her. I'm afraid he'd only do it if it came with money. Instead of paying off my house, can you give the money to him for her care?"

Kassie shook her head. "No. I'm sorry Edie. Saint made

his instructions clear. Your son saved my life. Emma and she would be about the same age. I can take her home with me. How do you feel about relocating? I can get you the best medical care and you can get to know your granddaughter. Even if she proves to not be Saint's, I'll make sure she has a home. If you don't want to uproot yourself, I'll make sure she comes to visit often."

Edie openly cried. "I knew you were good people. I'll do whatever I can. Theo needs to learn to be a man and it'll probably help if I'm not here to help him grow up. If you can help find Saint's baby, I'll do whatever I need to do."

Kassie rose from the table. "I'm sorry Edie. I need to make some calls. I need the name of the investigator you hired. I'll keep you posted as soon as I know something."

Michael patted Edie's arm as he walked out the door with a very determined Kassie.

CHAPTER TWENTY-SEVEN

Leo waited for Chase to examine the men. "So, what's the verdict, Doc?"

Chase read the chart. "Whiskey's vitals stabilized. Taco will be in a cast for a few more weeks. Ash's face went down, his nose is set, and his jaw needs to heal for at least another four to six weeks. Shadow's responding to the antibiotics."

"So?"

"It's time for us to get our asses back home," Chase grinned. "Whiskey's injuries still need supervision, Leo. He's got severe PTSD and insists he doesn't want to see Samantha yet. Ash needs counseling as well. I've observed him in his sleep, he has demons. We can use Ole' man Davis's cabin. There's four bedrooms. We can put Taco and Shadow up at my cabin. Saint has volunteered to stay with Ash and Whiskey. I'm assuming you'll want to be there too. I can assign Claire to start counseling, and I can check in on them daily. I don't know how you want to handle keeping them a secret." Chase waited as he watched Leo pace.

Leo ran his hand through his hair and sat in the black

leather chair next to him. Chase knew by Saint's posture he waited for Leo's directive. Saint anxiously awaited the clearance to get home, he worried about his mother.

"Saint, what's your thinking?" Leo jumped up and started pacing again. Saint twirled the toothpick in his mouth as he watched his leader hesitate.

"I say, it's their decision. I vote you let Claire assess them. She's qualified to determine what they need mentally and emotionally. I understand the guy's concerns of returning to their wives. First the shock of them returning from the dead. Then there are the children involved. The situation needs delicate handling. I'm unsure if I, personally, would want to meet my wife until I was assured I was stable enough to be around her. We dealt with PTSD issues after missions, and they are poster children for it. They might need some time to adapt back into society." Saint reminded Leo.

"That's a good idea. Where the hell is Liev? He's taking us to Germany. We'll fly home from there. We'll have to keep our association with these guys on the down low. I need to come up with a story on how we got out of the Caspian and to Germany. Ahmet and his niece have all the paperwork needed for visas into the US. Do you think you can help him with a job at the hospital? Agent Rhodes called in favors and will help them with visas. She left instructions for us to contact her as we leave for Germany. She'll arrange everything from there," Leo thought out loud.

"I'll go find Liev. What time should I tell him to be ready to go?" Saint stood and headed to the door.

"Doc?" Leo questioned.

"I can have the guys ready to go in an hour," Chase responded.

Leo smiled broadly, "Let's roll. It's time to go home."

Keeping Kassie

❄

Two hours later, the team loaded the plane. Chase secured Whiskey and made Taco comfortable with extra pillows for his leg. Shadow reclined in his seat and a small snore escaped every now and again. Leo sat at the small table writing his report.

Agent Rebecca Rhodes quietly planned for them to meet at a small private airport. Whiskey and Ash needed to be debriefed at some point. After hearing the state of both men, Rebecca volunteered to fly out personally to Serenity.

The trip required a couple of days before they'd make it stateside. Chase sat back in the leather seat and closed his eyes. His body hummed in anticipation of seeing Kassie. He never wanted to let her go again. A smile spread on his face. He knew what he wanted to do as soon as he got home. Making love to his woman was on the top of his list. Ladybug would also be ensconced in the pink room he painted for her. He knew Joe and Maddie would offer to take Em home with them for the evening, but he didn't want her going anywhere. Jake might even spend the night. He wanted all his family under his roof. His dreams for the mountain were slowly becoming a reality.

CHAPTER TWENTY-EIGHT

Homeless people scattered throughout the parking lot. People huddled around fire barrels. Some sold drugs, others attempted to cook over the heat. Kassie's heart fell in despair as her nurse's mind went to work thinking of different services available to lend a hand. Her attention drifted to the picture she carried of Saint's ex-wife in her hand. Edie gave her a description of the little girl.

"Kassie, did you take time to consider all of this? Caring for a child isn't like taking a puppy home. You already have Emma, the hospital, you wanted to go back to school, complete the set up the juvenile unit, and you're still in counseling and healing from what happened to you," Michael's concern radiated off him as he watched for danger as they walked deeper into the crowd.

Silently, Kassie scanned the crowd in hopes of spotting Clarissa and any potential threats at the same time. Victoria's training kicked in. This wasn't practice, it was reality. Getting injured didn't fit into her plans.

Keeping Kassie

Kassie glanced at Michael. "It's Saint's child. There's no way I can live with myself knowing she's here. It's the least I can do." Yanking the heavy metal door open, Kassie walked into the large building. Old blankets, sheets, and clothes divided the structure into rooms. The stench of sweat, urine, and drugs filled the air as they strolled each section. Drug addicts shot up and occasionally a mentally challenged person talked to themselves or yelled at others. Most steered clear of the trio, knowing by the sight of them, they didn't belong.

Kassie started to grab the railing of the stairs leading to the next floor when Michael's hand reached out. "Don't touch the railings. Let me go first, you stay in the middle, Victoria will have our backs."

Urine stained the floor, and their shoes adhered to the sticky and wet surface as they walked. The stench grew stronger the further into the building they walked. Kassie knew Michael wasn't happy about coming here. He struggled with the need to help a child, but as Chase's friend, she knew her safety concerned him the most.

Outside of Victoria and Ivan, no one had witnessed her newfound fighting skills. Of course, she still needed to learn a few things, but she wasn't helpless anymore. Victoria worked on her form and Ivan taught her to fight dirty. Between the two, they provided the skills she needed to survive a fight. Her skills with knife work impressed Ivan. In fact, she hid two on her body as she perused the partitions in search of Clarissa.

A loud noise in the middle of the room caught their attention. Two men fought, and a woman screeched. Kids huddled up in the corners. Older kids showed signs of despair while the younger ones cried. A thin woman in a pair of cutoff shorts and a tank top turned the corner. Kassie increased her pace. When she caught up, she saw the woman wore the same haircoloring as the one in the picture. The long blonde hair hung limp and appeared stringy and dirty. Black and blue needle marks decorated her arms and legs. She wore a pair of dirty flip flops which flapped as she walked to a cornered off section. Kassie followed her in. Michael and Victoria trailed behind her.

"Are you Clarissa Johnson?" Kassie asked sharply.

"Who are you?" The dirty blonde questioned moving closer to Kassie, invading her space.

"My name's Kassie. I've come to offer you help. Where's the child?"

Clarissa laughed, "Did Saint or his old lady send you? You tell that old bitch she's not getting the kid. She didn't even have enough money for me to get food for a week," she complained.

Kassie ignored her. "I need to see Saint's child, where is she?"

Clarissa apparently didn't get the response she wanted and decided to try a new one on Kassie. "How much do ya got? Then maybe, I'll tell ya where she's at."

Kassie stepped closer to the woman. Her face remained impassive. Her shoulders straightened as she stood toe to toe with Clarissa. Her breath wreaked from the rotting teeth and made Kassie want to gag, but she didn't make an outward sign of distress. "Tell me where she is, and I'll help you. I'll provide you with a clean bed, some fresh clothes, and all the food you can eat."

Boxes moved in the corner and a set of tiny eyes peered around them. "I'm hungry, mommy. Can the lady bring me some nuggets?"

Clarissa realized she lost her trump card. She angrily

Keeping Kassie

grabbed the little girl by the arm and tried shoving her behind the boxes. A fruitless endeavor since the trio saw and heard the little girl's plea.

"Get your hands off her," Kassie's sternly warned as the mama bear in her roared.

"It's my kid, I'll do whatever I want, and you can't do shit!" Clarissa wasn't prepared for Kassie to shove her aside onto a heap of blankets while she approached the stacked boxes.

"Hey!" Clarissa screeched as Michael barred her way from reaching Kassie. Grabbing Michael's shirt, she began to get loud until Victoria said something low to her and Clarissa's hand slowly let go and she sat on the blankets.

Kassie knelt at eye level and smiled. "My name's Kassie. What's your name?"

Rage filled Kassie at the fear in the child's eyes.

"I'm not here to hurt you. I'm here to help your mommy and you. You said you like chicken nuggets, I do too. I noticed a restaurant close by that sells them. Maybe we could convince your mama to walk with us and I'll get you some?"

The thin little girl stared as if Kassie offered her the world. Kassie noticed the child bore Saint's warm brown eyes.

"Let me see if your mommy will come with me and we can talk while you eat." Kassie turned to the woman sitting in the heap. "If you cooperate, I'll buy you a hot meal and we can talk."

Jumping up, Clarissa walked over to her daughter and yanked her from the boxes making them drop to the floor.

"I want fifty bucks now and fifty bucks when we're ready to leave, plus the food you promised the kid."

"Done. Let's go." Kassie handed her the money and

walked out of the miserable section and started down the stairs. She knew Michael followed behind Clarissa and her daughter and Victoria guarded their backs.

"McDuff's is that way." The girl offered as she pointed to the right.

Kassie turned in the direction of the fast-food chain. She held the door open allowing Clarissa and her daughter to go in first. Now seeing the state of the child in the light, she knew the situation was dire. The disgruntled manager of the store came forward.

"We serve paying customers only," he warned.

Kassie waved dismissively toward the employee, kneeled and softly whispered, "I have a daughter about your age. She likes apple slices with her meal. What do you like?"

"Just nuggets," the dirty little girl responded as she gawked at the sight of an ice cream cone.

Kassie followed her gaze and laughed. "How about I get you chicken nuggets and apple slices. If you eat them and tell me your name, I'll get you an ice cream cone."

"My name's Miya," the girl answered.

"Clarissa, please place your order. Get whatever you want to eat." Kassie assessed Miya as she did patients admitted to her care. Her clothes reeked and were as dirty as her little body. The shirt hung loosely like a dress on her tiny frame; two sizes too large. Her hair tangled around her head in knots. Miya's bones jutted out in several places, alerting Kassie to the fact the child was underweight and malnourished. The filthy tennis shoes contained gaping holes and missing one lace. Her skin carried several bug bites on her legs. Kassie's blood pressure spiked in anger for Miya's plight.

Michael and Victoria entertained the little girl as Kassie

directed Clarissa to a table across from them. "I'm sorry to tell you Saint's missing from a helicopter crash. He's presumed dead. I want to help you, Clarissa. Saint wanted only the best for you, and I assume he never knew about his daughter. I can help you into a drug rehabilitation center and provide care for Miya."

Clarissa began shaking her head. "I ain't entering no more rehabs. They don't do no good. Did Saint leave me any money?"

"No. Saint didn't bequeath you anything. I have the means to help you start a new life," Kassie offered.

"I know you think you're better than me, but I ain't stupid. You ain't doing this for me, you want his kid." Clarissa sipped at the large chocolate shake she ordered. Kassie noted no food. Clarissa's eyes remained glassy and unfocused. In the fluorescent lighting the needles marks contrasted against her pale white skin in deep black and purple. She smelled rancid. It was evident bathing remained low on Clarissa's priorities.

"I can help both of you," Kassie assured her. "I want to ensure Miya has everything she needs. You're her mother, don't you want her to have food every night and a safe place to sleep?"

Calculating, Clarissa stared at Kassie. "How much you offering for her? You look like you got money. How about a thousand dollars?" Clarissa leaned forward and her eyes calculated Miya's worth in Kassie's eyes. She licked her cracked lips in anticipation of receiving money. Kassie guessed where the funds would be spent.

"I'll take Miya and give you one thousand dollars to start a new life with. I'll check you into a hotel tonight and I'll rent an apartment for you. All payments to the landlord will be made by me to ensure you always have a safe place to sleep. If you sign over custody of Miya to me." Kassie watched Clarissa register the dollar signs as if her eyeballs turned into a Vegas slot machine.

"I want a car," Clarissa demanded.

Kassie nodded to Victoria. Michael brought over the legal document. "Once you kick the drugs and provide me with a valid driver's license. I'll provide you a car."

"How do I know you'll do what you say you're gonna do? You can't have her until I get the money!"

A thud sounded on the table as Kassie slammed a paper bag down in front of Clarissa. "I'll check you into a hotel myself. I'll have one of my men take you to a realtor to rent an apartment. Victoria can have clothes delivered to the hotel tonight and I'll even give you another five hundred if you let the girl leave with me tonight." Clarissa's hand greedily reached for the money. Her tongue slid between her broken teeth like that of a snake.

Kassie snatched the bag away. "You don't get it until you sign over custody. I'll leave you my information and if you ever want to clean up your act and stop doing drugs, the offer will always be there. Miya deserves to have a healthy mama present in her life."

A stunned Clarissa grabbed the pen and scrawled her name on the dotted line. She never looked back at the sweet innocent child scratching her legs.

※

FOUR HOURS LATER, a freshly bathed Miya sat in Kassie's lap as she clung to the windowpane fascinated by her first plane ride. Her eyes grew heavy, and her head went limp on Kassie's shoulder. Kassie picked up her phone and called

Keeping Kassie

Edie to inform her of the whereabouts of her granddaughter and provided her and Joe's contact information concerning her move to Serenity. She placed a call to Bryanna and peppered her with questions concerning Miya's more immediate needs. There were a lot of things she didn't know, but for her new daughter, she committed herself to learning.

CHAPTER TWENTY-NINE

Chase felt as if he was going out of his mind. The flight home detoured due to bad weather in Germany. Rubbing his temples to deter the headache threatening, Chase stared at the phone. He wanted to hear Kassie's voice. But after all the obstacles, he refused to add to her stress. They fought the Caspian Sea, survived their injuries, and now the storm prohibited him from holding his woman sooner.

Matthew contacted Leo. Kassie had boarded her flight and was on her way home from Alabama. Chase paced in the hotel room Ivan had reserved for them. Rebecca Rhodes worked her magic, and all their documents arrived as they landed in Germany. Leo left to inform her they arrived safely.

Whiskey struggled with being back in society. The bumpy flight and the building thunderstorm didn't help. Landing at the airport, crews surrounded them. The large number of people drove Whiskey's anxiety through the roof. Chase gave him meds to help, and he relaxed in the connecting room with Ash.

Keeping Kassie

Ash's reactions presented a conundrum. Chase knew people responded differently to PTSD, but Ash sat quietly with no signs of anxiety whatsoever. His behavior bothered Leo. Ash gave the impression everything was under control.

Leo stepped into the leader role the moment they left the plane. Issuing orders and getting his men settled, Leo excelled at prioritizing their immediate needs. The discussion continued about whether Catherine and Samantha deserved to know about their husbands. Whiskey adamantly refused to consider it. Only when the continual crack of thunder and clash of lightning sent him into a frenzy did he confess to Leo he didn't want to meet his son for the first time as a mere shell of a man. He begged for time to adjust to his current situation. Chase witnessed this time and time again when he worked at the VA hospital. He wasn't surprised by Whiskey's confession.

Chase worked out a patient care plan to help Whiskey. The biggest problem came into play because Samantha now lived in the town below and Kassie considered her one of her best friends. Samantha's strong spirit and opinions warranted them to tread lightly. Chase didn't relish her condemnation when she learned the team kept the information of Whiskey's rescue from her. Pictures hung all over her home and a small shrine showcasing the flag from his funeral graced the entrance. Whiskey's medals were proudly displayed, and he suspected she did it for LJ to remember his father.

Ash wrote on the whiteboard he didn't want to see Catherine yet. He offered no explanation, nor did he even ask about his daughter, Melody. As soon as they arrived at the hotel, they bunkered down in the suite. Leo assigned beds to Taco, Shadow, Whiskey and Ash. Saint used a cot in Taco and Shadow's room and Chase slept on another between Whiskey and Ash. Leo took the small couch in the living area.

Leo stood by the windows engrossed in the traffic of Harrisburg from the shared living quarters. Chase grabbed a bottle of water and joined him.

"Did you decide on calling Kassie?" Leo absently questioned Chase.

Chase noticed Leo's obstructed view caused by the rain coming down in gallons. Yet Leo continued to focus on the scene outside.

"No, I didn't. I don't want her stressed with any delays," Chase responded. "Do you want to talk about it?"

"Yeah. Probably a good call. I'm sure PITA reacted badly when she heard the news about us. It'll be better if you're there," Leo's voice seemed far away as he continued to fixate into the void.

"Did you contact Catherine?" Chase asked.

"There's no reason for me to contact Ash's wife. He's back now. Did you contact Jake or Joe?" Leo attempted to change the subject. Chase knew Leo remained conflicted about Catherine, and Ash's return complicated things.

"Jake wasn't answering his phone. I didn't want to leave a message. Joe's working on the hospital, and I haven't reached him. It goes straight to voicemail, and they don't recognize the number," Chase sighed. "Did you talk to Rebecca?"

"Yeah. She's getting flack in Washington. She'll call me back in a few. Our reunion back home might be delayed another couple of days unless she can figure out a way to stall," Leo responded.

"Damn it," Chase growled his unhappiness. Beyond ready to get home to his girls, the last thing he or the team needed was more bureaucratic red tape. "Why can't they

Keeping Kassie

meet us back at Serenity? We will fly home in another day," Chase grumbled.

"I know. If we want to keep future contracts, it's in our best interest to play their game. I'm sure they attempted to figure out how the Russian mob found us. Ivan's avoided Victoria's name coming up on their radar."

Chase nodded his head. "That's probably wise. I'm not gonna lie, I'm a bit anxious to discover them willing to guard Kassie. Matthew's still on it and I didn't sense any anxiety from his end. I'll feel better once we're stateside and we can find out what the hell happened."

Leo's new phone rang. Glancing down, Leo indicated to Chase "It's Rebecca."

"Leo," he answered the call.

Chase watched as Leo listened intently to Rebecca. Occasionally he nodded his head and grunted his affirmation. It wasn't until Leo grimaced and his eyes slid to Chase, he knew he disliked whatever the agent relayed.

Disconnecting from the call, Leo wasted no time.

"Bad news, we have a layover in Paris tomorrow. Rebecca Rhodes and Julio Hernadez flew in along with some Washington suits. Ivan Rostova will be joining them. Whatever's happening, Rebecca called Julio to meet with them. We'll be delayed another day," Leo explained.

"Shit." Chase finished his water and threw the bottle in recycling.

"One more day and then you can spend a lifetime with the woman you love. Have some patience, at least we aren't baking in the sun and have sand in our ass cracks," Leo tried to lighten the situation. Chase knew Leo's joke showed he was as anxious to return home and get all his own questions answered.

"What time are we bugging out?" Chase asked.

"Oh-six-hundred-hours, go get some shut eye," Leo commanded.

Chase quietly returned to his room. Laying on the cot, Chase tried to kibosh the building frustration. The sooner they were home, the faster the injured men could be settled and healing. Another delay threatened to make things worse for Whiskey and possibly Ash. Selfishly, Chase wanted to be on the mountain he missed over the last few months. He wanted to make love to Kassie and never let her go again.

CHAPTER THIRTY

Kassie called Catherine and Samantha to meet her at the cabin. Maddie ensured the girls were fed, and concern etched her face as she watched her goddaughter clean up the kitchen. She brewed a fresh pot of tea and coffee. Bryanna volunteered to bring some pastries from the shop and would be there by eight-thirty in the morning.

When the doorbell rang, Maddie answered the door letting the women in. After sharing hugs, Kassie indicated they all have a seat in the living room.

"Out with it. You act like you're about to jump out of your skin and I don't know if it's good or bad," Catherine complained. "Did you hear something?"

Kassie sat in the chair in front of the fireplace. "I haven't heard a single thing. I called you here because I need help. Saint's mama will be staying in Old Man Davis's cabin for a while."

Samantha's eyebrows shot up and her eyes widened. "Saint's mother is coming to the mountain. She lives in Alabama, doesn't she?"

"Yes, we have a tiny development. Saint has a daughter. I brought her home with me last night."

Maddie giggled as Samantha and Catherine's mouths dropped open.

Samantha blurted out, "I always knew he played the field. The southern gentleman slang and those big brown eyes and all those muscles—" Samantha exaggerated a shiver going down her body.

"I think we get the picture, Samantha," Maddie interrupted. Her eyes shot upward to the top of the staircase.

The little girl and Emma made their way down the stairs. Each clutching a doll in her hand. Approaching the women in the living room, Em spoke to Miya.

"Come on, Miya! Aunt Cat and Aunt Samantha are here. Where's Melody and LJ? I wanted them to play with us," Emma asked.

Kassie crossed the room and rubbed Miya's back as the little girl peeked around her leg at the women, "This is Miya. She's staying with Em and me."

"She'll be up in a few minutes with her grandma." Catherine assured Emma as she got to Miya's level. "Hello Miya, I'm Melody's mom, you can call me Aunt Cat." She smiled at the little girl.

Samantha bent down. "Hi Miya! LJ stayed the night with his grandparents. I'm Auntie Sam."

"I call her Aunt Cat." Emma pointed to Catherine. "Gran Carol is her mama. This is my gran." Emma clasped Maddie's hand. "My other gran's in heaven, and she watches over me. They can be your grans too."

Miya shyly smiled at the women while she walked next to Emma. She leaned into Em's ear and whispered something.

Emma deemed little Miya her responsibility. Her

Keeping Kassie

eyebrows furrowed as she concentrated on what Miya whispered.

"No Miya, if we're hungry we ask the grown-ups. I have a snack drawer in the pantry and in the refrigerator. Come on, I'll show you, and we can share!"

Emma dragged Miya to the kitchen. Rollo followed in the hopes of a few doggie treats.

Samantha turned to Kassie, "What can we do to help?"

Kassie smiled. She knew her friends wouldn't let her down. The doorbell rang again, Kassie rose, and opened the door for Bryanna. Carrying a basket of goodies, Bryanna stepped into the cabin. Kassie took the basket from her and indicated for her to have a seat in the living room.

A noise from the kitchen stopped the two women. Miya's eyes grew to huge saucers as she saw the basket full of wonderful treats. Emma peeked out from the pantry door.

"Hi Miss Bryanna! Did you bring chocolate chip cookies?" Emma questioned with drool practically running down her mouth.

"Now do you think I trucked all the way up this mountain and forgot to bring a batch of cookies for my favorite girls?" Bryanna laughed.

Miya took a step behind Emma and whispered in her ear. Bryanna's eyes followed the sweet duo.

"Now I don't think I've met you. What's your name sweetie?" Bryanna asked.

"Her name's Miya," Emma volunteered. "She wants to know if we can have a cookie."

"Thank you, Emma. Miya, do you like chocolate chip cookies?" Bryanna asked the little girl whose eyes remained glued to the basket.

Miya nodded.

Kassie handed the basket back to Bryanna as she walked

into the kitchen and poured two glasses of milk for the girls. Bryanna leaned down and let the girls make their selection before taking the basket into the living room. Kassie brought in tea and coffee pots.

"Oh my God, Bryanna. I don't know how you make these scones, but I'm hooked," Samantha crooned as she chewed the flavorful biscuit slowly.

"I'm in love with the individual cherry pies and those chocolate, butterscotch, and coconut creations," Catherine added.

"There's a little bit of each in there, help yourselves, ladies. I've already made my deliveries for the crews. I finished the morning rush and Becky stayed at the bakery." Bryanna took a seat next to Catherine as Carol and Melody opened the door and let themselves in.

Kassie returned to the kitchen and poured Melody a glass of milk as Emma encouraged her to get a cookie and join them.

The ladies went over the supplies they purchased for the hospital and the cabins while the kids finished their snack. Once the girls finished, Emma led the way back to her room to paint and play with dolls.

"I called you here to let you know I've taken in Saint's daughter. His mother suffers from some health issues and there was no one else. Miya's mom is hooked on drugs and Victoria, Michael and I found Miya in a warehouse in Montgomery. She's wearing Em's clothes today, but they're too big. She's a bit small for her age. I need to decorate the room right next to Em's for her. Her favorite color is purple. We need a bed, bedding, and furniture for her room. A few toys, and a doll of her choosing. Once we know what she likes we can add it to our list. I want her to feel at home here. I know you probably think I'm nuts, but Saint saved my life, and I wasn't leaving his daughter there." With all she had on her plate, she expected them to object to her taking on a new child.

"I'm headed into Seattle, I can find a bed and pick up the bedding," Samantha volunteered.

"I'll go with Samantha. She can drop me off so I can grab clothes if you can get me the sizes," Catherine added.

"Maddie and I can get the room together once you return. I think Henry's boy from the hardware store returned home from college. He helped paint the rooms in our cabin. We'll go over colors for her room and see if we can't get him started." Carol and Maddie nodded their heads in unison.

"I'm meeting Joe. I started putting the finishing touches on three of the cabins. It'll probably take me until at least four o'clock. Since Samantha doesn't have the experience, Bryanna has offered to teach us how to care for Miya's hair and skin. Since it takes a village to raise Em, LJ, and Melody, I figure we're adding Miya. I'm setting up Old Man Davis's house for Saint's mom. She's coming out next week to see if she wants to move here or we can set up a visitation schedule. She still lives in Saint's childhood home. I need to check if Becky wants an extra job to give it a thorough cleaning. We can't let Saint down."

※

WHEN THE LADIES left with their assignments, Kassie cleaned up the kitchen and Bryanna wrapped up the rest of the scones and pastries.

"Kassie, are you sure about this? I'm not trying to be mean, but have you thought about how there are people out there who won't think it's appropriate a white lady adopted a Black child." Bryanna refused to tip toe around the subject.

"She's a kid who needs a home. I don't care what color she is! Saint didn't care what color I was when he risked his life for us." Kassie's mouth formed a tight line. "Do you have a problem with it?"

Bryanna chuckled, "No. I don't. You aren't blind to the world we live in today. You're a single mom with one Black child and one white. Are you prepared for hushed whispers about you? Are you ready to listen to slurs about a child of yours? What if Chase comes home? Will he be thrilled to have Miya here?"

Kassie slapped down the dish towel in her hands.

"What exactly are you saying? I shouldn't take her in because small, minded people will judge me? Have you seen the internet pictures concerning me? I'm all over the news and not dressed in a few pictures. Do you honestly think I'll be ashamed because I took in a friend's child?" Kassie angrily questioned Bryanna. "She deserves a good life. I offered to help her mother and she refused. I wasn't leaving Saint's daughter to live in a warehouse full of junkies, homeless people, and God knows what else. Her father sacrificed for his country and last time I checked his blood was the same color as mine."

Bryanna walked to where Kassie stood. "Little miss Miya will be blessed to have you as a mama. I believe there is more to those pictures than meets the eye. It's none of my business. All I need to know is that you're a good person. I'll pick up some books for Miya. It's your job to help her embrace her culture. I'll help you, but you're already doing the most important thing."

"What?" Kassie's mind raced a mile a minute thinking about Miya's needs. How can she teach her about her culture? What could she do to protect Miya from hurtful comments?

"You love her. From what you told me on the phone, this is more care than she's experienced in her entire life. You've got this."

The two women hugged.

Kassie felt grateful for her circle of friends and family. Because of them, Miya's future brightened with the supportive group to care for her. With the addition of Edie, Saint's memory would come to life for Miya with stories about her father. If or when Clarissa decided to fight her demons, Kassie remained ready to help. Until then, Saint's daughter had a home.

CHAPTER THIRTY-ONE

Kassie parked the truck and smiled proudly at the newly built hospital. The inside and landscaping weren't finished yet. The exterior resembled a large log cabin home and appeared warm and welcoming. The back, made entirely of glass, showcased the surrounding mountains and the lake below. Around the back, a huge screened in deck housed picnic tables, and smaller game tables for checkers and cards. Individual outdoor lounging chairs lined the rail. Another patio shot to the side for barbequing. The teen unit was slightly smaller than the veteran's side. The game room on the lower level was wheelchair accessible. A huge professional kitchen gleamed in the center similar to the setup of Chase's home. Comfortable furniture, still in crates, covered the floor.

What excited Kassie most were the physical therapy rooms. A huge pool, a hot tub and all sorts of gear Elizabeth suggested, was ordered. Kassie added an additional room for prosthetics. She wondered if Chase would've approved of everything she'd done. Joe managed practically everything, but the project decisions rested on her.

Keeping Kassie

Joe knocked on her window, startling her. "Little Bit, you sittin' in the truck all day dreaming?" Joe teased her.

"I'm sorry, Joe. I wonder what Chase would say if he saw it. I miss him so much." Kassie opened the door and hopped down. "I want to see how the cabins turned out. I got all the finishing touches done last night. Did the workers hang the curtains?"

Pulling the last-minute homey touches from the bed of the truck, Kassie followed Joe down the path to the miniature subdivision separated from the hospital. Crews had completed three cabins and the next three were started. Eventually twelve cabins in a circle would house veterans not quite ready to be on their own but didn't need the hospital facilities.

She smiled as the sod covered the ground on the three furnished cabins. Kassie envisioned the structures for so long, it was exhilarating to see them come to life. Each contained two master bedrooms and baths complete with decks, a kitchen, and a shared living space. Kassie opened her bags and began placing pictures of Chase's parents and him with the story of how the commitment of one family made the dream of a hospital come true.

Kassie glanced up to see Joe watching her as she lovingly caressed the frame as her eyes welled up in tears. Joe offered comfort with a hug and held her while she quietly cried.

"Are you ready for tomorrow, Little Bit?" Joe pulled back from Kassie to stare in her eyes. His concerned face scanned hers to ensure she felt strong enough for what the morning brought.

"As ready as I'll ever be. I'm glad the town agreed to come for Leo's memorial. Afterward, they'll come back to the cabin and Ty will be catering. The workers brought the picnic tables over this morning. Do you know where Ivan and Victoria are? She sent a note saying something about an urgent business matter needing to be handled. She assigned men to stay with us, and left instructions on how to reach them if needed." Kassie closed the door to the first cabin and headed to the second.

"No. One of Ivan's men gave me a similar note when I came on site to meet the contractors. Don't let it worry you much. She seems determined to make sure you're protected."

Kassie laughed, "I received a list of workouts I need to complete before she returns."

"Well, I'll admit, I wasn't sure about all this, in fact, I wasn't happy about it. I worried about how you'd handle all of this. I believe Victoria has helped you to stay focused and Little Bit, you radiate strength and fitness. The exercises benefited you," Joe complimented.

"Thank you. I feel stronger mentally and physically." Kassie placed the pictures on the table, wishing she had met Chase's parents. Would they have approved of her? Especially with the pictures floating all over the internet. She grabbed the last frame and walked with Joe to the last cabin.

After setting everything out, she sat on the couch and regarded the picture she'd selected. Sophia Winters wrapped her arms around Chase in his Navy uniform. Her eyes held a twinkle and a hint of mischief in them. John Winters smiled at his wife, and it seemed to Kassie his entire world evolved around her. Kassie knew exactly how Chase's mom felt. Chase mimicked his father's habit with her. Even from the first moment, when she accidentally fell into his lap at Sharkey's, Chase took care of her as if nothing else mattered.

Working with Claire, Kassie recovered a lot of her memory from the time of her kidnapping and recovery. In every one of her recollections, Chase sacrificed his dream of building the hospital to be by her side. She refused to let him down.

"Have you seen Jake?" Kassie asked. "I tried to reach him. We need to talk about Chase. I promised Samantha if we haven't heard anything by the end of the month, I'd hold a memorial for Chase."

"Have you gotten any more information?" Joe asked.

"No. Samantha made me realize Jake and the town needed closure. They've known him longer than I have and if they need to say goodbye, I refuse to allow this to come between us. I hope Jake will listen to me," Kassie stated.

"Has Jake said something to you?" Joe's parental instincts kicked in by the tone of voice he used on Kassie.

"He left Taco's funeral early and the last time we spoke, he told me he'd plan the memorial for Chase. I know he's struggling. I hope this puts the tension between us at ease. Jake's as much a part of this family as you and Maddie. Chase loves him and I want him to know regardless of what happens, Em and I love him." Kassie closed the cabin door and walked up the trail with Joe.

"Jake's grieving, Little Bit. I checked on him and he's fine. A little gruff, but he's allowed to feel angry. Maybe tomorrow when he shows up to Leo's memorial, you can talk to him." Joe suggested as he opened the door for Kassie to climb into the truck.

Kassie slid in. "I don't know what I would've done without you and Maddie and this town. As difficult as it is to say, I'm glad Catherine sicced Leo on me. I don't want to even think about running with Emma again."

"You'll never have to worry, again. Now let's get home. Maddie made us po' boys for dinner and Miya's eating us out of chicken nuggets. We need to expand her tastebuds a bit. She didn't know what carrot sticks were." Joe shook his head. "In case I haven't told you, I'm proud of you for bringing her home."

"I was hooked the moment those eyes peeked at me from behind the box. I know addiction takes courage and strength to fight the allure of the drugs. Miya deserved to know Saint. I regret he never met her, she's a pistol. I'll make sure she has a family who loves her, even if she eats too many chicken nuggets and turns into one. Oh my gosh, Joe! We can nickname her "Nugget!" Kassie laughed. It fit Miya perfectly. Besides, the little girl was worth her weight in gold.

Kassie rolled down her window and let the cooler air enter the truck as she made her way back to the cabin. In September, the weather varied from day to day, but the evenings grew a bit chillier. The seasons changed, time went on, and people moved in and out of your life regardless of how prepared you were. She prayed with all her might Chase wasn't one of those people. She didn't think her heart could stand it.

CHAPTER THIRTY-TWO

Saint, Leo, and Chase helped the team off the plane. Three vehicles waited for them, thanks to Agent Rhodes. Their layover in Paris ended shorter than anticipated with Rebecca and Julio there to vouch for Leo's team. Ivan Rostova showed up with Victoria. Chase met her briefly at the hotel. Ivan offered information on the men the federal government wanted. His vague explanation on how his men found the team seemed to be enough for the feds. Or more likely, they didn't want to look a gift horse in the mouth with the information on the wanted men. The whole meeting took under two hours and Rebecca arranged a military flight back to Seattle.

Chase counted the time down the closer they got stateside. The team planned to head to Old Man Davis's cabin. Matthew and Michael agreed to meet them and stay with the injured team. Chase anticipated reuniting with Kassie, Ladybug, her family, and Jake. Leo volunteered to handle the supply run. Claire scheduled an afternoon session to assess Whiskey and Ash. Matthew busied himself setting up video calls for Taco's, Saint's and Shadow's families. As soon as they healed enough, Leo granted them leave for a month to reunite with their loved ones.

Once they landed in Seattle, the men hastened to get into the vehicles and headed to Serenity. They explained what became of the team after Whiskey and Ash's supposed deaths. Whiskey grew apprehensive as they went through the city. Leo informed him about Samantha's dad passing and moving them to Serenity. Leo updated Ash, explaining why his wife and daughter relocated to the small town with her mother. Ash nodded in understanding but asked no questions.

When they arrived, Matthew stood on the front porch and held the screen door open as Leo helped Taco up the stairs and Michael helped Whiskey. Shadow and Ash followed behind. Chase wanted to bolt across the mountain. Matthew's face pinched in frustration and anger, made Chase pause long enough to question him.

"What's wrong?" Chase asked as Leo joined him. Leo immediately picked up the weird vibes Matthew gave off.

"Welcome home. We've got a lot to go over but right now you need to head home. Shit went down and you won't like it."

Leo and Chase didn't waste any time.

※

KASSIE DRESSED in a blue dress and she chose flats for the short path to the Winters Family memorial at the top of the mountain. Her fingers traced the plaque she designed for Leo. It contained an engraving of the head of a lion. The plaque read, Derrick "Leo" Armstong, Navy SEAL, Brother, Protector, Uncle and Friend. Loved by his Forever Family.

Maddie and Joe stayed with the girls and Samantha and

Keeping Kassie

Catherine met up with Kassie for support. She wanted to go a bit early to place a small bouquet of flowers under her and Chase's unborn child's tree.

She kissed the girls goodbye and hugged Maddie and Joe. Bryanna and Ty pulled into the driveway and started unloading food. Bryanna hugged Kassie as she whispered words of encouragement. A close friendship had formed between the women and Kassie appreciated Bryanna's support. Getting into the truck, she headed to the top of the mountain.

The number of people already gathered surprised her. Matthew suggested two small shuttles to drive people from the town to the memorial and then over to Chase's for a reception. It helped control the traffic on the mountain and Jake agreed to oversee the details. The shuttles must've started early as Kassie noted most of the town gathered around the fenced off area.

Kassie checked her phone one last time to see if Ragu answered her text. She texted him the information for Leo's funeral, but he hadn't responded. Grabbing the wildflowers, and the plaque for Leo, Kassie exited the truck. As she got closer, she saw Catherine and Samantha arguing adamantly with Jake. She smiled tentatively. Jake's appearances at the cabin halted after their argument and she was unsure he would show. She knew he spoke with Joe at the construction site of the hospital, yet he ignored every offer she made for him to join them for dinner. Regardless of the hard feelings, Jake remained part of her family. With every step toward the group, Kassie began to feel like an outsider.

Her smile faded as she acknowledged people from the town. The crowd parted like the red sea. Remembering Victoria's advice, Kassie swallowed her emotions down and dealt with the task ahead. Walking straight to the reverend who stood with Jake and her two friends, Kassie intended to greet him. Catherine's mouth pinched into a scowl and Samantha tightly clenched her fists as if she wanted to punch someone.

"Jake, thank you for coming. Reverend Sheehan, do you mind speaking with Jake and I after the luncheon for Leo?" Kassie didn't understand why the Reverand seemed confused and her two friends appeared uncomfortable.

"Kassie, we aren't here for Leo's funeral. Chase's family lived on this mountain and has helped this town way before you or the team showed up. Chase only went on this mission because he felt he owed Leo for taking care of you. If it weren't for you, my boy would be at the hospital where he belongs. He'd be helping veterans and living the life he dreamed." Jake yelled at her.

Catherine shook her head and moved closer to Kassie as a show of support. Her arm wrapped around Kassie's back. Samantha whispered furiously to Jake. The reverend flushed an ugly purple. Turning toward the crowd, most of the people avoided her gaze. Others shook their heads and muttered angry words at Jake for deceiving her.

A second later phones began to ding and chime. It sounded like one large group text and Kassie was excluded. People checked their phones and turned back to Kassie. An uneasy feeling crept along her neck as her body began to feel numb. Kassie spied Rachel in the back of the crowd with a smug smile on her face.

Kassie narrowed her eyes and turned to face Jake.

"Don't do this Jake. You're obviously upset. We'll hold the memorial for Leo, return to the cabin, and talk to the reverend. We'll plan Chase's memorial together as a family."

Jake's bloodshot eyes narrowed as he weaved back and forth in his wrinkled suit, his tie askew. She caught the faint smell of whiskey on his breath. His chest puffed out as he turned steely eyes toward Kassie. "I'll not be memorializing my boy with you! If I'd known what I do now, I'd have kicked you off this mountain! You didn't deserve Chase. He deserved better. Now he'll never get the chance." Jake crushed the hat in his hand.

Samantha led him to a chair while Catherine grabbed bottled water from someone and made Jake drink as she took his pulse.

Kassie slowly backed down the aisle. Some of the men stared openly at her. Women held shocked faces as her eyes fell on them. She didn't have to imagine what the text contained. Kassie guessed Rachel plotted and schemed the entire event.

Humiliated and hurt from Jake's rant, Kassie dropped the wildflowers and took off at a run. Jumping back in her truck she slammed the gas pedal down and raced back to the cabin. She couldn't get air. The rock lodged in her stomach since the moment she learned of the helo crash threatened to come up. She desperately grabbed the steering wheel as tears blurred her vision as she navigated her way home.

As she drove closer, she realized Maddie and Joe would have questions and she wasn't prepared to provide the answers. The girls didn't need to see her like this. She slammed on the brakes, jerked the truck to the side of the road, and slammed it into park. Walking the rest of the way, she came to the barn. Pulling the door open, the memory flashed of her once prying it open to get Chase inside after the tree limb hit him in a storm. Now she sought refuge from her own tempest.

Rhett and Scarlett stood in their stalls. Grabbing the saddle and the stool, Kassie saddled Scarlett. Her hands shook badly, and it took forever for her to get it buckled. Leading the horse out of her stall, Kassie stopped long enough to shut the barn door. Mounting the horse, she steered Scarlett in the only direction she could feel Chase. With every gallop, her hair fell loose from the fancy chignon as hot tears ran down her face.

When she made it to the trail, she pulled Scarlett to a stop and tethered her to a shaded tree. Stumbling over the jagged path, Kassie made her way to where Chase proposed. Arriving at their special spot, Kassie finally let the bubble inside of her burst. Reality settled in. The helicopter hit the sea and the chances of survival were slim. As the days passed, she became obstinate and refused to listen to her inner voice which insisted to her that Chase had disappeared, forever. Kassie tried to be brave for her family, her friends and Jake. Terrified of what life looked like without Chase by her side, she screamed her frustration, fear, and anxiety over the mountain. She listened as it echoed down the valley. Sobs wracked her body as the intense pain rose to the surface.

"Chaaaaaase!" She screamed. "I can't do this without you. I'm not strong enough without you," she cried.

Silence greeted her. The emptiness enveloped her. The same feeling, she felt as she watched her sister die and leave her all alone...

CHAPTER THIRTY-THREE

Leo and Chase noticed his truck on the side of the road as they neared the cabin. As soon as Leo parked his vehicle in the driveway, people surrounded Chase as he exited the car. The townspeople patted his back or shook his hand, welcoming him home. Leo was immediately drawn into the fold as well. Rollo bounded up to his master barking and jumping at the sight of Chase.

Distracted by the sound of Rollo's continued barking, Joe and Maddie stood on the porch as Samantha and Catherine strained to see through the crowd. Jake sat on the wooden swing with his head hung down, clutching his hat.

Chase didn't stop as he headed toward the group on the porch. Samantha noticed Chase first, as his foot reached the bottom step.

"Chase!" She screeched as she ran down the stairs and met him halfway. He held out his arms to catch her.

"Where's Kassie?" Chase didn't mean to sound abrupt but the churning in his gut refused to stop. He made his way to the top of the stairs, taking the scene in.

Jake slowly walked to Chase in disbelief. Chase only witnessed Jake this distraught once in his entire life. When the love of Jake's life, Bonnie, died in a car accident during a snowstorm. When Chase's parents passed, Jake continued to be the pillar who held him up. Jake's body shook as the two men embraced tightly. Words escaped both of them as they realized how close this moment had been to never happening.

Maddie and Joe each took a turn welcoming him home. Maddie's eyes filled with tears as she stammered her shock upon seeing him. Joe squeezed his shoulder and smiled through his own watery eyes. "Little Bit will be so damn happy to lay eyes on you, son."

"I'll be happy to do the same with her, sir," Chase choked in answer. The emotions welled up inside of him as he reunited with his family and confirmed he was finally home.

Jake still grasped his hand while Maddie wrapped him to her side in a mama embrace as they watched Samantha and Catherine greet Leo. Catherine clung to Leo's neck as her nose reddened and tears tracked down her cheeks. Leo gripped her tightly by the waist but held her back from his body, making Chase scowl at his dumb assed friend.

"How did you make it back? They said you were dead. We had no idea..." Jake stammered, still in disbelief that his godson stood before him.

"I'll explain it all later. Where's Kassie?" Chase asked, desperate to greet her.

The group sobered for a moment before Joe took the lead.

Joe clasped his shoulder and steered him into the house, "I think it's best if we take this into the house, son." Chase followed the group inside and Leo shut the door.

"It's all my fault," Jake choked out. "I hurt Kassie something awful. She insisted you'd find your way back."

"What happened Jake? Joe? Someone tell me where Kassie is!" Chase lost his patience.

"Dr. Chase! Dr. Chase!" Emma squealed and she swiftly ran down the steps into his arms. Her arms clamped around his neck as he bent to pick her up. "Mama said you'd come home. She said to keep praying and have faith and you came home! Melody said you went to heaven. It made me sad."

Chase hugged the little girl tightly to his chest. His eyes closed as he wanted to remember this moment forever. "I'm here Ladybug." His hands slid to the back of her head as he peppered her cheek with kisses. "I've missed you too." His voice cracked. This was what his team fought to come home for. The love of everyone standing in this room. Emma's attention diverted to her Uncle Leo.

"Uncle Leo! Mama said you would make sure Dr. Chase came home to us! Good job!" She shot him a thumbs up and smiled widely. The room erupted in laughter at the precocious little girl as she launched herself into Leo's arms.

Chase turned back to Kassie's godparents and Jake. "Where's Kassie?"

Maddie and Joe shot dirty glances at Jake. Samantha gestured at Leo to wait until she escorted Emma and the little girl standing by the stairs back to her room.

"Oh my gosh, we need to get ready for a party to welcome Uncle Leo and Doctor Chase home! Do you think you can help me make some decorations?" Samantha asked. The girls' cheers filled the room.

As soon as the door closed, Chase turned to Jake, "What's happened?"

Catherine led Jake to a kitchen chair.

"I'm sorry, son. I blamed sweet little Kass because she refused to have a memorial for you. I rearranged the memorial she planned for Leo for you without her knowing. I thought she didn't want to face that we lost you. Then Rachel showed me all those terrible pictures of things she's done with other men—"

"Stop. Jake. You were supposed to take care of her. Not tear her down." Chase was beyond pissed, but he needed to know what happened.

"I'll tell you what happened!" Catherine's voice turned livid at Jake. Her hands clenched into fists and her mouth turned down in anger. "Jake listened to Rachel, who told him all about Kassie running around on you. She whispered to Jake about Kassie not grieving you appropriately when she held her faith the entire time. Isn't that right, Jake? You let Rachel into your head because you refused to listen to Kassie when she requested more time before scheduling Chase's funeral. The other families left her no choice but to go to theirs. Instead of paying attention to your heart, you acted without grace. You interrupted Leo's funeral and held one for Chase without his fiancée! If that wasn't enough to hurt, nearly the entire town got one massive text showing a very explicit Kassie! We have no idea where she is. Kassie ran to your truck and hightailed it down the road. We hoped she came back home. Somehow, I don't think she feels this is home anymore."

Chase turned to face his godfather. Rage boiled in his veins. He knew Jake took his presumed dead status hard, the evidence blatant by his blood shot eyes, rumpled clothes, and weight loss. What he hadn't expected was Jake falling for Rachel's lies or him not supporting the woman Chase loved.

"Is this true?" Chase demanded.

Keeping Kassie

Jake nodded his head in shame.

"Leo, I know where Kassie is. Saddle Rhett for me? I need to talk to Jake." Chase continued to glare at his godfather.

Maddie and Joe took the time to embrace Leo before he left to tend the horse while Chase escorted Jake to his bedroom for a private confrontation. "Before I left, I entrusted the most important thing in my life to you. I don't know what to say Jake, except I'm disappointed in you. I trusted you and you let me down. You broke trust with Kassie too. If this harmed her in any way emotionally, I'm holding you responsible," Chase didn't mince his words.

Jake visibly paled before his eyes. Gripping his hat tighter, he nodded his head. "I take full responsibility for my foolishness and as soon as you bring her back, I'll ask her for forgiveness. I'm sorry I let you down, son. She didn't deserve this."

"No, she didn't. And Jake, right now, I'm not feeling very happy with your actions, but you've always stood by me and I'm trying to refrain from saying something that could damage our relationship beyond repair. I need you to stay away from me until I can calm down." Chase watched as Jake flinched at his words.

His godfather helped him through all the hard times and even gifted him the land where he planned to raise his family. He barely reconciled the man before him as the person he grew up with.

"I understand, son. Please tell her I regret everything. When she's ready to see me, I'll apologize for my actions," Jake somberly stated.

"First, we're going out there and talking to our neighbors. You'll assure them this misunderstanding was a huge mistake." Chase led the way out of his room and out the front door. A sharp whistle from him brought everyone to a halt.

"I'm standing here before you to tell you exactly what you need to know. My Kassie was a victim of James Stanton from Texas. The pictures texted to you were shown at a trial in which Kassie testified as a witness. I grew up with all of you and some of you raised me to become the man I turned into. Kassie suffered through hell and since she arrived, the hospital my father dreamed of for this community has become a reality. Kassie even included a small intake clinic. You don't have to drive all the way to Seattle anymore for urgent medical needs. We can handle them right here. She planned to use local businesses to help build the hospital, for our town to profit and grow. If you are the people I know you to be, you'll forget about whatever you saw in the text and remember the woman who will become my wife and your friend. If you can't, then you aren't the town I thought you were." Chase scanned the crowd.

Mrs. Meyers, the town librarian, and church pianist began to speak. "Son, I don't know what you're talking about. I thought we gathered to welcome you and your men home. Your lovely girl saw me walking home after my car refused to start last month and I had ice cream melted everywhere! She gave me a ride and thirty minutes later all the groceries in my sack that had been ruined showed up at my door replaced. You made a wonderful choice." The crowd grew louder echoing the same sentiment about his girl.

Leo stood patiently holding on to Rhett as Chase made his way through the crowd. As he mounted the horse, he heard Jake speak from the front porch.

"I apologize for my actions, and I owe Kassie a huge apology. I got caught up in my anger and my common sense

Keeping Kassie

deserted me. She refused to give up on Chase when I refused to listen to reason. I hope you'll understand." The older man's eyes met Chase's. Chase knew he was talking to him, but right now, Jake wasn't the most important person on his list. He needed to find her. Rollo followed along the horse, his tail wagging happily. His master had come home.

CHAPTER THIRTY-FOUR

Kassie pulled her knees to her chin and stared at the valley below wondering what to do next. Her entire life revolved around the mountain. She wasn't about to abandon Chase's dream. The more she thought about how things occurred, the madder she got. Kassie knew Jake. He'd struggled with Chase's disappearance from the start. Sniffing, Kassie swiped the tears from her face. Wishing she'd asked Victoria to show her some mafia moves to destroy Rachel.

Kassie's refusal to discuss the opportunity for Jake to say goodbye to the man he raised probably rankled. Rachel went in for the kill. She intended to address that matter later. Right now, she imagined the town had held their funeral for Chase and was making their way to the cabin.

Maddie and Joe popped into her head. They'd worry after hearing what had occurred. She pulled out her phone, ignoring the missed calls and texted Maddie and Joe. She required some time alone to get herself together. Tears flowed as she thought about Chase. How he always seemed to know when she needed him and never doubted his love

Keeping Kassie

for her. Now she sat wondering if they'd ever get the chance of a life together.

❄

Relief flooded Chase as he spotted Scarlett tied to the tree. Chase tied Rhett and started up the path to his and Kassie's special place.

Reaching the opening, he caught a glimpse of Kassie. His breath caught. She resembled a young girl as she sat in the exact spot where he'd proposed. Her head hung down, and her shoulders slumped. He knew she had been crying. Not wanting to startle her as she sat near the edge, he softly called out, "Princess."

When she didn't respond, Chase said her name louder, "Princess."

Kassie's head slowly raised, and she closed her eyes as if his voice gently caressed her.

"Princess." This time, Kassie stood and waited to see if she had heard correctly.

Chase took a step forward and Rollo nudged her leg, "Kass."

The noise and Rollo caught her attention. She inhaled a big breath as she turned and blinked her eyes a couple of times as if she thought she conjured him up in thin air.

"Chase?" She whispered as her head shook in disbelief. If she closed her eyes, he'd disappear.

"It's me, Princess. I'm right –"

Kassie's body slammed into him before he said anything else. Her arms clung to his neck as he picked her up. Her legs wrapped around his waist. Her head moved to his shoulder as he peppered tiny kisses in her trail of tears. Truth be told his eyes watered too. His hand ran through her thick locks, and he held her in place by the back of her head.

"I didn't give up, I believed in you. I didn't give up. Where were you? What happened, they told us the helo crashed? I was so worried about you. I was scared" Kassie said into his shoulder, her voice muffled as she held him tightly.

Chase gently caressed her back and spoke softly, "I'm home, Princess. I've missed you, Kass. Shhh," Chase soothed the sobbing Kassie. He walked to the closest tree and let Kassie's body slide down his. Sitting on the ground, he pulled her onto his lap. His eyes swept up and down her body.

She cupped his face with her hands and wiped away his tears while he took the edge of his shirt and wiped her face.

Kassie's hands stroked the stubble on his jaw as she took him in as if she couldn't believe he was truly there.

"You're home. I prayed and prayed. How's the team? Is everyone here?" Kassie's eyes widened as she searched his, clearly worried about the other men.

"Everyone's home. We've had some injuries—" Kassie immediately pulled away to inspect him.

"Where are you hurt? Oh my God, I rushed you. Did I hurt you?" Kassie frantically tugged at his shirt.

Chase took her hands in his. "It's fine, Princess. Calm down. Let me hold you for a moment. I've dreamed about this every night for months." He nestled her back into his shoulder. Her hair smelled of wildflowers from the mountain. His hand roamed over her arms and back, surprised at the formed muscles beneath her clothes.

"I saw Ladybug. I swear she grew a foot since I left. How are you?" He inquired softly.

Chase felt Kassie snuggle further into him as Rollo lay under a tree watching them.

"I'm fine, Chase. I wasn't the one who flew thousands of miles away from home and crashed in the ocean. I'm even better now that you're here," Kassie stated.

"I've stopped at the cabin, Kass. Talk to me." Chase kissed her forehead and waited for her to speak.

Kassie paused, "Then you know what happened. Jake's listened to Rachel, and I'm sure she took advantage of a grieving man. It was only a matter of time before someone in town discovered those pictures of my sister. It's not important. All that matters is you're home and everyone else is too."

"By the grace of God, sweetheart. I've thought of nothing else but getting home to you." Chase leaned in and slowly captured Kassie's mouth. He took his time getting reacquainted. She tasted like the mint tea she loved. He wasn't in any hurry to let her go and relished the feeling of her body against his. A gentle breeze rustled through the trees, and he became acutely aware that his mountain was welcoming him home.

Kassie's hands roamed his chest as she moaned into his mouth. He knew exactly how she felt. He foolishly left the blanket on the horse with the intention of getting to Kassie as fast as possible after Jake's revelation. Now he regretted it. He grabbed her hand which snuck its way up his shirt.

"Kass, we have to stop. The blanket is back with the horses, and I don't think I can be gentle right now." Chase returned her kiss as she became the aggressor.

"I don't want you to be gentle, Chase. I need to feel you, now." Kassie yanked his shirt above his head. Her eyes grew darker as she took in his tattoo and the bandage on his upper arm.

"Kass, we don't have protection. I wasn't prepared—" Kassie put her fingers to his mouth.

"Chase Winters, when I make love to you, on this mountain, you'll know you're finally home." She smiled as her words echoed the ones, he said to her when she fought her way back to him.

"The chances of my getting pregnant diminished with Roger. I don't want you worried about being gentle. I don't need your tenderness. I want you to officially be home." Kassie stood and pulled the dress over her head. Her hair fell all around her as she spread the full skirt out on the ground.

Chase's mouth watered. Kassie's smooth stomach featured toned muscles. Her arms were well defined. The soft Kassie he kissed goodbye a few months ago now looked like a miniature warrior princess. His eyes skimmed over the pale pink lacy bra and matching panties to see the conditioned thighs. She smiled a siren's smile as she crooked her finger and beckoned him closer to her.

Chase pulled her in for another kiss and got a shock when his feet swept from underneath him, and he landed flat on his back. Kassie giggled as her hands fell to his belt buckle. She unzipped his pants and stood to tug the offending garments down, tore off each of his shoes, and threw them over her shoulder.

She straddled his hips and lay on top of him. Her mouth captured his, her tongue licked his lip, and she gently nipped it. Her hands ran through his stubble and down to his shoulders. Her touch alone drove him crazy. Her bottom wiggled over his cock while her mouth captured his nipple, her tongue stroked as she sucked. The sensation going straight to his cock as he moaned. His mind went completely blank as her tongue lathed his abs and her teeth nipped him here and there.

Kassie changed. Her confidence showed in her eyes and in her actions. He always took charge in their lovemaking and seeing Kassie assert her rights as his lover, did something for him. Oh, he would still be in charge, but it amused him to let her have her way. She resembled a kitten learning to bare its claws. No matter, he'd pounce when she finished exploring. This new facet of Kassie definitely turned Chase on.

Kassie's eyes never left his as her fingers slid the straps of her bra down her shoulders. The insecure woman who worried about the scars on her legs disappeared. A growl caught his attention. Did Kassie just growl at him?

She abruptly stood and slid the delicate panties from her hips and let them fall to the ground. She straddled herself over his hard staff. He lay completely entranced. A flirty smile appeared on her face as she thrust her chest out as she undid the clasps and slid the bra down her arms before flinging it into the trees. Placing his cock to her center she slowly slid down on top of his shaft. She felt tight, warm, and slick. Chase moaned loudly as she moved immediately into a faster and harder rhythm.

"God Kass, you feel amazing. I've missed you. You're beautiful," he uttered. Her hands kneaded his chest and raked through the jet-black hair. Kassie threw her head back and closed her eyes. Unlike her usual soft moans and sighs, Kassie's moans sounded deep and guttural. She ground herself further onto his shaft, causing his eyes to roll back into his head.

Grabbing her waist, he rolled her over. He wanted his time to explore too. Kassie wasn't having it. She tilted her hips and wrapped her legs around his waist.

"Kass, I won't be able to hold on, it's been a long time..." Chase gritted out as he attempted to keep from embarrassing himself. She made him feel like a teenager having sex for the first time.

"Welcome home, Chase. I have made a few changes since you left. I missed having sex with you. I'm not fragile, you don't need to hold back. I can take as much as you give." Her statement nearly undid him.

Raising up, Chase no longer worried about the forcefulness of his thrusts as Kassie's hips met his. She traced his nipple with her tongue as she pulled on the other.

"Geez Kass! Are you trying to kill me?" He shifted his hips to find her sweet spot as she mewled out her pleasure. His breath came in hard pants as he tried to stave off his orgasm. He was hell bent on taking care of her first. Gritting his teeth, he raised up, reached for her nub, and pinched.

Kassie's eyes widened as she went over the edge. She screamed his name, and he chuckled as it echoed down the valley. Her juices made her even more slick as he increased his pace. Her fingers dug into his back drawing him closer to her.

"I love you, Chase. I want to feel you come inside me. I need you." Her pants quickened, and she tilted her hips and tightened herself around his shaft. She closed her eyes as the second orgasm hit at the same time Chase went over the edge.

Chase leaned over her and marveled at the transformation in his woman. "I love you, Kassie. I don't want to wait to marry you. I know you probably want a huge wedding and everything. I won't argue with you, but I want you bound to me forever. Even if it means we go to the justice of the peace tomorrow," Chase didn't mean to blurt it out, but he knew the moment he flew home, he wanted her name to change from Kassie Stanton to Mrs. Kassie Winters. He wasn't barbaric, but he refused to let James Stanton own any part of her. She was his. Chase yearned to make it official.

"How about next weekend? I don't want some big fancy wedding. I want our family, the town, and I want to do it here on the mountain. Maybe at sunset." Kassie wasted no time in her response, shocking Chase.

He moved to let her up. Going after his pants. She sat up, totally unconcerned with her nakedness. He gathered her panties and located her bra snagged to a tree limb. Returning to her, he sat down in the opposite direction as he drank in the sight of the mountains. Placing a kiss on her shoulder and running his hand down her arms, he chuckled as she shivered at his touch.

"Are you sure? You aren't doing this to please me?" Chase waited as she slipped her bra on, and he helped her clasp it. He nipped her neck, making her laugh.

"No, I'm doing it for us. Do you think we can do it here? This is where I knew I was home, and you found your way back to me here. It's as if the mountain made this place for us," Kassie mused.

"There's an access road on the opposite side. If we used the shuttles I saw down by the cabin, we could make it work. Kass, about the town—"

"Don't go there. You're home and right now, everything is right with my world. Tomorrow we can worry about the town." Kassie slipped her panties on and stood to dust out her dress before pulling it over her head.

Kassie's eyes got round. "Chase, where's the team?"

"I set them up in Old Man Davis's cabin. They need to recuperate. Leo's at our cabin." Chase told her as she finger brushed her hair.

"I need to talk to Saint. Can the horses get us there or do we need to get your truck?" Kassie now seemed rushed.

"Princess, you aren't allowed to go to the cabin. I need you to stay away from there," Chase's voice firmed. He refused to ask her to hold the secrets from her friends.

"I can't. It's imperative I speak with Saint. They can't stay at the cabin. Saint's mother will be here this weekend. I've offered her the cabin." She bit her lip, and he waited while she worked out the problem in her head.

"She can stay at our cabin," he offered.

Kassie shook her head. "Maddie, Joe and Miya are there."

"Who's Miya and why are Maddie and Joe in our cabin? I told you to give them my parent's place." Chase followed Kassie down the path to where the horses stood tied to the trees.

Kassie stopped abruptly, "Chase, I'm not trying to sound secretive. From now on there aren't any secrets between the two of us. I wasted time, terrified to tell you things for my fear of losing you. It's important I speak with Saint."

"If I allow you to go to the cabin, you'll have to keep something from your friends. I don't want to ask you to do that," Chase explained.

"Miya is Saint's daughter. I'll explain it all later. I've gone to their funerals, Chase. I've done all of their requests except for yours and Leo's. I need to be reassured with my own eyes they returned safely. They're my family too."

His red head was stubborn and persistent. Chase sighed, "I need your word. You can't talk to Samantha or Catherine about it."

Kassie nodded her head. "I swear."

"Then let's go, Princess." Chase helped get her settled on

Keeping Kassie

Rhett and tied Scarlett to the saddle. After months apart, he wasn't ready to let Kassie go yet. He mounted behind her and steered the horses toward the cabin.

CHAPTER THIRTY-FIVE

Chase helped Kassie off the horse. Shadow walked out of the cabin door and stood on the porch, favoring his side. Kassie squealed as she ran toward Shadow.

By the time she reached him, Kassie had given Shadow a once over. Gently hugged him, Kassie babbled, "I missed you. How badly injured are you? Did you get medical treatment immediately? What tests did they run?"

Shadow, not one to show emotions, pulled her tightly in and held her close. Even from where Chase stood, he witnessed his friend choke up at Kassie's mothering.

Saint walked through the entrance. Kassie wasted no time welcoming him home. Her arms wrapped around his neck as she kissed his cheek.

"Miss Kassie, it's good to see you too." Saint's voice cracked as she echoed his greeting.

Kassie started toward the door when Saint blocked her way. Kassie grabbed his hand as she tried to drag him inside.

"Saint, I need to talk to you. It's important. I need to check Taco's leg. Chase told me about it." Kassie made another move to pass him when Saint blocked her again and lifted his chin to Chase.

"Leo's on his way, I called him as we rode over." Chase assured Saint as Saint attempted to communicate they were under orders to keep Ash and Whiskey's existence a secret.

Chase's truck pulled into the driveway driven by Matthew and Leo pulled in behind him. Kassie bounded down the steps and jumped into Leo's arms. Leo swiftly caught her in his and twirled her in a circle. Chase chuckled at the two of them. It wasn't that long ago Kassie would've loved to strangle Leo on sight. If any other men greeted Kassie as hard as these guys did, Chase knew he'd tear them apart. These men protected Kassie when he couldn't. They loved hard and their loyalty was forever.

Leo set Kassie apart from him and placed his hands on her shoulders. "Chase says you need to talk to us. You understand that when you enter the cabin, you're involved in our secrets. You didn't sign up for this, PITA. I need your word that what you see or hear doesn't leave this cabin."

Kassie licked her lips, "I promise Leo. I'd never put you or the team in jeopardy."

"I know. I can't stress to you how important this is. Are you prepared to keep secrets from your family and friends?" Leo asked.

A worried Kassie shifted from one foot to the other. "I understand."

Leo put his arm around Kassie and hugged her to him in a brotherly fashion as he walked her back to Chase. When they reached the porch, Kassie smiled widely at Saint. "May we go inside?"

The men all followed her lead.

"Oh Taco," Kassie dropped to her knees on the floor in front of him. "Are you in pain? Do we have your x-rays?

What do you need to get more comfortable?" Kassie fussed over him.

A movement from the hallway caught her attention. Ash scrutinized Kassie and he nodded his head in greeting. Kassie turned to Leo and Chase before slowly rising and walking toward the unknown man.

"Hello, I'm Kassie. Chase is my fiancé. I'm assuming you must be part of the secret. Your poor face." Kassie gently inspected his jaw with her fingertips. "What are they giving you for pain?"

Chase rattled off Ash's medications as she investigated the injured man. "Kass, Ash saved me and Michael a few years ago."

Kassie thoughtfully studied the man. "Thank you. If it wasn't for your service, I would've never met Chase. So, you saved my life too. What can you eat?"

Leo spoke for Ash as he endured Kassie's compassionate inspection. "PITA, Ash's jaw makes it painful for him to talk and chew. He's mainly stayed on a liquid diet and very soft foods."

"You poor man. I imagine the MRE's sucked. When I get back to the cabin, I'll bring you some of Maddie's jambalaya. Bryanna made some soft rolls for the reception this morning and they are beyond heaven. Tomorrow, I'll bring you a poultice Bear showed me how to make. It'll help with the pain and swelling." Her nose scrunched up adorably as she made her plans and a mental list of what she needed to do. Chase loved seeing her work again.

Ash gently squeezed her hand in acknowledgement. It was the first time he had engaged with anyone since he was rescued. Maybe the mountain could heal Ash too.

Chase took Kassie's hand and Leo followed as they took her into one of the bedrooms in the back.

"This is Whiskey." Leo softly told her. Whiskey's eyes popped open as he felt the movement beside the bed. He swung his fists in the air as he shouted and searched wildly about the room for the enemy.

Chase pulled Kassie behind him as Leo spoke calmly to the wild-eyed man in the bed.

"Whiskey, it's Leo and Doc. You're in a cabin on Serenity Mountain."

Whiskey stopped thrashing at the sound of Leo's voice. His chest rose heavily as his eyes darted around the room until they settled on the one person he didn't know.

Kassie walked around Chase and sat gently at the end of the bed. "My name is Kassie. I'm engaged to Chase--I mean Doc. You're completely safe here on the mountain. Chase brought me here when Leo and the team watched over me. I'm a nurse practitioner, you'll see me from time to time. Can I get you anything to make you feel more at home?"

Whiskey propped himself up against the headboard. He glanced at Leo then Chase. "I thought I died and went to heaven. Damn, Doc. She's an angel." Showing every sign of embarrassment, Whiskey addressed her, "I'm sorry, I hope I didn't scare you. I haven't gotten used to my surroundings yet."

"Oh, I wasn't scared. Leo's overseen me for months, nothing's scarier than him in a bad mood." Kassie rolled her eyes toward Leo making the men laugh. "What can I do to help make you more comfortable? I found a weighted blanket helped me and nightlights, lots of nightlights. Have you tried bone broth, yet? It will provide protein to add muscle mass. I'll send some over with honey from Bear. A cup of hot tea soothed me, especially when I couldn't tolerate anything heavy on my stomach."

Whiskey nodded. "A nightlight so I can find my way to the bathroom wouldn't be a bad idea."

Chase and Leo listened as Whiskey admitted to Kassie, he wasn't tolerating certain foods and Chase recognized the request for the nightlight as Whiskey's own fear of the dark.

"May I ask your real name? Were you part of the team who saved Chase and Michael?" Kassie asked.

"Yeah, I belonged to the team," Whiskey responded. "My name's Liam."

Kassie's eyes flared in recognition of his name. "Your Samantha's, Liam," she whispered as she put two and two together. "Then who is Ash?" Kassie turned and faced Leo.

"Ash is Catherine's husband," Leo's voice held a finality to it.

Chase watched as Kassie's demeanor changed. "I see. Whiskey and Ash were over there all this time?" Kassie waited for confirmation from Whiskey.

When he nodded, she took his hand and gave it a gentle squeeze.

Kassie licked her lips before she turned to Leo. "These men need to be fully quarantined. Did you do blood work? Those areas are known to carry all kinds of parasites and diseases. We'll need to follow up every few weeks. Whiskey, I know you're settled, and I hate to ask you to be moved again, but I think I have a perfect place for you. In fact, I think it would suit everyone here. It's private and you can sit out on your own deck and feel the fresh air from the privacy of your bedroom—"

"Princess, I want to keep him on the mountain. Claire will be here this afternoon. We can't take them to my parent's cabin." Chase shook his head, confused. What was Kassie thinking? Kassie's nose wrinkled as she concentrated on the immediate needs of the team.

"I don't know what possessed me, but I instructed crews to work around the clock. You haven't seen the hospital site yet. I finished three cabins. They have two bedrooms each. Shadow and Taco in one, Leo and Ash in the other. Saint can stay here or room with Whiskey." Turning her attention back to the thin man in front of her, Kassie explained. "I think you'll find the rooms more to your liking and secure. You can have as much privacy as you need and when you feel up to company, you can use the common areas. I'll have the crews halt construction on the subdivision and concentrate on the hospital."

Chase placed his hands on Kassie's waist. "You've been quite busy. She's managed to supervise the hospital construction and got herself acquainted with not one but two mafia families who got us home." He worried he'd find her broken and stressed. The woman in front of him defied the odds and exuberated confidence. Now if only he could figure out what was going on in her head.

"Seems to me she plowed a few fields since we got home." Leo teased as he took in her dirty dress and guessed what she'd been up to.

Chase watched as a blush crept up Kassie's neck and cheeks as she leaned in and playfully smacked Leo on the chest. "No one is at the site today because I didn't want any noise during the memorial. We need to get them moved immediately. Claire needs to be notified." Kassie stood and headed back to the living area. Not bothering to say goodbye to Whiskey. Chase shrugged his shoulders as he and Leo followed her out of the room.

"I'm sorry, Saint, I need to speak with you privately." Kassie's voice changed from friendly to professional. "Shall we speak out on the porch?"

"Sure." Saint followed Kassie out the door.

Leo shrugged and Chase grinned at Saint as he slapped him on the shoulder. "Come on man, I think you need to have a seat for this one."

Kassie bit her thumb nail as she paced the wooden floor. Finally, she stopped in front of Saint. "I know Matthew's setting up a video feed for you to talk to your mother and you haven't reached her yet. I followed your instructions. Your brother is an ass by the way."

Saint chuckled as he braced himself in the chair for what Kassie had to say.

"Princess, I think you better tell Saint, or he'll think something's wrong." Chase crossed his arms and leaned against the cabin next to Leo.

"Well, I did as you requested. But Edie asked if she could use the money for someone else. I wasn't aware you were married before," Kassie stated while promising him with her tone, the discussion on the topic was far from over.

Saint started to stand when Chase's hand touched his shoulder.

"Miss Kassie, please tell me you didn't give the money to my ex-wife." Saint's eyebrows slanted in a deep V as he scowled.

"I did, not for the reasons that you might think," Kassie gushed. "I tracked her down at a warehouse in the middle of Montgomery."

"Kassie, what were you thinking, going down there! The men let you..." Saint continued voicing his frustration.

"Michael and Victoria were with me. That's not important. I found your wife—"

"Ex-wife," Saint corrected her.

"Right, anyway, Saint, I didn't go to see her, I went in to get your daughter. You're the father of a very beautiful, precocious little girl. She's Emma's age and it fits the timeline. She has your eyes," Kassie softened the blow.

Saint swallowed hard and his eyes nearly bugged out of his head.

"I offered to get your ex-wife rehab and she refused. I set her up in an apartment, bought her food and clothing. I gave her one-thousand dollars if she'd give me custody of Miya."

"Miya." Saint whispered. "Her name is Miya."

"Yes, and she's staying with us. Bryanna helped me get everything she needed. Emma, Melody, and LJ have taken her under their wings. Your mama's coming this weekend. She's decided to move here to give Miya a part of your family. You can use the cabin with Edie and get to know your daughter." Kassie smiled.

Saint stood. Taking Kassie's hand, he pulled her toward him. "You don't have to tell me what you saw but I'mma gonna have a few questions about this later. Do you think I can see her?" Saint's voice held trepidation at the thought of seeing his daughter.

"Absolutely, she's sharing a room with Emma while we got hers painted and she's settling in. I think it might be a good idea since she's gotten used to us, if you let her stay with Emma and visit with her, until your mama arrives."

"Kass, I didn't know Miya even existed. You took my daughter in... I don't know what to say... you planned to raise my child."

Kassie seemed confused. Chase smiled to himself. She didn't even know how incredible she was. She had a heart of gold. She saw a need and fixed it.

"Of course, I took her, Saint. You're my family. Miya belongs here too. Of course, I'll sign legal custody over to you. If you continue in this job, I'd suggest you at least leave me or someone with some sort of guardianship when you're on a mission—" Saint grabbed Kassie into a huge hug. Tears ran down his cheeks.

"If you don't up and marry this angel, I'm gonna steal her away," Saint teased.

"No need. We're getting married next weekend," Chase announced.

"Good for you. I can't think of anyone more deserving." Saint shook Chase's hand.

"Do you think we can load the guys in the vehicles and get them settled in? Then we can introduce Saint to his daughter." Kassie's eyes dropped to the ground, and she fiddled with the buttons on her dress. A sure sign Kassie hid something.

CHAPTER THIRTY-SIX

Kassie remained quiet as they drove to the other side of the mountain. When they drew closer, he felt her eyes on him. When they turned on the dirt road, the hospital he'd always dreamed of, stood proudly before him. He stopped the vehicle taking in every detail. He knew Joe supervised the teams, but Kassie built his dream. She showed in every single homey detail. A giant flag flew high and proud in the circular drive. It didn't resemble a medical facility. It reminded him of one giant log cabin home. He knew anyone who crossed the threshold of the hospital would instantly be adopted into the family. Pride welled up for the woman beside him. His throat closed with emotion; words failed him.

Leo let out a long whistle. "PITA, you did good. Real good. You make us all proud."

Kassie took Chase's hand and gently squeezed. "Maybe this evening, we'll have time for a tour. Go to the left of the drive to get to the subdivision."

Chase slowly drove past the hospital as Leo peppered

Kassie with questions. "Did Matthew vet the workers? How many men did you hire?"

Kassie rolled her eyes, "Matthew background checked everyone. Ivan showed him a flaw in the system, and he revamped his entire security protocol. I don't recall how many workers. Joe managed the hiring. I concentrated on the hospital and subdivision first and we cleared the area for the training facility you discussed with us before you left. Now you can provide some input concerning your office and if you needed bunks for the team."

"You started on my training facility? I didn't see the finalized plans, but damn Kassie if you designed it anywhere near with as much detail as you gave the hospital, I'll be pleased." Leo sat in awe of Kassie's accomplishments.

Chase rounded the bend and took in the three completed cabins and three partially constructed ones. He pulled into the first driveway.

"This is Taco's and Shadow's cabin," Kassie announced. "The next one is Whiskey and Saints. It has the best view of the lake and mountain, Whiskey. I think you'll feel right at home."

"Thank you, Kassie. It's a beautiful place." Whiskey quietly took in the scenery. The mountains surrounded them and reflected in the lake behind the structures.

Kassie helped Whiskey get settled in his room, while the men unpacked their supplies. "These are blackout curtains. Inside the walk-in closet, I placed a cot. If the storms bother you, you won't hear them in there, I soundproofed them. All the outlets have a nightlight, if you prefer to go without them, flip this switch on the wall."

She pointed to the wall. "There's also a security system. The code is one, two, two, four. The blanket on the foot of the bed is weighted. Four men remain stationed here per

Matthew's instructions. If you pick up the phone and dial zero, it will call two of them. Nate and Alek will bring you whatever you need. The cabin is stocked with condiments and the basics already. If you'll give me a list of food items you like, I'll have it here by this afternoon."

Chase watched Whiskey take in the room. Kassie remembered everything they had discussed late one night before he left on the mission. The attention to detail astounded him. When he walked by the coffee table, he noticed the picture of him and his parents. Picking it up, he read the story Kassie attached detailing his dad's dream and now his.

"If you need me, Leo or Chase can reach me." Kassie informed Whiskey.

Whiskey slid the glass patio door open and stood on the balcony overlooking the lake. Kassie followed him while Chase stood in the doorway.

"Is my Sunshine and little boy close by?" Whiskey quietly asked Kassie.

Pulling out her phone, she scrolled through snapshots of his wife and little boy. One held Samantha with LJ, another showed LJ on a horse with the girls, and Kassie captured Samantha with her head tossed back laughing as she held a glass of wine.

"She misses you. When I arrived in Serenity, I was terrified. Samantha became the first person I trusted. She told me we may not be able to change the past, but we can take all the good parts and keep them close to us. She talked about you. Your parents stay involved with LJ too. He's a firecracker and keeps us on our toes." Kassie softly told him as he flipped through the pictures.

Whiskey's fingers traced the picture of Samantha and he smiled at his boy. "They can't know I'm here. I don't want her to see me this way. I'm weak. I'm not the man I used to be. You can't tell her."

"You have my word." Kassie took her phone. "I was kidnapped, and I understand you aren't the same person. I felt the same way about Chase. I didn't know until later he stayed with me the entire time. Love is what got us through. If you give it a chance, this mountain will heal you. It's up to you to decide when you're ready. Don't discount the love Samantha has for you. It can help heal you if you let it." Kassie left Whiskey on the deck. Chase's hand clasped in hers.

"I think Leo can handle getting the men settled and get the grocery lists to me. It's time Saint met his daughter," Kassie announced.

"I'm ready to get reacquainted with Ladybug too." Chase closed the door and walked Kassie up to the truck. Once she settled in, he climbed in next to her and held her hand.

"In case I forget to tell you, I'm proud of you, Princess. I worried once they assumed we died, you'd struggle. Never in my wildest dreams did I consider you'd accomplish all you have. Baby, words can't express the gratitude I feel for everything you've done."

"It wasn't all me. The entire family pitched in. Victoria and Ivan's men have helped tremendously. Joe and Jake poured over the plans and supervised. Catherine, Samantha, Carol, and Maddie helped get the cabins ready. I wanted it to be everything you told me about when we ate lunch at Pike's Place. Your face lit up when you talked about your dream. Keeping busy helped me to cope with waiting for you. If it turned out you died, I knew I'd find you where we fell in love, here on this mountain. Now we can build the rest of it together."

Keeping Kassie

Chase leaned over and placed a soft kiss on Kassie's lips. "You amaze me."

Saint opened the passenger door. He changed into jeans and a T-shirt. Despite his put together facade, he seemed as if he'd jump right out of his skin. His leg bounced up and down and he kept wiping his hands on his pants.

Kassie smiled and patted his leg. "She'll love you. I showed her your pictures and told her how you protected me."

"I don't know anything about girls. How am I gonna talk girl stuff with her?" Saint wondered aloud as he ran his hand over the top of his head.

Leo slid into the seat next to Saint. "Whiskey decided to rest and try out the weighted thing. I wanted to come along to meet Miya if that's all right."

"Man, I need all the support I can get," Saint answered.

Kassie turned and laughed, "You'll be fine. You helped me with Emma a million times, and they're very close in age. It takes a village to raise a child and she's got everything she needs. A safe place to call home, food in her belly, and people who love her. I'll have to warn you, Clarissa made a bad habit of feeding her fast-food chicken nuggets practically at every meal. We're slowly getting her to try different foods. We call her Nugget, and she thinks it's about the chicken, but we agreed she's worth her weight in gold."

"Let's go meet this little Nugget." Leo exclaimed as he gave Saint a friendly shoulder pat.

"I'm ready." Saint sat back in his seat. A wide smile grew across his face.

Chase pulled out of the driveway and headed home.

CHAPTER THIRTY-SEVEN

Most of the visitors at his home left after the luncheon and Ty and Bryanna directed the clean-up. Food sat on the table, wrapped, and waiting to be delivered to the community food bank, several elderly, and Victoria and Ivan's men.

Kassie went upstairs to get Emma and Miya. Melody played with them since Catherine helped put the kitchen back together.

"Miya, come here sweetie. I need to talk to you. Em, Dr. Chase and Uncle Leo are downstairs, why don't you—" She didn't even need to finish the sentence as Emma and Melody threw down their dolls and took off down the stairs yelling their names.

Kassie sat on the floor and Miya crawled into her lap. Kassie kissed her forehead. "Do you remember me showing you pictures of your daddy and told you we were searching for him?"

Miya nodded.

"Well, we found him, Nugget. He's downstairs right now and is excited to meet you."

"Is he gonna like me?" Miya's eyes got wide as she cuddled further into Kassie. "Will I live in a big building like I did with Mama?"

Kassie held her close. "No, Saint plans to stay on the mountain with us. He lives not far away from here, and we'll get to see each other all the time. When he goes to work, you can come stay with Em and me."

"So, I won't get a room of my very own?" Miya's worried face broke Kassie's heart.

"I'm sure your daddy will make sure you have a room. Remember I told you your Granny planned to come visit? She'll help you pick out stuff to go into your new room. And when you come here, you can sleep in here with Em or you can sleep in the room we painted for you."

Miya dropped her eyes to the floor. "If he doesn't want me, do I have to go back to my mommy?"

Kassie turned Miya so her little face could see her own. "Miya, your daddy wants you very much. Your daddy is a hero and a very brave man. He helps save people. He might bring you here when he has to work, but he'll always come back for you." Kassie tweaked her nose to make her laugh. "So, what do ya say, shall we go meet him?"

Miya held Kassie's hand as they descended the stairs. Her purple dress matched the purple barrettes in her hair, and she held the purple teddy bear tightly in her other arm.

Kassie watched Saint's face as he drank in every single detail concerning his daughter. His eyes registered the emotion he felt as she descended the stairs. When she stopped at the bottom, Saint bent down to Miya's eye level.

"Hi Nugget, my name's Saint. You can call me Saint or Daddy, whichever one you like. I heard you like chicken nuggets. Did you know they're one of my favorite snacks?"

"Really?" Miya cautiously asked.

"Yes, I love 'em. I like to dip mine in barbeque sauce. How do you like to eat yours?" Saint attempted to make the little girl in front of him comfortable.

Emma walked up to Saint and put her arms around his neck. "I missed you, Uncle Saint. Miya likes hers with ketchup. Tomorrow, we're dipping them in ranch dressing with our carrots."

Miya dropped Kassie's hand and drew closer to Saint, seeing how comfortable Emma seemed with the man. "Do you like carrots?"

"I sure do!" Saint exclaimed.

Bryanna walked over to Saint and the girls. "I got four leftover chocolate chip cookies. Do you know anyone who wants to take them off my hands?"

Saint's eyes wandered over the woman who stood in front of him. Bryanna smiled as she took Miya's hand and Emma followed. Bryanna turned and beckoned Saint to join the girls.

Kassie watched as Leo, who held Melody, closed his eyes and gave her one more hug before setting her down to join the group.

Leo said something low to Catherine, and they disappeared out the front door. Kassie slid into Chase's arms. She felt him stiffen and glanced up from watching the girls to Chase's face. His jaw set, he drew her tighter to him as if to protect her. Jake slowly approached them.

"Kassie, darlin', I don't even know what to say. I apologize for all the grief I caused. I take full responsibility for my actions." Jake stood tall and straight, ready for Kassie to dismiss him entirely.

"I trusted you to care for Kassie, Jake. Instead, you went behind her back and listened to the one person in the world

Keeping Kassie

you shouldn't have. The damage you caused is inconceivable. It was unfair to Kassie."

Kassie only heard Chase speak in his steely voice one other time. When he learned the truth about her and Emma. Kassie cringed knowing what it felt like on the receiving end of Chase's disapproval. What Jake did hurt, but he grieved the loss of the man he considered his son as much as she fought to keep searching.

Kassie stepped in. Placing a hand on Chase's chest, she stopped him before he said something he might regret in anger. "Chase. It's been difficult for all of us. Jake, I'm disappointed you took Rachel's word without discussing the situation with me. The fact you entertained any of her lies hurts me. I won't allow this to ruin the team's homecoming. We are blessed beyond measure to stand here together. We will set aside a time to talk rationally, but tonight we are going to rejoice they are home safe and sound."

Jake's eyes stayed glued to the floor until Kassie finished. "You are wise beyond your years, young lady." Jake tipped his hat at his godson. "I realize I've made a mess of things. I'll make it right."

Kassie stepped forward and gave Jake a hug. His arms slowly came around her waist and held her tightly.

"I don't know about you, but I'm craving a cup of tea and one of Bryanna's goodies. Would you like a cup of coffee or a drink, Jake?"

Jake warily waited for Chase to say something. Chase slowly stared Jake down, but for the sake of peace, he attempted to let it go, for now. Jake extended a hand and Chase shook it.

"It's good to have you home, son. I'll take a raincheck, Kass. I need to get back to town." Jake swiped at his unshaven beard and exited the cabin.

Catherine returned and gathered Melody's things. "Welcome home, Chase. I'm happy everyone made it back home." Kassie started toward her friend when Catherine subtly shook her head as she managed to hide her face from the rest of the group in the cabin and made a hasty exit.

Kassie decided to call her once her company left for the evening.

Maddie interrupted her thoughts. "We were getting ready to deliver this food. I have enough left for supper tonight for Joe and I and the girls. Since Victoria isn't staying at the cabin, we'll have a sleepover over there." Maddie slyly suggested.

"I thought Victoria's business would be finished by now." Kassie stated.

"I briefly saw Victoria and she said she'll be back by this weekend." Chase interjected as he wrapped his arms around Kassie. "Just long enough for you to tell me how you got involved with two of the biggest mafia families in history." Smiling down at her, Chase added, "Kassie and I have an announcement. We're getting married next weekend."

Maddie and Joe rushed forward to give their congratulations followed by the others.

"We don't want to wait. I'm sorry, Maddie. I know you and Carol made all kinds of plans," Kassie apologized.

"Nonsense, Little Bit. We were young and in love once too," Joe brushed Kassie's apologies away. "Whatever you decide on, we'll make happen."

"Honestly, we want to say our vows in our special place surrounded by our family and friends. With things the way they are, we don't have time to order a wedding dress and Seattle is out of the question, we'll need to go through my wardrobe and see what will work," Kassie explained.

"Princess, I don't want you to sacrifice anything. We can

wait—" Chase was interrupted by Kassie putting her fingers to his lips.

"I'd marry you naked. What matters most is everyone we love will be there." Kassie stood on her tiptoes and placed a kiss on his lips.

Giving her attention to Leo, Kassie began directives with the food. "Maddie, Leo can take the food to the men and the food bank. I'll send Victoria's men with the deliveries."

Joe chuckled, "I think Little Bit has everything in hand. Saint, why don't you walk the girls over to our cabin and Leo, we'll help you get settled with the food."

Kassie and Chase stood on the porch and watched as Maddie and Joe headed to his parents' cabin. Saint walked with the girls. Miya giggled as Saint threw her up on his shoulders. Emma climbed up him like a monkey. Leo nodded his thanks to Kassie. The men loaded the truck with food while Kassie placed a grocery order online. She and Chase would check on them later this evening. For the moment, all was right in her world.

CHAPTER THIRTY-EIGHT

Chase closed the door and watched as Kassie turned and headed toward the bedroom. Her dress fell to the floor as she walked into the kitchen, and she sent him a flirty smile over her shoulder. He didn't need more of an invitation.

Picking her up in one scoop. She giggled and wrapped her arms around him. Her soft lips met his. She tasted of chocolate and cherries from Bryanna's cookies.

"I want to make love to you, Kass. All I thought about was getting back home. I know we have a ton to talk about, but for the next couple of hours, it's the two of us."

He sat Kassie on the stool in front of the vanity now covered with her things. He turned the water to warm as he unbuttoned his shirt.

He returned to Kassie. Her head hung down, and her hair hid her face. Getting on his knees, he gently pulled back her hair and tucked it behind her ear. Then he saw the tears.

"What is it, Princess?" he said softly.

"I hoped. I didn't give up," Kassie choked. "You're really

here. I can feel you." She traced the outline of his jaw and her fingers slid down to his tattoo and she outlined the pattern. "I fell asleep tracing this pattern on your pillow. I missed you, Chase. After today, I have to admit I worried you weren't coming home to me."

Chase swiped away the tears with the pad of his thumb. "I'm here. I'm real. I'd go through it all over again to be right here with you in the end."

"How did you escape the helicopter crash?" She whispered.

"Shhh. We can talk later. Right now, I need to take care of my girl. It's been a long damn day and I need to feel you." Chase slid the straps of her bra down and removed her panties. His gaze never left hers as he removed the rest of his clothing.

Taking Kassie's hand, Chase led her to the shower. Steam filled the room and surrounded them as if they were the only two people in the world. Kassie grabbed a tie from the edge of the shower and pulled her hair up. Chase led her into the water, letting it run down their bodies. Grabbing the soap, he leisurely caressed her shoulders and arms. Kassie placed her hands on his chest and leaned to place tiny kisses on his cuts. She peeled the soaked bandage from his arm. When she seemed satisfied the wound was healing correctly, she bathed it in kisses.

Turning her around, he washed her back and shoulders, marveling at the muscle tone Kassie developed in his absence. She was still soft, but her newly developed muscles hid a strength you couldn't see on the outside. Kassie followed his requests in his letter. She went on with her life. She didn't break. She stayed strong for him and their family.

Kassie grabbed his soap and created a lather. Turning back toward him, she rubbed the soap into his shoulder and chest. Her hand followed the hair on his chest to the lower part forming a V. She scraped his balls gently with her nails. Chase leaned his head back and groaned. He pulled her to him letting the soap glide over them. His hands cupped the cheeks of her ass. His cock stood at attention and wanted his turn. After weeks of thinking about Kassie, he wasn't rushing this now. He contrived to treasure every inch of her.

"Chase, I don't know if I can wait too much longer." Two blue pools of innocence stared back at him.

"We got a little dirty earlier, I thought you'd like to shower. I want to make love to you in our bed." Chase hummed and closed his eyes as she gripped his cock and began a steady rhythm going up and down.

"Why can't we do both?" One eye popped open as he peered down at her. A sly grin appeared as she rinsed him off and dropped to her knees. Her tongue swiped at the precum at his tip and her warm mouth covered the head of his cock.

Chase groaned loudly as his hand gripped the back of her head. Kassie's warm, wet mouth continued to suck and lick up and down his shaft. Afraid she'd hurt her knees, Chase reached for a towel at the edge of the shower door and dropped it on the floor. He indicated for her to use it. She grinned as she scooted on the towel, shaking her head. Kassie slowly sucked, and teased as her nails grazed his sack. Chase's eyes rolled back into his head.

"I don't know what you were up to while I traipsed around the desert, but I wholeheartedly approve," he growled as she took him further down her throat.

"I want you. I need you, Chase," she breathlessly told him.

"Fuck it." Chase pulled her up, shut the water off and

opened the door to the shower. Picking her up he strode across the bathroom and threw her on the bed.

Kassie shrieked. "I thought you wanted to take your time?" Her eyes held mirth as he leaned over her. He shook his head spraying water over the two of them. He pulled the rubber band from her hair.

"The sheets! They'll be soaked!" Kassie laughed as he nipped the inside of her thigh. Holding her legs, he stared down at her center like a man who hadn't eaten in days.

"I changed my mind." Chase splayed her legs wider and settled in. His tongue glided up between her delicate folds, eliciting a sigh from Kassie. She tasted like the sweetest honey. His tongue delved deeper as he couldn't resist her scent and taste. Kassie jumped as his finger slid inside of her and curled upward.

"Chase!" She exclaimed as she squirmed under his ministrations.

Chase growled and held her in place with his arm as he took what he wanted. The knowledge that her heart belonged to him and the following week she'd be legally bound to him forever, made him feel content. He'd give his life to protect her and Em. They were his everything.

Raising up, he slid his fingers slow and deep inside her as his other hand caressed her breast. When he pinched her nipple, Kassie's back arched off the bed.

"I want to touch you" she pleaded. Kassie watched as his fingers moved in and out of her, playing her like a fine instrument. Yeah, and he knew exactly what cord to play.

His fingers curled inside her and she panted hard.

"Come for me, Kass. I want to watch you fly," Chase whispered.

Kassie let go. The ripples of her orgasm made her eyes heavy, and a sated smile rested on her face. She glowed like a temptress with the halo of curls surrounding her in disarray. One section lay over her breast with her delicate pink nipple peeking out.

Chase slowly climbed Kassie's body placing kisses and nips which sent shivers down her spine. His mouth closed over her nipple while he played in her now soaked folds. Positioning himself over her, he lined up at her entrance when her hand came up and stroked his jaw.

"Welcome home, Chase. I love you." Kassie softly kissed his chin and along his jawline as he sank deep into her.

"I love you, Princess." Chase closed his eyes reveling at the feel of her around him. She felt slick and warm. He inhaled the scent of her hair. It smelled exactly as he imagined all those nights in the desert with lavender and rosemary. Recalling the smell alone had given him the strength to push forward on those long nights when the team trudged exhausted from camp to camp. No one voiced it out loud, but the doubt lingered in all their minds, on whether they would make it back home.

Her hips thrust upward to meet his. "Don't hold back, Chase. I'm not made of glass."

Her words floated over him. He'd never hurt her, and after everything she experienced, the last thing he wanted to be was rough. He needed her like nothing else he had ever felt before. Maybe it confirmed he survived and was finally home. Her words set him free. He thrust harder and fought to maintain some control. He wanted to crush her to him and sink so deep, the mere thought of it sent shivers down his spine.

"Let go, Chase. I'm your home. Let go." Kassie leaned forward and gripped the back of his neck as her tongue explored his mouth. He thrust harder. She moaned and met each stroke. Kassie's nails dug into his back as she pulled him down further. Her hot sheath tightened around him as he plunged deeper. She closed her eyes.

"It feels sooo good. Yes...Chase..." Kassie urged.

He leaned down and bit her shoulder as he let the reins on his control go. The fragile Kassie he knew didn't exist, she turned into a fighter. She'd shown him that all along. Her hands slid down to his ass, encouraging him to go even deeper. Kassie panted, and screamed his name as she went over, taking him with her. Her walls clamped down on his cock and milked him.

A pleasurable sigh left Kassie as she loosely hung her arms around his neck.

He pressed his lips to hers. "Stay here, I'll be right back."

Walking into the bathroom, he returned with a warm cloth and gently cleaned between her legs.

"As much as I love the feel of you, baby, we need to use condoms." He placed the towel on the floor next to the bed and kissed her stomach. Her hand came up and massaged the back of his head.

"It doesn't matter. I went for tests while you were away... Chances are extremely unlikely." Kassie turned her head to avoid him.

"Hey. We have a family. If you decide you want to expand it, then we'll figure it out together." Chase brushed the hair away from her face. "I'm not worried about you getting pregnant. I'm more concerned you've teamed up with two mafia families. Matthew told me James attempted to grab Em. I want to concentrate on getting him back behind bars where he can't hurt you."

"Victoria saved us. She's taught me how to protect myself and Ivan has worked with Em." Kassie sat up further against the pillows. Her hair fell all around her. Her cheeks remained rosy from their love making.

Chase placed his hand on her side. "I'm home now. Leo and I will devise a plan. I don't want you to worry about it." His hand roamed her arms and landed on her stomach. "I can't argue with the results. Your body has changed. I'll have fun learning all these new muscles. You not only feel stronger, but the confidence in yourself increased and I'm happy to see it."

Kassie met his eyes. "One day, James will catch us off guard and he'll strike. When he does, I need to know how to protect us. I won't be helpless again. I won't leave Em vulnerable to him and I refuse to go down easily."

"You won't be going down at all," Chase sternly told her.

"James left a message for me. He said he only asks once. I heard Phillip say that to my sister, Chase. He's already asked once. He'll take what he deems as his and destroy anything in his path. I'm in his way. It's only a matter of time before he comes after us again."

"When James and Phillip hurt your sister, they took the one thing away from her she needed the most to defend herself. If James thinks he's taking you or my daughter, he'll have to get through me and our family. Maddie, Joe, Jake, and the team. You might as well count Catherine and Samantha too." Chase was determined to figure out a way to get James away from his girls.

"Don't forget Victoria and Ivan. You need to know I made a deal with Victoria. If she helped me, I'll walk away when she asks. I plan to keep my promise, Chase. James has hurt and killed innocent people. He's destroyed lives and sold humans like cattle. Em will never be safe. I'm not playing God. But if the opportunity happens, I'll be happy to send him on his way for judgement," Kassie vehemently explained her position to Chase.

"Taking a life isn't easy, Kass. Even when they deserve it.

You fought nightmares for months and I've seen the nightlights again. I know it would eat at your soul. Let the team and I handle this."

Kassie pursed her lips, refusing to argue with him on the day he returned home. "I've faced the fact I may have to live my life without you. I ran through the woods with a terrified little girl to escape James. Matthew put his life on the line to borrow time for us to escape. I can't promise you I'll sit back and let you handle everything. When the time comes, Emma and I will defend ourselves. If you must choose between me and Emma, always choose her. Promise me, Chase. I made Victoria promise and now I'll ask you. Save Em at all costs. She's the priority."

"I promise I'll save Emma." Chase vowed. He neglected telling Kassie he refused to leave her behind. He'd sacrifice himself before James Stanton would take her or Emma.

CHAPTER THIRTY-NINE

Kassie examined Ash's jaw. Rollo sat at her feet watching the man warily. A low growl emitted from the dog. Immediately, Kassie chastised him.

"I'm sorry, he's having a difficult time distinguishing friend or foe these days." Kassie scratched Rollo on the back of his ears. "Your jaw healed nicely. How's the pain on a scale from one to ten?" She turned his face from side to side examining the work done by the Russian physician.

"It feels better. I'm damn glad I can chew. I've missed having regular food. What was the dish you brought us last night?" Ash shifted as Kassie reached for her stethoscope.

"It's called shrimp remoulade. Maddie's made it for our family for years." Placing the stethoscope on her ears, Kassie listened to Ash's breathing. When she was satisfied, she wrote the data on a piece of paper.

"Where's Leo and Chase? I thought Chase was doing the exams," Ash asked as Kassie checked his eyes and ears.

Kassie frowned, "They're plotting and planning."

"Ahh, I take it you don't approve. Is this about that guy Stanton?" Ash sat back when Kassie finished.

Keeping Kassie

"Yes." Kassie didn't mean to be short with Ash. In the four days since they'd been home, Chase treated her like she was helpless. Every morning, she stuck to the routine Victoria set up for her. She practiced with Ivan's man and thanked her lucky stars Chase didn't come with. Her morning shower with Chase got her motor running and started her day right. They shared breakfast with her family and usually Matthew and Leo popped in for a bite. Chase held meetings with the men while she started her warmup by running and met with Alek.

"Do you want to talk about it?" Ash stood and made his way over to the pastries Kassie set on the table.

Kassie countered, "Do you want to talk? Why do you and Whiskey insist on staying hidden from Catherine and Samantha? I don't understand. I was only separated from Chase for three months and almost lost my mind. I know Whiskey doesn't want Samantha to see him because he doesn't want to appear weak. I don't understand why you refuse to see your wife and daughter."

Ash sighed. "It's been three years. Whiskey and I have changed. I imagine our wives have too. Is it fair for them to drop their lives and take care of us?"

"I know Samantha. She'd drop anything to care for Whiskey in a heartbeat. I don't know as much about you. When I finally started to open up to Catherine, men hunted me and found us. We haven't discussed much about her life before I came into it. I know she tells Melody you died a hero protecting your country," Kassie stated.

"How did you meet Chase? Why are people hunting you down? Did you rob a bank or something?" Ash questioned her.

Kassie hesitated. Catherine's words rang in her head. *I was married to a man who wasn't good. He separated me from my mother and threatened me. When they told me he died, they thought I cried because I loved him. I cried because I was free...*

The conversation played like a movie in her head. Since Kassie met Ash, seemed part of the team somedays and yet other times, he isolated himself from the group. He remained polite and helpful when she visited the cabins. If Leo and Chase distrusted him, they wouldn't have brought him to Serenity.

"What? Don't you trust me? Did Leo tell you I wasn't part of the team? Maybe he thinks I'll slow the team down." Ash swiped the stubble along his jawline.

Kassie hastened to reassure him, "Leo hasn't said anything. We've been too busy to chat since you guys showed up. Leo plans to train men here on the mountain to do security jobs and such. I'm sure, once you're healed, he'll talk to you about it."

"But you don't trust me," Ash stated.

"No, it's not that I don't trust you. It's a long story and I can't...don't want to discuss it in detail. James Stanton is the mafia boss who killed my parents and hurt my sister."

Ash patted her hand. "It must have been difficult to be involved with all of that."

"I was on the run for two and half years from James and landed in Seattle. Catherine asked Leo to help me."

"They were together?" Ash questioned.

"No. They're just friends. I don't think they talked much until she asked him to help me." Kassie had attempted to call Catherine. Chase wouldn't allow her off the mountain, and Catherine's calls went straight to voicemail, or she claimed she was busy helping her mom and cut the call short. Kassie suspected Catherine avoided her. She would see her the next day to discuss the wedding, so she'd corner her then. Kassie planned to ask Catherine the

Keeping Kassie

same tough questions she demanded of Kassie not so long ago.

"Leo helped you keep your identity?" Ash pushed for more information as he tried to put the pieces together.

Kassie laughed. "Not exactly. He assigned Chase to me. That's how we met. I didn't like Leo at first."

"Was it Leo's wonderful personality that won you over or his stunning good looks?" Ash joked.

Kassie chortled, "Chase and Leo took care of Emma and me. It was such a traumatic time. I don't want to talk about it." Kassie turned to place everything back in her bag. She couldn't pinpoint exactly what made the alarm bells go off in her head, but they were dinging loud and clear. Every member of the team had asked Kassie questions and challenged her at times. Ash's questions caused an uneasy feeling in her gut. She wondered why he never asked to see pictures of Catherine or Melody. He didn't inquire about Melody's school or why they lived in Serenity. Rollo must've felt the same way as he stuck to Kassie like glue in Ash's cabin.

"You talk about him like he's a saint." Ash half-heartedly joked.

"He's human. He's suffered loss." Kassie straightened and checked her watch. "I need to check on Whiskey. Then I need to return home to see Maddie. She's in total wedding planner mode." Kassie let out a groan as Ash chuckled.

Pulling out a sheet of paper, Kassie indicated the exercises listed. "Here's your homework and I'll see you bright and early tomorrow. Three times a day and if you behave, I'll bring you homemade beignets in the morning."

"Yes, ma'am. I'm not about to pass those up!" Ash insisted as he helped her load the items in her car.

Kassie waited for Rollo and closed the door. They made

their way to Whiskey's cabin. Claire called and asked Kassie to remind Whiskey of their appointment in the afternoon. Kassie wanted to convince him to shower and get dressed. Whiskey ate what food she brought but he struggled with loud noises. He was constantly checking the windows and doors. Kassie called through the door and waited for Whiskey to open it. When he finally acknowledged her, she knew Whiskey struggled through another rough night.

Bloodshot eyes, hair sticking up in all directions, and two-day old clothes indicated Whiskey suffered from his imprisonment. As he allowed her in, she watched his eyes scan the surrounding landscape seeking the enemy. The stark differences between the two rescued team members were night and day. Ash showered daily, noises didn't bother him, and he asked a million questions, yet nothing about his wife or child. In fact, he seemed more interested in Kassie and Leo's connection. When Kassie visited Whiskey, his eyes traveled wistfully to her phone. She pulled out the device, tapped her code in and swiped to the photos. He lovingly stroked Samantha's face and smiled at pictures of LJ and Emma's antics. Kassie tried to capture as many pictures as possible when she saw Samantha or LJ so she could take them to Whiskey. Kassie patiently waited until Whiskey's focus came back to her.

"Good morning, Whiskey. I brought you some pastries, eggs and biscuits. Leo said you need to eat," Kassie added softly. He tended to do better when he thought the instructions came from Leo. Kassie was determined to put some weight on the man. She held out a bag with bacon and sausage. She discovered the man was a carnivore.

Whiskey took the food and set it on the table. Pulling the chair out, he held the material to his nose and inhaled deeply. He placed it on the table and stared at it.

"Eat it while it's hot, Whiskey. I have plenty of time." Maddie wasn't expecting her back for at least another hour. She related to him the most. Like her, he refused to see Samantha because he didn't want her to see him as broken. Kassie remembered pushing Chase away for the same reason.

Kassie hoped when her friends learned her secret, they'd forgive her. It sucked not telling them, yet she understood at least Whiskey's point of view, and respected Ash's.

Kassie started the coffeemaker. She knew Leo made it nightly to run in the morning. After the first two days, Kassie figured out Whiskey became overwhelmed over something as full as a pot of coffee for himself. She waited for the coffee to brew and placed a big fat double chocolate donut on his plate with a half a plate of eggs. She waited as she held out a fork.

"A shower sounds like a great idea today. I equipped all the bathrooms with a seat. Chase used one in his own shower while he recovered, and I love to sit and soak in the shower when my leg gets stiff. I imagine sitting under some hot water might feel good for those aches and pains in your legs." Kassie spoke conversationally.

Whiskey's eyebrows arched in surprise, and he kept shoveling food in his mouth as if she would take it away at any second. She remembered the feeling all too well. Roger forced her to choose meals for the day and most often than not, they were empty plates. She shivered as she brushed away the thought.

"Claire will be here after lunch. I'll place a note on the door to help you remember it's okay to answer the door for her. Did the new clothes fit? If not, I can exchange them for a different size."

Whiskey finished the eggs and took the cup of coffee

Kassie offered him. He closed his eyes as he inhaled the aroma. "They fit," he replied.

"Oh good, then you'll have something to change into. Would you like me to shave your beard today? We can start by letting me cut it and you can decide if you want to keep it or get rid of it all together. I brought the scissors like you asked." Kassie reminded him as she took in the scraggily beard down to his chest. In almost every picture, Whiskey was clean shaven or had a five o'clock shadow.

Whiskey stopped eating. "I don't know if I can handle you behind me to shave and I can't do it myself. I shake too much."

"I can stay in front of you. I'll use scissors first and if that's as far as we get, there's always tomorrow." Kassie went about the kitchen putting new snacks in the cabinets to entice him to eat. She knew he opened the drawers to check everything.

Leo stayed there at night and knew better than to open the top drawers. Whiskey needed to relearn how to choose items he liked. Whiskey developed an obsession with Bryanna's pecan bars.

"I wish Leo was here. Are you sure the men gave you permission to come alone?" Whiskey stressed about having an episode and hurting her.

"I'm positive. Plus, Rollo is here. Trust me, he's as protective as one of the guys. Did I tell you how he saved me from becoming coyote food? I assure you I have no intention of letting you beat me at cards today. I thought we could play a couple of hands of rummy." Kassie sat at the table across from Whiskey, showing him, she held no concerns about him injuring her.

"Sunshine and I used to play rummy. We paid for her father's medication and some weeks we couldn't afford to go out and we played cards every night." Whiskey smiled as he told her.

"Well, you better brush up cause she's a card shark now. Every time we play, I swear she knows exactly what cards I have in my hands," she complained.

Whiskey's soft laughter was a welcome sound. "She's very competitive."

"You don't say," Kassie chided.

Whiskey ate the donut in three bites and finished off the eggs and half the bacon. Kassie mentally high fived herself. Rummaging inside her purse, she pulled out a bag of disposable razors, shaving cream, after shave, and scissors. Walking to the bathroom she grabbed a couple of towels.

"What if I hurt you?" Whiskey asked her quietly.

"What if you don't? I'll sing my way through this shave. What do you want to hear?"

"I don't know, I haven't listened to music in a long time," he confessed.

Kassie's voice started low as she started the lyrics of "I'll Stand By You" as she held up the towel and slowly wrapped up his shoulders and lap. Again, she held up the scissors as she sang along to "Scars to Your Beautiful" Whiskey closed his eyes and gripped the edge of his chair. She stopped to get a bowl of hot water and removed the towel from his lap to get rid of trimmings.

He peeked up at her when she laid the cloth back over his legs. Kassie held out the shaving cream and gestured for his hand. She sprayed some in his hand and waited as he rubbed it on the fresh stubble. She started singing, "Honest" and switched to "Baby I Am." while the razor revealed the man he used to be. She held a hot towel out and he groaned as she placed it on his face.

"You're good at this. Is Doc aware you have these skills?"

Whiskey bantered. His confidence grew as she worked. The key to Whiskey was easy. Don't make any sudden moves and she always let him know when she was moving on to something else.

"You did such a great job, I brought you a reward," Kassie announced.

"What is it?" he asked wearily.

Kassie pulled a used phone from her bag and placed it in the palm of his hand. She demonstrated how to turn it on and where to locate the photo file.

"Don't use this for calls. Leo is setting up special cellphones for the team and your name was added to the list. In the meantime, this holds all the pictures I have of Samantha and LJ. When I take more, I'll text them to your phone so you can open them whenever you want."

Whiskey held the phone to his chest and squeezed her hand. Overcome with emotions, he whispered, "Thank you."

A knock at the door made Kassie and Whiskey turn as Leo and Chase walked in. Leo sat next to Whiskey as Chase narrowed his eyes at Kassie. She lost her composure for a minute before she finished picking up the shaving items. She knew she was in trouble. She lied about Chase and Leo giving her permission to stay with Whiskey alone. Chase expressed his desire for her to stay away from Whiskey until Claire cleared him of violent episodes. He didn't want her to get hurt.

"I'd think my bride had other stuff to do with the wedding days away. Yet here I find her with another man. I don't know if I even recognize him." Chase teased.

Leo rifled through the box of treats. Kassie smacked his hand. "Those are Whiskey's. You already ate your share at my house."

"Come on PITA, you know Saint stole the last of the crullers. And I didn't get a Boston crème either. How come Whiskey got one and I didn't?" Leo whined.

"Fine. You can have one. Now I laid out some clothes in the bathroom, Whiskey. Why don't you try the shower?"

Whiskey stood, "Thanks." He retreated to his room, and they heard the shower water turn on.

"You're good with him, PITA." Leo complimented her.

Kassie cleaned up the mess and rinsed out the bowl. "I understand what he's going through right now. I've decided I don't want to go to medical school. I want to stay a nurse practitioner. I can still cover things at the hospital and be home to spend time with Emma. Two doctors in the family might be too much."

"Are you sure, Princess? I don't want you to sacrifice for any of us. We'll work it out if you want to go back to school." Chase watched her carefully. He observed her a lot lately. He needed to adjust to a new confident Kassie. She knew what she wanted, and it was time he knew it too.

"I'm happy. I can work with my best friend and alongside my husband. I love what I do. I can work with the veterans, but I want to be involved with the teen unit. I've continued therapy with Claire. My needs are factored into the equation. Becoming a doctor means more school, more time away, and longer hours. I started this as your dream. Now I realize it's our dream. I want to be by your side. I'm not settling, there's a lot to be done and this will give me the flexibility to manage it."

"Doc, I think your girl has figured herself out." Leo smiled.

"Yes, I believe she has." Chase smiled as his arm wrapped around her. "I'm proud of you, baby. You amaze me and I love you."

Kassie winked at Leo as she stepped into Chase's embrace. "I think I need Chase for a couple of hours. There's a super-secret meeting we need to hold."

Leo laughed as she closed the door to the cabin and Chase helped her into the truck. She didn't need to tell him where they needed to go. Chase started the truck and headed in the direction of their spot. Life didn't get any better than this, right?

CHAPTER FORTY

Kassie sat with Catherine and Samantha on the couch. Maddie and Carol stood in front of the glass windows and resembled two commanding generals.

Carol suggested, "We have a lot to plan. Let's see what's on our to do list and then we'll prioritize."

Maddie nodded her agreement, "An excellent idea. Food, dress, and suit for Kassie and Chase. What about the wedding party? What will they wear? Flowers, we need flowers. Cake, rehearsal dinner and where will we hold it? I know you mentioned holding the ceremony at your special spot, what about a backup plan if it rains?"

Catherine nodded. Samantha said, "We need to organize all of it."

Kassie swallowed hard and pasted a smile on her face. Bryanna set a platter of cake samples in front of Kassie and sat on the couch to show her united support. Kassie crammed the first miniature cupcake in her mouth and closed her eyes as the flavors of the carrot cake exploded in her mouth.

"At least use a napkin," Maddie chastised as Kassie stuffed the almond cake in her mouth and proceeded to lick her fingers clean. A moan escaped as she licked her lips and eyed the red velvet sample.

Realizing the other women stopped talking, Kassie put the cake down. "What? Do I have to decide on one flavor, Bryanna, or two? Maybe three?"

The women laughed as Kassie sat confused as to why she was the butt of the joke. She failed at this bridal stuff. Maddie shook her head, and Carol's hands rested on her hips. It didn't take an idiot to realize this was a bad sign.

"What flavors were you thinking?" Bryanna asked.

"Chase would love carrot cake. My favorite is the almond. Although, I have to admit, I had the fudge thingy at the bakery and it's simply divine. Is anyone else going to try the samples?" Kassie held out the tray and the ladies each took a cake from the assortment. Oohs and ahhs filled the room as they debated on which flavor was the best. Kassie rubbed her forehead to stave off the stress headache that was threatening to form. If she couldn't decide on something as simple as the cake, how long was this wedding planning going to last?

Bryanna stepped in, "Kassie it's your wedding. Some brides have a small cake to cut then serve an assortment of cupcakes or a selection of other cookies, pies and cakes. What do you want to do?"

Kassie straightened on the couch. "Can I do the last thing? Chase and I can slice a red velvet cake and then have a dessert table?"

Bryanna wrote down Kassie's choices and placed it in the folder.

Maddie cleared her throat. "One item down and a million to go. For the rehearsal dinner, we could use Ty's restaurant or rent something in Seattle." Maddie shook a pen as she ticked things on her list.

"Maybe we should start at the beginning with the ceremony. What about the bridal party?" Carol chimed in.

"Chase and I decided to keep it simple. Leo and Catherine agreed to be the best man and maid of honor." Kassie smiled, pleased she had the answer to that question.

"What are the wedding colors so we can match the tux and dress?" Carol asked.

"Colors?" Kassie echoed.

Maddie rolled her eyes. "Little Bit, what color would you like Catherine to wear?"

Kassie cringed as she turned toward Catherine, "What color do I want you to wear?"

Catherine covered her mouth to disguise her laughter. "Remember, we discussed blue."

"Oh yeah, blue!" Kassie sounded gleeful as she answered two questions in a row.

"Flowers, I think Kassie should carry white roses. Or maybe ivory?" Maddie pondered the question as Kassie made faces behind her napkin, making the women on the couch giggle.

"How about sunflowers? They would pop with the sunset." Carol suggested.

"Oh, that's an excellent idea. Let's move on. Rehearsal dinner at Ty's or Seattle?" Maddie picked up her list to examine her options.

"Seattle traffic will be a disaster at that time of day. Ty's a better option. Plus, he makes a lovely creamy parmesan dressing." Carol scribbled on the notepad.

"Good now that's settled, let's go to the reception." Maddie and Carol bent their heads together over the list, oblivious to the rest of the women in the room.

Victoria sat in the overstuffed chair by the fireplace and wisely stayed quiet. Maddie begrudgingly accepted her presence but didn't like it.

Finally, Kassie held up her hands. "Maddie, I'd like to have the rehearsal in Bear's barn. It smells heavenly with all the herbs he has drying in there. When I went to Saint's funeral, they set out this lovely long table and everyone sat together as one big family. As far as flowers go, I want to carry a bouquet of wildflowers from the mountain."

Maddie pursed her lips. Carol took a seat while she waited for Maddie to blow a gasket.

"Little Bit, I want your wedding day to be special. We didn't think we'd ever get to see this day. I want it to be perfect," Maddie explained as she pushed her hair back into her normal bun. "I never envisioned you eating in a barn."

"Kassie did you pick out what dress you want to wear?" Catherine asked, trying to change the topic.

Samantha brought over several dresses for her to try on. Nothing seemed appropriate. "No, I haven't decided on a dress. I'm sorry, ladies. This is not my thing. I don't care what I wear. I just want to marry Chase." Kassie blew back her hair which fell in her face. "After this last year, Chase and Emma, and all of you, are the most important people to me. If you're there, the rest doesn't matter."

Maddie stood back and cleared her throat. "All right, Little Bit. I'll talk to Bear and get the barn set up. Victoria, can I borrow a couple of your men to help decorate and guard the area?"

"Yes, I know just the ones to help," Victoria agreed.

Kassie's mouth hung open as she watched Victoria take direction from Maddie and within minutes, they locked down the details for the rehearsal dinner. Maddie nodded to

Keeping Kassie

Victoria, and she picked up the phone and spoke to someone on the other end.

A few minutes later, Joe walked in carrying a huge white box with a big red bow. He set it on the kitchen table and stood back.

"I know you don't like attention put on you, Sugar. This is the one day everything will be about you and Chase. Victoria helped me retrieve this and I think it'll solve your biggest problem of what to wear." Maddie nodded to the package on the table.

Kassie walked into the kitchen. Samantha, Bryanna and Catherine followed behind. Kassie shot a glance at Joe. He shrugged and smiled at her. Pulling the red bow, Kassie lifted the lid and pulled aside the tissue.

A gasp left her as she held up the dress. She hugged it to her chest. Happy tears fell from her cheeks. She gently laid the dress down and ran to put her arms around Maddie.

"You remembered, Maddie. How did you get it?" Kassie returned to the dress and fingered the delicate lace bodice with seeded pearls and rhinestones.

"What is it, Kass?" Samantha asked.

"It's Mama's dress. When my sister married Phillip, Maddie gave her a choice. My sister wanted a designer dress. I never dreamed I would have it to wear at my wedding." Pulling the dress out, the women gushed at the delicate design and the long veil.

"I wanted you to have something of your parents with you. They loved you, Sugar." Maddie caressed the dress. "I've already altered it to fit but we'll need to try it on for last minute adjustments. I asked Victoria to pick it up for me on her way here," Maddie explained.

Kassie grinned at Victoria, who remained seated. "Thank you, for getting it for me."

"Maddie insisted upon it. I'm the delivery service." Victoria smiled. Kassie knew, for her, they had made a tentative truce.

"Mama gave me the best present ever. She and daddy gave me you and Joe. I don't know how I'd have survived without you. You're the reason I fought to come home. You're my second mama, Maddie. I love you for all you do." the two women hugged.

Kassie walked to Joe. "You've always watched over me, Joe. I can't think of anything better than you giving me away. It'll be like you and Daddy are right beside me."

"I'd be honored, Little Bit. Chase is a good man. Your father would approve," Joe choked.

Kassie kissed his cheek and they held on to one another.

"Let's get this wedding planned. So, LJ will be the ring bearer and then Emma, Melody, and Miya will be flower girls. Do they have dresses?" Catherine asked as she pulled the veil from the box and the women clustered around Kassie. Samantha gathered her hair and figured out the best style to complement the dress.

"Miya wants purple, Emma chose white, and Melody picked pink. Their dresses arrive tomorrow. Bear said he'd provide lavender lemonade, tea, soda and Ty agreed to bring a full bar," Carol piped in as her phone dinged from text messages.

"I guess the reception is last. Can Ty cater it? We can buy a bunch of picnic tables from the hardware store in town and set them around here. Between the deck and the trees, there's plenty of room. Then we can donate the picnic tables to the school and the park and place a few at the hospital," Kassie wondered out loud.

"Don't forget the most important item!" Samantha

exclaimed. "Have you and Chase decided where you're honeymooning?"

Kassie shook her head. "Honestly, we're happy to be home. The hospital is taking up a lot of time, and we don't feel comfortable leaving the mountain when we can't account for James's whereabouts."

The group grew quiet.

"You only get married once and it's a shame you can't even have a honeymoon," Catherine sympathized.

Kassie put her arms around her best friend.

"Cat, we are blessed to have our family around us, especially now. James won't be around forever. Chase and I will take some time off. Michael's practice has occupied most of his time. He'll be coming up this weekend. Matthew doubled security and the closer the wedding becomes, the less I see of him. I'm hoping with the return of the team, Matthew can devote time to finding José and his mom, and a couple of other people. Elizabeth called, she gave her notice last week at the hospital and she'll start the interviews for administrative staff positions. It'll be nice having her on the mountain."

"Ivan is annoyed with a couple of his men, he assigned them flower picking duty. Maddie and Carol, please give me a list of what they need to gather. Has anyone seen Jake?" Victoria joined Carol and Maddie as they gathered the dress to take to Kassie's bedroom. She needed to try it on.

"Chase talked to him about the wedding. I know he's planning on coming, he's avoided us like the plague. I'm hoping I can pull him aside at the wedding. I don't want this looming over us."

"He's licking his wounds, Little Bit. Jake's fine. I saw him yesterday. He feels awful about how things went down and even though he apologized, he feels guilty for how he handled it. Give him time," Joe advised.

※

A HALF HOUR later Kassie slid the dress over her head and Maddie buttoned the tiny white buttons along the back. She excused herself to give Kassie a moment alone.

She took a moment to view herself in the bathroom mirror. The dress fit perfectly. The sheer sleeves, beaded with pearls and a few rhinestones, shimmered as she twisted around in different angles, taking in her mother's gown. The beads were designed to catch the light but not enough to distract from the details of the gown. The embroidered bodice contained lace and seed pearls, and it flared into layers of tulle. Not puffy, yet not fully straight. It complemented Kassie's frame perfectly.

One detail on the dress made Kassie stop. She sat in her favorite reading nook and let the sun hit the sparkles on the sleeves. Her eyes followed the pattern of embroidered flowers. Lilies, roses, shamrocks, and… marigolds. Her mama sent her a sign. Chase sent Kassie marigolds during her recovery and told her they reminded him of her strength. The bridal bouquet request contained the sentimental flowers.

"Thank you, Mama, for sending him to me. I promise as I make my vows, I'll remember no matter what, I need to carry the strength to pull us through the rough times. I wish you, daddy, and sissy sat in the front row to witness my marriage. I miss you so much." Kassie spoke out loud as she peered over the mountain. "I know you're here with me. Emma and I will always keep you alive in our hearts. If you see Sophia and John Winters up there, please tell them

Keeping Kassie

thank you for raising the man I love more than life. I promise to always love and cherish him."

Taking a deep breath, Kassie opened the door to the waiting women. Joe left the dress fitting to the ladies. Collective ooh's and aah's came from the women as Kassie walked into the room.

Maddie sniffed. Kassie hugged the woman tightly. Tears filled her eyes. Maddie stepped in for Abigail Reynolds, her best friend in the whole world, to ensure Kassie's wedding went smoothly. Samantha choked back a sob and Catherine dabbed her eyes. Victoria handed the women tissues as she swiped at her own watery eyes. Kassie hugged each of them and started to giggle.

"This is a wedding, why are we crying?" she asked through her tears.

"Because you're stunning Kass. Chase will flip when he sees you walk down the aisle." Catherine laughed through her tears. "I can help get the decorations done and get the girls ready."

"Kassie and Emma will dress together. Saint's mom arrived, and I'm sure she'd appreciate some help with Miya if you want to get dressed at their cabin instead of coming back into town. LJ and I will return with Kassie and Emma." Samantha coordinated everyone and set up times for hair and makeup. Leaving Kassie and Emma last.

"Wear a button-up shirt the day of the wedding, we can avoid messing up your hair. I'll still have everything we need for last minute emergencies. Chase mentioned he wants you to take pictures before the wedding to allow time for you to relax. The only ones after the ceremony will be of you and him. He requested pictures of him, and Emma done before the ceremony. I'll have a touch up bag on me for everyone."

"I don't know what I'd do without you. Elizabeth said

she's coming straight from her apartment to the wedding. I think I'll have Michael bring her, he's already in Seattle anyway." Kassie grabbed her pen and paper and started making a last-minute list.

"Where are the men? I don't think I've seen much of them since they got back." Samantha grabbed the veil and started arranging pieces of hair away from Kassie's face for effect.

"Working out some details from their last mission. It's all confidential," Kassie added. "Cat, help me out of the dress?"

Catherine nodded and followed Kassie to the bedroom. When the door shut, Catherine began undoing the buttons. "You look beautiful, Kass. I can't wait to see you on the big day," even Cat realized she sounded phony and cringed at her own words as Kassie turned around to face her with a frown.

"What's going on? Have you spoken to Leo since he returned? I saw you leave after he asked you to talk on the porch. Are you all right?" Kassie worried for her friend. Leo seemed miserable when he thought no one could see.

Catherine sat down in the reading nook and stared out the window. "Leo informed me, he will be busy with setting up his company and felt with the amount of time he'll be gone, it might be best to remain friends. He sounded very professional about it."

Kassie ran her hand up Cat's arm in a soothing gesture. "Don't read too much into it, Cat. The mission went wrong, and they barely made it back. Maybe Leo needs space to think, you remember how he gets caught up in his own head, sometimes."

Caterine shook her head. "No, he made it perfectly clear. The funny thing is, I resisted him and refused to talk to him about...stuff and he insisted I give him a chance. When I thought I'd never see him again, I realized how precious life is. If he came back, I'd consider giving us a chance. It's like he did a one-eighty."

Kassie regretted she couldn't share what Leo's true problem was. How do you go about telling a widow of three years her dead husband was alive? And the man who loved her, stepped aside because he felt it was the right thing to do. For once, Leo had his head stuck up his ass. Kassie planned to earn her new nickname after the wedding.

"You mentioned your husband worked on the same team as him. Were they close?" Kassie wanted to get answers from Cat's perspective.

"I think Leo considered them close. Ash hated him. Leo was constantly at my house because he became best friends with my brother. When Ash and I got together, he became extremely jealous of Leo. The night I broke up with Leo, I was with Ash. It made team family nights awkward to say the least. Ash resented any time Leo came near me. Before long, my circle got smaller and smaller. Then Melody came along, and he controlled what time I spent with my parents. When my father died, Ash pitched a fit when I went to the funeral and left Melody with a sitter. He timed how long I spent at the service. The marriage became more toxic every time he returned from missions. I wish I had recognized all the signs of abuse and spoke with Leo, but it's too late."

"What if you told Leo now? Do you think he'd understand?" Kassie asked.

"What would it matter now? The bastard died. I'll never let another man control me."

Kassie nodded. The sinking feeling in her stomach grew stronger as she thought about the information she kept from her best friend. She wondered if friendship survived when one friend didn't know her promise to hold the confidence, had the potential to hurt the person she loved the most. Kassie learned a long time ago, secrets always had a way of coming out.

CHAPTER FORTY-ONE

Chase woke Kassie up with a tender kiss on her shoulder. The sun shone through the window, peeking above the mountain. Kassie appeared restless the last couple days. He put it down to last-minute wedding planning. Tomorrow, they hosted the rehearsal dinner and the next day, she became his wife.

Kassie groaned and shifted allowing her body to meld into his with her face buried in his chest. "Good morning. Don't talk too loudly, Maddie's probably waiting at the door to stuff food in me and go over the menu again. Can't I go with you to check on the team?" She batted her eyes coquettishly trying to win her way.

"You're supposed to be having your bachelorette spa day. Surely, all the plans are finalized by now," Chase whispered.

"At least Emma, Miya, Melody, and LJ enjoyed themselves between cake testing, cookie baking, and whipping up frosting with Bryanna. They're thick as thieves. Taco seems in good spirits. He's leaving after the wedding to see his folks. Shadow's staying here. I asked Matthew to do some digging to find Avie Rahimi for him. He located her and Rebecca Rhodes wasn't happy when Shadow's letter and check showed up. How did they even know? Maybe I don't want to know. What about Whiskey and Ash? You can't keep them hidden forever." Kassie traced Chase's tattoo. Deep in thought of what her friends' reactions might be.

"Claire assessed Whiskey and Ash. She set up care plans and suggested therapies for each of them. Both expressed the fact they gave up believing they would be rescued. They reconciled themselves to their fate. In some ways, Whiskey wishes he died in the explosion. It's not fair to throw them into unknown family situations without the proper tools to cope." Chase played with the silky curls laying on her shoulder and placed sweet kisses along Kassie's jawline.

"I was prepared to wait forever for you. I knew the chances slimmed with each passing day and I needed real proof to accept it. Leo's team confirmed the deaths of Whiskey when a grenade went off. Ash's new team confirmed his death on a separate mission. Their wives grieved and moved on. They've created entirely new lives for themselves. What if they want a divorce?" Kassie questioned as she bent her neck, allowing Chase more access.

Chase raised his face to see Kassie's face. "I know I've asked you to withhold information from your friends. I've appreciated you checking in on the men. Both seem to come out of their shell for you. Maybe because you understand the experience more than others. Is there something on your mind? Have they said something to you the team needs to address?"

Kassie propped her body up on her elbows allowing the sheet to fall. She smiled as Chase's gaze lowered. His finger traced the outline of her breasts sending a shiver through her.

"I don't want to keep secrets from you. Every time I do, I

put our relationship on the line. I vowed to work through my feelings with you and stop running. What I say to you in this bed, stays here. Not with the team," she warned him.

"Princess if I repeated what you said in bed, the team would be fighting to be in my place," Chase joked as Kassie playfully threw her pillow at him.

Grabbing her wrist, he pulled Kassie on top of his chest, allowing her tresses to act as a curtain away from the world.

"Talk to me, Kass. What's on your mind?" Chase knew something bothered her by the questions she asked about the two men. He assumed it involved her friends.

"When Cat called Leo and asked him to help me. I assumed he was an old friend. When he went on the run with Emma, Cat, and Melody, I sensed a connection between them. At one time, I asked Cat about Leo, she said nothing could happen between them. I've seen them checking out each other when they think no one's watching. When Cat approached me about running from something, she told me she married a man who hurt her. What if Ash hurt Cat?"

Chase sat up and leaned against the headboard. "Did she say Ash hurt her?" Chase kept his anger controlled. Kassie may be the key to forcing Leo to admit his feelings for Cat.

"She never said exactly what occurred. He stalked her even when he left for missions. She wasn't even allowed to see her mom," she explained.

"Did he threaten or hit her?"

Kassie shook her head as she laid her head on his chest and listened to his heartbeat. "She didn't say it, but I bet there was more to it. Cat's reluctant to talk about it. I've heard her speak to Melody about her father. She told her Ash died protecting his country."

Chase sighed as a timid knock sounded from the door. "Let's not say anything until we get more information. I'll see what Leo says and maybe question Ash. Claire may have some insight too." Chase got up and slid a pair of exercise shorts on as Kassie watched. Her heated gaze did nothing but add fuel to the fire. He hoped for some alone time. By the way the knock sounded, a miniature of Kassie stood on the opposite side.

Kassie wrapped her robe around her as Chase opened the door and Emma and Rollo came bouncing in.

"Mama, Gran Maddie said breakfast is getting cold, and she has something to show you."

Kassie rolled her eyes to Chase. Swinging Emma up in his arms, he kissed his soon to be bride and whispered, "Just say the word, I can have Leo plan a mission to Vegas in under an hour."

Giggling, Kassie knew they would never give any of this up. This was their life, and they were blessed.

CHAPTER FORTY-TWO

The guys planned to spend time at the cabins to allow Whiskey and Ash to join in on the celebrations. A night of card playing, good whiskey, and cigars awaited them.

Kassie and her tribe planned an evening at the spa. Samantha stocked up on wine and Ty and Bryanna made hors d'oeuvres and treats. Bryanna thrilled Kassie when she accepted the invitation to join the group for an evening of pampering. After some resistance, Maddie, Carol, and Saint's mother, Edie, agreed to join the women. They argued the younger women needed time alone, but Kassie wasn't having it. They were her family.

Victoria and Ivan volunteered to watch the girls and LJ to allow everyone to join in on the fun. Disappointed, Kassie confronted Victoria.

"I want you there, Victoria. You're part of my family now too." She argued.

"You and I will have plenty of time to do our own pampering day. Let Maddie have you to herself. I want to be her friend as well, but we can't until she stops seeing me as a threat," Victoria explained to Kassie.

"She asked you to get Mama's wedding gown for me. Surely, her opinion has changed." Kassie knew Maddie's reserved behavior around Victoria had lessoned and deemed Victoria exaggerated Maddie's feelings.

"Go. Have a wonderful time. Ivan and I will enjoy an amazing time with the kids. I always wanted a houseful and for a little while, I'll get my wish." Victoria ushered Kassie down to the car where her teams escorted her and guarded the little party. Ivan's men discreetly scouted the area.

An hour later the group of women laughed as their feet soaked in scented water and flowers. Catherine and Samantha made question cards asking for a lot of personal details. As the bride, her title required her to answer first. It took a couple of glasses of wine to relax her enough to answer things in front of Maddie.

Edie sent them into hysterics when she described her wedding night. "I got in bed and turned off the lights. Mr. Johnson lay next to me and says, 'Edie, honey, are you scared?' I said no, I ain't, I'm just cold is all! He turned the lights back on and said Edie, I ain't saying you scared, but I ain't never heard of anyone coming to bed with their coat on!" The women howled in laughter.

Carol Reese sat forward. "Well, I learned about sex before the wedding night."

"Mama!" Catherine's mouth hung open at Carol's admission.

"In my day the hot and spicy book of my time was a little book called *Peyton Place*. Well, my daddy worked as a janitor for the school. Some of the older girls brought their copies of the book and snuck them into the bathroom. We obviously couldn't walk the school halls carrying such a scandalous item. We wrapped it in a book cover made of brown paper bags, to resemble a normal schoolbook. Then we'd go in during our breaks to read the sinful story. One day, my daddy came in and slapped that outrageous book on our table. I asked Daddy, did you buy it for me? He said Yes, Carol. I know you young girls snuck the book and read it in the bathrooms. If you have any questions, I'd rather you learn it here. So, here's your own copy and if you have any questions, you can ask your mama or me. Well, the next day at school, I proudly walked the halls as everyone knew I owned my very own copy. A few days went by, and we sat and ate dinner. My father inquired if I had finished the book. There was no way I could gobble that book up when I received so much attention at school. I committed myself to only reading two chapters a night. There was just one thing which stumped me. So, I looked him dead in the eye and said, 'No I haven't finished the book. They keep talking about this character called the pulsating member and for the life of me I can't figure out who it is!"

The women lost it while Samantha got up and poured more wine.

"What did your father do?" Kassie asked.

"I must give him credit. He wiped his face with a napkin and said, Carol, it's a discussion not appropriate for the table. After dinner, your mama will explain to you who the pulsating member is. He scooted back from the table and left the room!"

The women held their stomachs as they cried in laughter. Samantha started giving Kassie a pedicure as the other women dried their feet and helped themselves to snacks. Cat handed Kassie a plate.

"So Kass, give us the deets. Was your first time with Chase everything you imagined it would be?" Cat wiggled her eyebrows up and down making the room fill with giggles.

"As usual, Chase took care of me first. It happened on Christmas Eve after we fought terribly. I neglected to tell him something important. I thought he would drive me to Leo, himself. Instead, he made love to me next to the Christmas tree and made the moment extremely special."

"Aww." The women exclaimed as Kassie blushed.

"You couldn't find a better man, Kass. He'd walk through fire to get to you." Catherine's voice was wistful. "I had that once. Hold on to it, fight for it, and never take it for granted." She raised her wine glass and the group clinked glasses.

"I love you. All of you. Thank you for supporting me. I'm grateful for each of you and what you bring to my life. Three years ago, I never thought I'd have this ever again. I couldn't find more supportive friends in the entire world."

Samantha raised her glass. "To Kassie and Chase. We pray your marriage is blessed. May you always find your way back home."

The clinking of glasses filled the room. Happiness hung in the air.

CHAPTER FORTY-THREE

Chase kissed Kassie's shoulder as she sat at the vanity debating on what jewelry would complement her form fitting blue dress. Chase loved when she wore the color to bring out her blue eyes. She picked the dress with him in mind.

Chase lowered himself on his haunches next to her and gently placed a box in front of her wrapped with a blue ribbon and a marigold stuck between the knots in the bow.

Kassie beamed her pleasure at the sweet surprise. "Chase, you didn't need to get me anything. I'm excited about tomorrow and exchanging our vows. I wish my family and your parents could be here to enjoy the day with us."

"They're here in spirit. I understand Maddie got your mom's wedding dress for the ceremony. I'm sure your mama would be pleased to know she played a small part in your wedding. I saved these for a special moment, and I don't want you to feel pressured to use them tomorrow." He pushed the box closer to her with his finger, encouraging her to open it. "My father spent months designing my mother's ring. When I proposed to Rachel, something prevented me from giving her this. The night of our rehearsal dinner, my mother sensed something was wrong. As usual, she allowed me to make my own decisions, but she left me with some advice. She said I needed someone strong, someone who knows how to love unconditionally, and needs me as much as I need her. Someone loyal, faithful, and willing to fight me as much as love me. Kassie, she was describing you. When I slide the ring on your finger tomorrow, part of my dad will be there with us. My mother loved the way my dad represented the mountain where they planned to build their life. The big sapphire represents the mountain, and the smaller diamonds are placed to represent the lake. The leaves designed into the band represent the leaves from the trees and the tiny sapphires are the flowers. My mom was moved by my dad's thoughtfulness. On their first Christmas, my mother, who never asked for anything, asked my father to design a pair of earrings to match her wedding ring."

Kassie tugged on the ribbon letting it fall onto the vanity as she slowly opened the box. She gently pulled an earring from the holder and held it in her hand. "Chase, it's exactly like the ring but it has pearls added." Kassie delicately stroked the design in awe.

"When my dad gave my mom the earrings, it consisted of two sapphires to match the ring and the leaf design. Every Christmas, my dad added pearls and diamonds to represent the blessings in their life. The diamond in the center next to the sapphires represents me. The pearls are blessings that complement the bigger blessings. For instance, my parent's friendship with Jake and Bonnie, the town, my dad's practice, and my mom founding the community center. The other diamonds couldn't exist without the pearls. The gems you see here," Chase pointed to the smaller diamonds. "Represent their home, my graduation and on my dad's last

Christmas, he added the bottom diamonds because I finished my time in the Navy, and we planned to start building the hospital together. He died before I returned home from being held captive." Chase whispered, "My mom never got a chance to wear them before she passed away a few months later. I give them to you today, because you are also part of the last diamond. You helped build our dream. You blessed my life and made me happy beyond my dreams. My mom would want you to have them."

Kassie's eyes filled with tears as her thumb caressed his jawline. "I would be honored to wear them. Chase, I'm going to wear them tonight and tomorrow. I decorated empty chairs to represent the ones missing from our special day. The earrings and the dress allow our moms to be part of the ceremony. I'm wearing the pearl necklace my daddy gave my mama on her wedding day, and Maddie sewed a blue heart from one of my sister's shirts inside my dress. They're here with us, cheering us on. Their love will live on forever with us." Kassie could tell her enthusiasm over the gift had pleased Chase as he placed a kiss on her temple and pulled the remaining earring from the box to hold while she fastened the other to her ear.

"Are you ready for tomorrow? No second thoughts? I'm a bear to live with..." Chase teased.

"Nope. You're stuck with me. Did you take your tux down to the cabin? You have everything you need? Maddie's insistent you can't stay here tonight. Something about it being bad luck," Kassie sighed. "I sleep better when you're here..."

"I have no intention of leaving you alone in that bed tonight. The guys and I have a plan," Chase's boyish grin covered his face as he whispered in her ear.

"What about Maddie?" Kassie softly asked.

"I won't tell if you don't." Chase kissed her behind the ear. "We haven't had a moment to ourselves. I'm voting to rethink the honeymoon."

"We can't. What about James?" Kassie tried to keep the disappointment off her face, but Chase knew her well.

Chase turned her to face him. "James Stanton won't ruin our wedding day. Matthew has taken care of securing the mountain. Michael will help when he arrives. Victoria and Ivan's men will be scattered. There's no way he can get to us. Not even at Bear's. Trust me. No one gets to Bear's place without someone knowing."

Kassie nodded. "I know. I have this feeling..."

Chase pressed his mouth to her lips as his tongue teased hers. Kassie leaned in as his hands slid down her waist to her bottom. Chase groaned into her mouth.

"What you do to me woman. We need to leave. I swear you better be naked under that dress of yours because I want to consummate our marriage right after our vows. I swear Maddie needs a job in security. I even *think* about making love to you, she needs something from the barn, or Joe needs help. Yesterday she sent me to Jake's to pick up a tux for Rollo. Who puts clothes on such a manly beast?"

Kassie giggled.

"Everyone's waiting. Let's go enjoy the party and you'll have to at least pretend to be disgruntled about us not sleeping together. Maddie has eyes in the back of her head."

Placing his hand on her waist, Chase walked her out of the cabin and into the SUV.

❋

CHASE HANDED A GLOWING Kassie a glass of wine as the townspeople slowly drifted in. Her blue dress brought out her eyes. She kept her hair long and swept up one side. His arm went around her in obvious pride.

Seeing Jake, Kassie smiled and excused herself from her fiancé's side. Reluctantly, Chase let her go but only when she nodded in Jake's direction.

Kassie smiled and exchanged greetings with neighbors who came to wish them well. Between the hospital and their wedding, the town made it the event of the century. Kassie didn't mind. Chase's family loved and encouraged community service. These people helped shape the man Chase had become and were extended family of sorts. Word had gotten back to Kassie; Jake made his rounds through the town explaining what he said was out of line.

Kassie was determined to pull Jake back into the fold. He only came to the hospital meetings Joe held at the site. Jake avoided the invitations to coffee meetings in the gazebo. Kassie missed seeing him.

"Hi Jake! I'm glad you came." She wrapped her arms around him and hugged him.

"Hi, Kass. You look beautiful. So, I guess you're all ready for the big day?" Jake fiddled with the hat in his hand. The tension radiated off his stiff shoulders and he stood as if Kassie would shame him in front of everyone.

"Not quite. I waited for you to come up to the mountain. I've missed you. I wanted to ask a favor from you." Kassie held onto his arm as she walked him to the giant table toward the rest of the family.

"I want all the family represented tomorrow. I have miniature bouquets I want delivered tomorrow to Chase's parent's grave, your Bonnie, and our baby's grave. I know they'll be with us."

"You want me to place flowers on my Bonnie's grave?" Jake asked, clearly confused.

"Why yes, Jake. Bonnie was part of Chase's family and now she's part of mine, just like you. I'm making them in the morning from the flowers from my bouquet. It's an important task and I didn't want just anybody to do it," Kassie waited for Jake's reply.

"Yes, I can do it for you. I'll pick them up in the morning." His chest puffed out. "If it means that much to you."

"Thank you." Kassie winked at Chase as Joe and Maddie walked over to greet Jake. Seeing Bryanna talking to Ty, Kassie made her way over to them.

"I sent the checks for everything this morning. Both of you have outdone yourselves. Two days in a row of this and everything smells like heaven."

Bryanna smiled and hugged Kassie. "I think you wrote the check for more than the amount we quoted you. We'll deal with it later. We did this out of friendship. Not because you have a ton of money."

"I didn't do it for that reason. There's an empty building between yours and Ty's restaurant. I thought the extra funds made a good down payment for a community kitchen. I could send some of the teens to come and help at the restaurant and bakery. If we placed more of those cute little tables out front, the seniors in the community would have a place to go. There will be a few more people on the mountain and you and Ty work well together." Kassie watched as Ty shrugged his shoulders and Bryanna shook her head.

Kassie slowly made her way back to Chase. Slipping her arms around his waist, she contented herself to staying there the rest of the night. Leo and Michael approached the couple.

"Wow, I didn't know Bear had it in him. This is amazing." Leo took in the transformed barn. "I'm surprised he agreed to do this. He's usually crabby," Leo grimaced.

"Ha! You calling someone crabby!" Kassie exclaimed as the group laughed. "Where's the rest of the team?"

Leo and Michael parted. Matthew drank a beer. Taco sat at the end of the table with his leg extended. A pretty blonde held his attention. Shadow stood next to a raven-haired beauty. Noticing Kassie and Chase watching, Shadow gave a chin nod as the blonde giggled at something Taco said. Shadow rolled his eyes. Kassie stifled her giggles into Chase's chest.

"If you would have told me a year ago my life would be like this, I would've thought you were insane. I love you, Chase Winters." Kassie tilted her head as Chase leaned down to place a soft kiss on her mouth.

"I love you, Princess. Unlock the sliding doors by our bedroom exactly forty-five minutes after I drop you off at home," Chase whispered in her ear and let out a slight growl.

The clinking of glasses grabbed everyone's attention. People made their way to the long community table and stood in front of their seats. Joe stood at the makeshift podium.

"On behalf of Kassie's parents, Nathan and Abigail Reynolds, Maddie and I along with Chase's parents and Jake, welcome you to this joyous occasion." Jake joined him on stage. "If everyone will raise your glasses to toast the happy couple." When everyone held a glass in their hand, Joe continued. "We wish you the very best. Chase, you are the son we never had, we welcome you into our family. Kassie, you are a blessing beyond measure. Emma fills our hearts with joy. Tomorrow, we gain a son. Jake will have a daughter and a granddaughter. The love you two share is strong beyond measure. May you always remember the strength each of you carry. Tomorrow, you will be one. Carry the bond throughout your lives together. Trust one another, be good to each other, and remember love is always worth fighting for. To Chase and Kassie." Joe raised his glass.

Kassie clinked her glass with Chase and leaned in for a kiss. Turning, she tipped her glass with Leo, Shadow, Samantha and Catherine. People began to take their places when someone clapping brought a murmur through the crowd.

A very drunk Rachel stumbled into the barn. Dressed to the nines, in a pant suit, heels, and her blonde hair sleek and shiny, she started toward the happy couple.

Kassie felt Chase stiffen as soon as she recognized the woman's presence.

"Congratulations to the happy couple. This town is full of hypocrites. A week ago, you saw the pictures of this woman. You saw how she is with other men, and you all sit here like she's some perfect little angel." Jake stood and headed toward Rachel. Chase's hold on Kassie tightened. Leo stood and was already headed in the direction of the drunken woman.

"Stop." Kassie's voice rang through the air.

Chase stared down at Kassie. "I'll handle her, don't let her ruin tonight."

Kassie shook her head, "Trust me."

The silence in the barn was deafening. Everyone held their breath as Kassie walked toward Rachel. The woman sneered as Kassie approached her with her head held high. Sophia Winter's earrings caught the light as Kassie's determined stride bounced the long tresses behind her shoulders.

"Rachel, this is a private party, and you weren't invited. You've had too much to drink. It's time to leave. You aren't welcome here."

Rachel laughed and tossed her hair over her shoulder. "You think you're so much better for him than me? At least I can give him children. You can't even do that."

A collective gasp came from the crowd. Kassie inhaled as if Rachel struck her. Only certain members of her family held the knowledge of Kassie's inability to have children.

"It takes more than blood to be a family, Rachel. I feel sorry for you. You'll never understand loving someone means you sacrifice some things for others. You don't understand love will always find a way. If I can't have more children, we have Emma. We are a proud auntie and uncle to LJ, Melody, and Miya. Chase doesn't love me because I'm perfect. I'm far from it. Chase loves me even with my scars, my fears, and my inadequacies. I don't think you love yourself, Rachel and until you learn how, you'll never find what Chase and I have."

Matthew grabbed Rachel's arm and practically dragged her from the barn. Chase came behind Kassie and wrapped his arms around her as they listened to Rachel screech her way along the drive until a truck door slammed and an engine started.

The group cheered, hooted and whistled as Chase picked Kassie up and gave her a resounding kiss. "Well said, Princess. I'll love you to the day I die."

"Whatever you do, make sure that is a very, very long time from now," Kassie whispered in his ear as he escorted her back to the table. Everyone bowed their heads for grace. It was time to move on.

CHAPTER FORTY-FOUR

*L*eo pulled the ladder from the woods. "SITREP," he whispered into his coms.

"Doc kissing PITA on the front porch. Eagle Eye is waiting at the door. Eagle Eye two, leaving Ladybug's room." Taco reported from the bed of the truck.

Shadow slipped onto the porch and signaled to Saint he made it. He moved to the side as Maddie checked the lock on the glass doors in the kitchen. Grabbing the tea kettle, she placed it on the stove. Grabbing two cups, she set about making a pot of tea.

"Eagle Eye two is making tea," Shadow whispered.

"Stay in holding pattern. Doc is getting into truck, PITA entering house with Eagle Eye one," Taco responded.

"Set timer for ten minutes boys," Leo ordered.

❄

"Would you like a cup of tea before bed, Little Bit?" Joe asked Kassie as he locked the door.

Kassie yawned. "No, I think I'll go straight to bed. I want to be fresh for tomorrow. Did Em go to sleep okay?"

Maddie placed the cups on the kitchen table and returned to the kitchen to grab the teapot.

"She conked out before the third page in the story. Saint is dropping Miya and Melody off here and helping Catherine with decorating tomorrow. Victoria and Ivan said they will be here bright and early. They may head up and help decorate too. Joe and I will get ready in our cabin and Victoria and Ivan insisted on staying with Edie and Saint. If she plans to stay in Serenity, we'll have to put our heads together for a more permanent arrangement." Maddie, in her own way, gave Victoria her stamp of approval.

"I sure hope Rachel didn't ruin your evening, Little Bit." Joe shook his head at the thought of Rachel.

"I meant what I said. I don't think she's ever loved anyone to know what it feels like. I feel sorry for her in a way. Not enough to be best friends or ask her for dinner or anything. After everything, Rachel's like an annoying mosquito who needs a good swat."

The older couple chuckled.

"Well, I'm off to bed," Kassie yawned. "I can't believe how tired I am."

"Don't worry about Em. Sleep in tomorrow, you'll need your rest. Tomorrow will be a big day and very long." Maddie gave Kassie her motherly advice.

Kassie kissed Joe's cheek and then Maddie's. "I love you, both." She practically skipped her way into her room, leaving the older couple to enjoy their tea.

Kassie unlocked the sliding glass doors. Running to the bathroom, she counted the minutes before Chase appeared. She slipped out of her clothes, showered, and slid into the blue negligee Samantha gifted her the day before. Running a brush through her hair and brushing her teeth, Kassie pulled the blankets down to the end of the bed and propped herself on pillows in a sexy pose as she waited for her man.

Not even three minutes later Chase slid his body through the sliding glass doors. On seeing Kassie, his eyes grew dark. He started toward her when she indicated the door. Realizing he forgot to shut it, he ran quietly back and slowly slid it closed. When he turned the lock, it clicked loudly in the room. Chase held his breath.

Kassie giggled.

"Shhh..." Chase admonished. "I never thought I'd be sneaking into my own house."

Kassie stifled the laughter at Chase's harried appearance. It felt like they were in high school with Chase sneaking into her room. "Is this what you act like when you're on missions? Cause I thought you guys were suaver than that."

"Do you know I risked certain death climbing a ladder on a mountain with Leo trying to shove his thumb up my ass to push me up before Victoria's men caught us. It's one of the toughest missions I've ever accomplished." Chase whined pathetically, causing Kassie to laugh harder.

"You're finally here. What's the rest of your mission?" Kassie batted her eyes.

"Come here." Chase tugged on one of the soft curls, pulling Kassie closer. His nose touched hers. "You are my love, my life and my home."

"You are mine," Kassie responded as Chase slid his fingers through the strap of her lingerie.

The heat of his gaze scorched her. An ache spread lower in her belly as he slowly grabbed the end of the garment and pulled it over her head.

"I look forward to many years of worshiping your body. Knowing it's mine as I'm yours. You're stunning."

Kassie smiled as she concentrated on getting his dress shirt unbuttoned. She sat up on her knees and slid his shirt off his shoulders and down his arms. She let the clothing fall to the floor.

"No panties?" Chase sat back surprised. Samantha always provided matching sets.

"I didn't want to waste time." Kassie breathlessly told him as he slid his fingers inside her silken folds.

"You are soaked, Princess," Chase whispered.

"I've dreamed of this since you told me to unlock the door," Kassie admitted.

Chase stood and picked Kassie up and placed her on the edge of the bed.

Kassie's hands stroked his abs and followed the path of hair disappearing into his pants. Her hand pressed against his hard on. "It appears you've thought about this too," she teased.

"Hmmm," Chase stared at Kassie as his hand caressed her cheek and moved to her neck, lightly massaging it.

Kassie's head dropped back, and Chase leaned forward creating a path of kisses and nipped along her shoulder. Kassie gasped.

"Shhh. I plan to make love to you tonight and the last thing I need is Eagle Eye two to find me in here. She made it clear my bed was located on the opposite side of the mountain." Chase chuckled as he caught her mouth, devouring her.

He tasted like whiskey and mint. She smelled a mixture of cedar and fresh air on him. It fit him because he had become the air she craved. She needed him to breathe, to live.

"Eagle Eye two?" she whispered.

"Maddie," he responded.

Kassie smiled. She'd have to tell Maddie someday. Right now, she focused on Chase.

Chase tugged her nipple and sucked it into his mouth. His other hand roamed to the other breast and his thumb skimmed the tip of her nipple causing a soft moan to escape Kassie. Pushing her back among the pillows, he propped her legs on the side of the bed. Her ankles touched her bottom as she lay displayed in front of him. The gleam in his eyes as he stroked her and put his fingers in his mouth, set Kassie on fire.

"You taste like honey." Chase told her as he got eye level with her pussy and dragged his finger up and down her clit. When she started to move her hips to the rhythm of his hand, Chase held her hips down.

"We're going slow tonight. I know tomorrow, knowing you're mine, I won't be able to promise you I can control myself. I want you to be Mrs. Chase Winters in every way."

"I'm already yours in every way." Kassie whispered.

Chase stood and removed the rest of his clothing. Kassie admired the contour of his abs. The patch of black hair trailing down to his thick cock. His well-defined thighs, and his ass might have been chiseled by a sculptor.

"Are you satisfied my soon to be wife?" Chase stood in front of her.

"The view is worth admiring, but I'm far from satisfied." Kassie sat up and swiped the precum off the tip of his cock. She licked her lips in anticipation as she leaned forward and swiped her tongue across the head.

Chase groaned.

"Shhh," she grinned. Watching his face, her mouth covered him, and she began to suck. Her hand slowly pumped him up and down. His hands grasped her by the hair.

Her hand cupped him and squeezed his sack as she continued to take more of him in her mouth.

Chase closed his eyes and hummed.

His cock grew strained as Kassie took her time exploring every inch of it. Chase let out a low growl and pushed her back on the bed. He leaned down and sucked on her clit. Kassie's back arched in response. He licked and sucked; a finger stroked her from inside.

Kassie panted, as another finger joined the first and Chase increased the pressure of his fingers. His mouth remained relentless. As she neared the precipice, he nipped the inside of her thigh. Jolting her back to the beginning.

"Please Chase, I need to come," she softly mewled.

"Not yet, Princess. Not until I'm inside of you." A third finger slid inside her and he stretched her. His fingers curled upward as he raised up and sucked on the pale rose nipple. Kassie gripped the back of his head. Her mouth parted slightly as she closed her eyes reveling in the feel of his touch.

"I need you inside of me now." Kassie pleaded as he changed the position of his fingers. Taking her back off the ledge.

Chase leaned over to his nightstand and pulled a condom from the drawer. Kassie took it from him and ripped it open with her teeth. Her body coated in sweat, and he hadn't even entered her.

Kassie gripped him as she placed it on the head of his shaft and slowly slid the condom down.

She lay back and opened her legs wide.

Chase crawled over the top of her and settled at her entrance. In one full stroke he entered her deeply. Kassie cried out. Chase captured her mouth stifling her moans. His thrusts became hard and deep. Her hips rose and met his. Her fingers dug into his back, as she clung to him, letting him take her higher. She'd follow him anywhere.

The pressure built inside of her. The ache grew deeper in her belly. She reveled in the warmth and slickness Chase brought out in her.

Chase slid out of her. Kassie tried to pull him back. She growled in frustration making him chuckle.

"Turn to your side," Chase ordered.

Kassie immediately did as he asked. Desperate, she'd cry if he pulled out of her again.

Chase spooned her and lifted her leg into the air. He slid his cock inside of her. His hands cupped her breasts as he tugged and pulled on her nipples. Kassie found the rhythm.

"Chase!"

Her head turned and she sought his mouth. His tongue captured hers in a war of passion.

"Come Kassie. Come for me, baby." Chase demanded as he thrust deeper and gripped her hips, grinding her harder on top of him.

Kassie's breath caught. The orgasm hit her like a freight train. Her mouth fell open in a silent scream as she rode the wave. Her eyes closed as a pleasant humming sensation ran through her body. She was barely cognizant when Chase pulled her onto her hands and knees.

Kassie wiggled her ass as he slowly entered her from behind. They hadn't tried this position. Chase's hand on her back stilled her movements.

"Easy, Kass. It will feel different this way," Chase soothed.

His cock pressed forward making her feel full. Chase grabbed her hips and moved in pace with his cock. It didn't take long before Kassie waited to go over the edge. She pushed back against him, grinding her hips. She panted harder, as she glanced back at Chase.

His jaw clamped shut. His head fell back, and his eyes closed. As if sensing her watching him, he opened them and smiled.

His hand moved from her hip and pinched her clit. Kassie's head fell forward into a pillow as she clenched down on him. Chase gripped her as he followed her into oblivion.

Chase slid out of Kassie. She saw him enter the bathroom to discard the condom. He brought back a cool washcloth and wiped her face and body as she lay like a limp noodle.

When he finished, he climbed into bed behind her and spooned her. The last thing she remembered was him whispering, "I love you."

※

Joe closed the door to their bedroom upstairs. He gazed out the window and watched as the SEAL team completed the mission.

Maddie wrapped her arms around his waist from behind.

"Did they deliver the package?" she asked quietly.

"I believe so. How early do you think I need to have coffee on the deck tomorrow? Eagle Eye one, indeed. If that's our country's finest, we sure are in trouble, Maddie." Joe chuckled quietly.

"Oh Joe, we were young and in love once. When did you discover their mission?" Maddie slipped into her nightgown.

"I wish Abigail could see her. His love for her makes her more beautiful by the day."

"Abigail and Nathan are here with us. They wouldn't miss this for the world. I discovered the master plan when Saint and Leo tried to take Taco to the bathroom. I happened to be entering as Leo wanted to do rock, paper, scissors, to determine who held Taco's ...let's just say he informed them he didn't need help. That's when they made that ridiculous secret plan."

Maddie laughed as Joe pulled her close.

"And who says only the young get to have fun?"

CHAPTER FORTY-FIVE

Kassie stirred as Chase placed a gentle kiss on her lips.

"Happy wedding day, Princess," Chase whispered.

Kassie's eyes popped open, and she smiled from ear to ear. "It's finally here. I'm becoming, Mrs. Kassie Winters."

"I can't wait. Joe and Maddie are stirring. Emma woke up and they convinced her to let you sleep in. I called Leo for an extraction."

Kassie's mouth formed into a pout. "This evening can't get here fast enough. Where are we going tonight after the reception? I forgot to ask."

"It's a surprise. Samantha has everything in hand. I'll see you this evening. I have some things to do before the ceremony. Remember the photographer will be there early to take all the pics except for the ones of us together."

"I remember." She pulled him down close enough to wrap her arms around his neck. Her thumbs gently caressed the stubble along his jawline. "I love you, Chase Winters."

"I love you too, soon to be Mrs. Kassie Winters." Chase gave her one last kiss before sliding out the glass door. Kassie hugged herself as she got up and tiptoed into the bathroom. A single rose lay on her vanity. Picking it up, Kassie inhaled the sweet scent as she thought about Chase and their night of lovemaking. Smiling to herself, she realized he'd stopped treating her like a fragile flower. She was stronger. She was his equal in every way. She anticipated her life with him on the mountain. She didn't expect everything to be perfect, but she prayed they lived a long and happy life together.

Making her way back to her room, she realized she was too excited to go back to sleep. She felt as if she wanted to run down the mountain and back up again. Joy bubbled up inside her.

Pulling the robe from her closet, she went in search of Em. Maddie poured tea while Emma and Joe made pancakes.

"Oh, Sugar, I thought you'd sleep in." Maddie chastised her. "It will be such a long day."

Kassie kissed her cheek. "I can't sleep, I'm too excited." Helping herself to a cup of tea and honey. She kissed Emma and watched as she flipped a pancake.

"Mama, Melody and Miya said when you and Dr. Chase get married, I'll get my very own daddy." The excitement in her voice bubbled over.

"Yes, Dr. Chase will be your daddy. We talked about this Em. Remember Chase and I talked to you when we went for a horseback ride?" Kassie placed the plate closer to the stove for Emma to place the pancake on it.

"I remember. Melody says her daddy died cause he's a soldier. Did my daddy die too?"

"Ladybug, I'm sure hungry. Do you think I could grab the pancake right there? It looks like a horse. Then I can say

I was so hungry I ate a horse." Joe redirected Emma much to Kassie's relief.

Emma's laughter filled the kitchen as Maddie topped off Kassie's tea and patted her arm. Kassie refused to let Emma's father ruin the day. Emma would never know James Stanton if she had anything to say about it.

❄

"The photographer will be here shortly after the first ceremony. Victoria's man will detain him until the ceremony is finished and give the all clear. Shuttles won't run until we are done with pictures. Leo, make sure she arrives on time, but don't rush her. I want her to stay relaxed and happy today." Chase went over the last details of his surprise.

Leo groaned, "You are as nervous as a cat on a front porch filled with rocking chairs. We've gone over the details a million times. We are a SEAL team. Surely we can manage getting a bride to her wedding."

"I know, Leo. I want Kassie to know I accept that she has to play her sister's role from now on, but I'm marrying Kaitlyn. The night I found her in the cemetery talking to her parents and sister gutted me. It's important she knows I love *her*." Chase ran his hand through his hair as he paced the deck overlooking his mountain at Whiskey's cabin.

"How did you convince the minister to perform two ceremonies? Everyone else is aware of the situation except the minister and Bryanna. How did you handle it?" Leo glanced back to see if Whiskey made his way out of the bedroom closet. Kassie had been smart to make it into a decompression room for the men to use to calm down. He'd give him another ten minutes before he checked on him.

"Bryanna doesn't know. She's new to the town and we

don't know her well enough. Plus, she'll be busy setting up the catering until the other ceremony begins. The minister wasn't hard to convince." Chase checked his watch for the one-hundredth time.

"How did you accomplish it?" Leo waited for Chase to spill the beans.

Chase stopped pacing and leaned against the corner of the deck; his arms crossed as he faced his friends. "I blackmailed him."

Leo laughed, "Did you catch him with a woman? He drank the wine in the back of the church. Come on, man, what did you have on him?"

Chase wiped his mouth and confessed, "I'm going to hell for this. When I went to the church to discuss the wedding, I may or may not have witnessed the upstanding minister practicing his sermon on morals in his underwear. I didn't intend on blackmailing him. He was embarrassed and claimed it was hot in the church because the air conditioner had broken. No one informed him I was scheduled to meet with him, and he thought himself completely alone."

Leo leaned in, fascinated by the tale, "Well, what happened next?"

"I presented our situation to him, adding some embellishments so he wouldn't know the real story. I thought of sweetening the deal by asking if we could donate a new air conditioner to the church as a way to ensure he never talked about a second ceremony. He isn't allowed to discuss personal matters anyway, but I offered," Chase explained.

"Why did you blackmail him then?" Leo scratched his head.

"As soon as the offer left my mouth, he got all flustered and assured me that he wouldn't repeat it to another living soul and begged me not to tell anyone of his indiscretion. I never intended to say a word. It was freaking hot in the church, and I offered a way to help him. Apparently, he considered it blackmail," Chase concluded.

Leo slapped his knees and hooted at Chase's unintended blackmail before going back to playing cards.

❄

Ash rounded the corner and smiled.

"I'll show them," he muttered to himself. "Leo ruins everything. He ruined my team, my life, and my plans. I'll get even with him. He'll lose everything. I'll make sure I crush everything Leo's built."

CHAPTER FORTY-SIX

Kassie checked the clock again. Maddie and Joe left to get dressed in their cabin. The team gathered to help set up the wedding site. Bryanna and Ty directed men on where to place the picnic tables. It seemed like everyone was on time except for her. She scheduled the men to leave for Samantha's in half an hour. Victoria and her men scoured the mountain while Ivan directed security for the shuttles to get people to the wedding. Where did her security detail go? Kassie called Leo. When he didn't answer, she went down the team list. Hoping one of the men stayed with Whiskey or Ash, she called Whiskey's cabin.

"Hey Kassie. Whiskey's in the shower. Wanna leave a message? Congratulations on your wedding day, by the way." Ash answered the phone.

"Hi Ash, I wondered if any of the team stopped by there? I'm supposed to leave for Samantha's and my detail hasn't shown up. I can't get anyone to answer their phones," Kassie explained.

"Chase picked up Leo and they headed to the wedding

area to help decorate. Saint drove to Bear's house to grab honey for Ty, then planned to join them. Taco said something about taking a nap so he could enjoy the evening. How about I take you? Leo parked his truck here, and the windows are tinted. No one can see me, and I've heard about the town, I want to get a peek. I can stay in the truck while you and Em get gussied up. Ivan's got men crawling all over the area. I haven't met Samantha, she won't recognize me," Ash offered.

Kassie hesitated. Ash acted nothing but kind toward her and if Leo suspected something, he'd insist she stop going to the cabins to check on the men.

"I'm still part of the team, aren't I?" Ash asked.

"Of course, I don't want to go against Leo's orders about keeping you a secret," she explained.

"Like I said, no one can see inside the truck, but if you feel uncomfortable, I can take the truck up to Leo and Chase. Leo's worked shorthanded before."

"No. I'm being silly. It must be wedding nerves. Em and I will be ready and waiting on the porch. Can you come over now?" Kassie didn't want to burden anyone when everyone worked so hard to make the day perfect for them.

"Sure thing, let me give Whiskey a heads up, he can let the guys know and I'll be on my way." Ash assured Kassie as she heard him grabbing the keys to the truck.

Kassie hung up the phone. "Em, let's get your shoes. It's time for Samantha to do our hair and makeup."

"Do I get makeup too?" Emma ran into the entryway and grabbed her shoes from the closet.

"I think Samantha has some pretty pink lip gloss that will be lovely with your dress. Where's your bow?" Kassie asked as she made her way into the closet and pulled one of Chase's blue dress shirts from the hanger. Slipping her T-shirt over her head, she buttoned up the shirt, inhaling Chase's scent. It seemed permanently ingrained in every article of clothing he wore.

"I'll get it, Mama!" Kassie heard Emma's feet pitter pattering to her room and running back down.

"No running on the stairs!" Kassie called out to her daughter.

Grabbing the knife Victoria gave her, she shoved it in the inside of her shoe. Ushering Emma outside, she watched as Ash pulled into the driveway. Kassie helped Emma inside and climbed into the seat next to her. Ash backed down and headed toward town.

Kassie watched as Ash's head swiveled back and forth. He didn't talk as he scouted the area. Kassie noticed his sidearm. Leo didn't mention giving him or Whiskey guns, but then he really didn't discuss team business with her. Maybe she overreacted. Ash and Whiskey were stuck at the subdivision, and she imagined they were bored. Jameson guarded the cabins with Alek. They'd notice if Ash disappeared with Leo's truck.

Ash pulled into Samantha's driveway as Kassie directed. Kassie exited the vehicle and assisted Emma.

"Kass, is everything all right?" He asked as she gathered her things. Emma was already opening the door to greet LJ.

Kassie flashed him a smile. "I have wedding day jitters. You know, it's almost time and I think it hit me."

"Everything will be fine. I'm right out here and can see the door from here. It's your big day, go get your hair done, and enjoy every minute. Chase is a lucky man." For a moment, Kassie thought she saw a flash of regret cross Ash's face. Something dropped in her gut.

"I will. Thanks." Kassie shut the truck door. Her mind raced. When she got into Samantha's, she'd call Leo. She didn't want to worry Chase unnecessarily. Ash didn't do anything the other team members hadn't done on several occasions when they acted as security detail. Shaking it off, Kassie opened the door and let herself in.

Dead silence greeted her. Emma bounced nonstop all morning, excited at gaining Chase as her daddy. She didn't stop talking. When she visited LJ, Samantha and Kassie knew exactly where the kids played in the house.

She took a deep breath and called out to Em. Kassie walked by the reception desk and slid the envelope opener up her sleeve.

"Samantha?" Kassie walked into the salon.

Samantha struggled against the tape holding her to one of the salon chairs. Blood ran down her forehead as Jameson stood behind her. Kassie's gaze shifted to where Samantha's eyes focused and filled with fear.

A man held an unconscious Emma. LJ stood on a chair where another man held a knife to his throat. A drop of blood dripped off the tip of the knife. LJ's mouth moved under the duct tape and tear tracks covered his sweet cheeks.

"Hello, Kaitlyn."

The hair on the back of her neck rose. Victoria spent days teaching her to trust her instincts and she failed. Kassie straightened and recalled all Victoria taught her. She needed everything to save Samantha and LJ. James wouldn't kill Emma. Her on the other hand...

CHAPTER FORTY-SEVEN

Chase worked on setting the lanterns down the path while Catherine added the candles. Victoria placed wildflowers from the mountain in each. The bouquets made from wildflowers waited at Saint's cabin. Catherine added the finishing touches to the empty chairs that represented the missing members of their family.

Leo avoided Cat by staying on the opposite end of the wedding set up with Saint, placing chairs in a row. He seemed bored out of his mind. Chase noticed his set jaw and when Leo thought Cat wasn't paying attention, he glanced her way. After the wedding, Chase planned to tell Leo about Ash and Catherine. Maybe Leo knew more than he thought. One thing for sure, Leo wouldn't leave Cat or Melody with anyone who abused them.

Leo's phone rang at the same time as Saint's. Leo pulled out his phone and answered.

Saint shook his head. He hung up the phone and dialed someone else. Leo issued orders. Chase dropped the lantern and walked brusquely to where the men stood. Catherine followed behind.

"Doc, don't get worked up. Two of Ivan's men were found dead in the field right outside town. Someone jumped them. Joe can't find Kassie and Em. He wanted to know who was assigned the security detail." Leo continued texting and then dialed Ivan's number.

"Kassie and Em were due at Samantha's." Catherine chimed in. Chase pulled out his phone. Samantha's phone went to voicemail. He ran his hand through his hair. His gut screamed. Not today, this was their day.

Leo ran to Victoria and Chase saw the two start making calls. Chase missed what Leo said. Blood pounded in his ears. Fear spiked from his toes to his head for Kassie and Em. Leo hung his head and walked toward him.

Chase's phone rang. Caller ID showed Carol Reese. She screamed into the phone. Chase's body went numb. He didn't need them to tell him what he already knew.

James Stanton took his girls.

Leo exchanged a look with Saint.

"Chase, we'll get them back. Let's get the weapons from the cabin."

The trio dashed to the truck and peeled down the mountain.

They loaded the truck quickly as a flustered Edie looked on. Leo fishtailed out of the driveway and gunned the gas.

"Keep your head straight, Doc. We saved them before; we will do it again," Saint offered his support.

"Kassie will sacrifice herself for Emma. James tried to grab Em, he has no use for..." Chase couldn't bring himself to say the words that threatened to choke him.

"Damn it, Doc. Kassie isn't a freaking fragile flower. She's smart. She'll figure out a way to stall until we get to her."

They closed in on the small town of Serenity and turned

onto Samantha and Jake's street. The vehicle slammed to a stop. Chaos was everywhere.

CHAPTER FORTY-EIGHT

Kassie kept her face blank. *Never show your emotions, when you do, you give the enemy fuel to add to the fire to burn you. You don't want to burn, Kassie, you want to be the flame.* Victoria's words echoed in her ear.

"Hello, James. I think your heart attack must have deprived the oxygen to your brain. For a moment, I thought you called me by my sister's name. This is between me and you. Let the kids go. Samantha has nothing to do with this."

James pinned Kassie with a stare. Before... she would've trembled where she stood. Not today. Emma's life and the life of her friends hung in the balance.

"Take the girl and put her in the car." James ordered as he waited to get a reaction from Kassie.

"Move her and you'll lose an eye. I've learned a few things since you did all those horrible things to me. I'm not the scared little girl you knew, James. You aren't leaving with Emma. She's my daughter." The man holding Emma began to move. She couldn't afford to let Emma out of her sight.

"I said, don't move. After all, I only ask once." Kassie cocked her head toward James.

James shot daggers at Jameson. "Did you know she was Kaitlyn? He said she was the twin. I'd hate to think you knew and didn't tell me."

Jameson stared confused, "She's Kassie. I'm sure of it."

"How sure are you, Jameson? Would you bet your life on it? How would Kaitlyn know about James Stanton? I know he doesn't have enough money in his bank account to pay any of you what he promised. In fact, he's broke. I will be happy to share the balance of his bank account," Kassie goaded.

"Take the girl to the car." James seemed unsettled. "Then come back and kill them." James tilted his head at Samantha and LJ. "You better hope you're right, Jameson. I'd hate to think you've disappointed me."

"LJ, honey, close your eyes. That's it, sweetie. Don't open them until your mama or I tell you to. We're playing a game and I need you to do what Aunt Kassie says." Kassie took her sight off James long enough to watch LJ's face squint. Kassie stepped to her right.

"If she makes one more move, Jameson, kill the bitch sitting in the chair and her kid in front of her."

Kassie heard Samantha struggling against her bonds. She screamed against the tape. Kassie tuned out all the noise. She felt Ivan's breath on her neck as he taught her how to throw knives.

The man holding Emma started forward and Kassie threw the letter opener and the man dropped Emma as he fell to the floor. Before the weapon she flung hit its mark, Kassie bent to her shoe, lightning fast and threw the knife into the face of the man holding LJ. The man stood suspended for a moment before he fell over.

Out of the corner of her eye, Kassie saw Samantha

attempting to rock the chair back and forth, causing her body to spin in Jameson's way. He grabbed the arms of the chair to subdue her when Kassie grabbed a jar of one of Samantha's creams and threw it at Jameson's head, hitting him right between the eyes, knocking him backward.

She grabbed his gun as a shot went off. Kassie kicked out. Jameson dropped it on the floor as his hand went to hold his forehead, and she wasted no time aiming it at James.

"One more step toward Emma and I'll plant one between your eyes. LJ, keep your eyes closed," Kassie warned.

James pulled a knife and held it to Emma's tiny neck. "He assured me she was Kaitlyn. Her nerdy twin was a nurse. She wouldn't have the guts to kill a man. Kassie was a crazy bitch, she'd do it. Is she Kassie or Kaitlyn?" James demanded to know.

"I don't...know." Jameson stammered.

"If I had a gun, I'd shoot you myself. Your mother was beautiful, but she wasn't the brightest bulb in the box. I told you to get close to her." James angrily grabbed Emma's arm.

"Don't grab my daughter again, James. We can work something out if you like. I have the ten million dollars you're missing from your bank account for starters."

James's eyes widened. Kassie watched him, disgusted, as he practically salivated over Emma.

"A child is a ton of work. Ten million dollars provides you a way to get out of the country," Kassie bargained, knowing James wouldn't release Emma or leave the money.

"Give the gun back to Jameson. You'll come with us. I'll let you and Emma go as soon as you give me the account numbers," James offered.

"No. Give me Emma first. Then I'll give the gun to Jameson," Kassie ordered.

James's eyes narrowed. Kassie saw he disliked being told what to do. She waived him away from Emma as he slowly put her down. Not to be outsmarted, James maneuvered himself closer to LJ causing Samantha to whimper. He held the knife to the little boy's side while Kassie edged her way to her daughter. She bent down and picked her up.

"I'll carry my daughter. I don't want you to even touch her," Kassie snarled.

Kassie waited until Jameson stood. She held the gun out with the barrel pointed down. He took her wrist and tapped it twice before taking the gun. Kassie eyes flickered to meet his. His head shook slightly, and he winked. She didn't know what he tried to convey but she didn't plan to trust him ever again.

Kassie walked down the hall. Ash sat in the driveway and would notice when they walked out. James must have read her mind as he jerked her arm toward the kitchen.

Turning to Jameson, he ordered, "Take care of them and bring me the gun."

James waited for tears and pleas as he scrutinized her face. Kassie held Emma tight. The only sound came from Samantha screaming through the tape and two shots rang out. The second shot cut Samantha's yelling short. Kassie jumped at the sound of the gun, but her face stayed perfectly blank.

Surely Ash heard the noise? He'd be here any minute. She needed to stay calm regardless of the despair that overwhelmed her.

Jameson walked into the kitchen and handed James the gun. Kassie tried to shout a warning before James aimed the gun at his own son's chest and pulled the trigger. Jameson stumbled backward and fell to the floor.

"You disappointed me, Jameson. Your mother thought she was clever when she named you after me. She was amused no one ever pieced together it meant James's son. You never replaced Phillip. You didn't fool me when you gave the excuse about your car careening out of control when I sent for Emma. You didn't deceive me this time either, showing up as I arrived to do the job myself. No son of mine would turn on me. You might as well be dead." James gripped Kassie's arm and shoved her out the door.

Kassie reminded herself that by now, Maddie or Joe would be searching for her and Samantha. They'd call the team. Whiskey knew Ash brought her down the mountain. Leo and Chase would find her. She and Emma needed to stay alive until then.

The register of a shot gun permeated Kassie's thoughts and she turned to see Jake standing behind James.

"Turn around slowly, asshole. You ain't taking our girls anywhere." James turned and fired. Jake's rifle went off and missed James. Blood bloomed from Jake's chest. Kassie placed Emma on the ground. She heard the raspy sound of air escaping. Jake struggled to breathe.

"Jake, slow breathes. Chase is coming." Kassie pressed his hand to his chest and squeezed.

James grabbed her arm and tugged her up. "I have one bullet left. Pick her up and get in the car."

Jake grabbed Kassie's hand. "So sorry, Kass..."

She nodded her head and bent to pick up her daughter, now grateful Emma stayed drugged. She didn't want her to see the carnage her real father left behind.

James shoved them in the car, and it took off down the

road. Kassie watched Serenity fade from her view through the rear-view window as James made calls and issued commands. This was supposed to be her wedding day. She closed her eyes and called out to her parents and sister, praying they would intercede and help her protect Emma.

CHAPTER FORTY-NINE

Chase fell by Carol Reese, a former nurse, who worked on Jake. Trying to seal off the wound with plastic wrap.

"Jake! Hang on!" The EMTs pulled the stretcher across the yard. A bag dropped down next to him, and he began inserting an IV.

Jake's pale blue eyes met Chase's. "Go get the girls. I'm sorry, son. I let you down."

Chase cupped Jake's face in his hands. "Don't you die on me old man. Emma needs you to teach her how to ride her new pony. Jake, I need you. You have to help me with the hospital. Kassie has all those kids coming, she's gonna need your help." Chase helped them get his godfather on the stretcher. "Carol, go with him!"

Leo tapped his shoulder as they ran into the house. Samantha held LJ tightly. Blood dripped from her forehead as she kept her son from seeing the blood on the floor and the two dead men lying across her salon. Saint didn't hesitate as he picked Samantha up with LJ in her arms and cradled them to his chest. He walked to Jake's porch and set them on the wooden swing.

Saint gently tugged LJ from his mama. "The EMTs will check him out and I'll bring him back."

"What happened, Samantha?" Leo questioned.

"They broke in and grabbed LJ before tying and gagging me. Emma ran in and they stuck her with something in the neck. She was breathing. I couldn't warn Kassie, they threatened to kill LJ," she hiccupped. "Kassie killed those men. She threw the knives like a ninja or something."

Chase checked Samantha's head and determined it needed stitches. He ordered Leo to grab an EMT. "Samantha, did he say where he was taking her?"

"No. She offered him ten million dollars to leave Emma. He said he'd let them go once he got the money. Kassie went with him when he told Jameson to shoot us. Jameson came in and shot at the wall and then shot the gun again and covered my mouth. He said, tell Victoria and Leo he was James's son. His name literally means James's son. His second son."

Chase ran off the porch and grabbed Leo. "Where's Victoria? Where's Ivan?"

"We're right behind you." Joe and Maddie stood with them. Maddie cried while Joe held her. Victoria and Ivan seemed oblivious to the medical personnel. Maddie held her hand up to her mouth when the second stretcher came out covered in blood. She cried out in anguish.

Chase signaled for Victoria to follow him through the house. Jameson lay slumped against Samantha's kitchen cabinets. Red smeared where Jameson slid down on impact of the bullet. He'd lost blood and his skin turned a dusky pale. Shadow leaned over him asking questions.

"Does he know where they took them?" Chase impatiently asked. Every minute counted. He didn't trust James to keep Kassie alive.

"He says, he took them to the same place he held Victoria. There're tunnels under the house. It exits into the woods, by a shed." Shadow murmured something low to Jameson.

Victoria and Ivan exchanged glances. Ivan grabbed his phone and began speaking in Russian while Victoria spoke with the team. "Two helicopters will be here in ten minutes. They're stocked with everything you'll need. I'll give you both helicopters and we'll join you. Your job is to get Emma and Kassie. Then you walk away. I need your word. James is mine. I promise he won't darken your doorstep again," Victoria instructed.

Leo nodded.

Chase stared at Victoria. "He has no need for Kassie. He wants Emma. You knew this."

Victoria didn't bother to deny it. "I prepared Kassie with everything to stay alive. She knew this day would come. She told me to remind you of your promise to her."

Chase's head jerked up. He gripped his hair and paced waiting for the helos. Leo grabbed him by the shirt, "Damn it, focus, Doc. You aren't going in half-cocked. We do our job as always. You know our team. We saved your ass. Taco's pulling up Stanton's house plans, Victoria can show him where the tunnels let out. We can get in through there."

Chase nodded to let Leo know he had heard him.

"What the hell is my truck doing here?" Leo raced toward the truck and opened the driver's door. Ash slumped over the wheel, unconscious. Leo felt for a pulse. "Hang on, Ash."

Chase checked for wounds and found a lump on the

back of Ash's head. "He took a bump on the head, he's knocked out."

Saint ordered a second medivac while the EMT loaded Jake, and Carol joined them, as she kept her hand on the wound. Jameson would be next, but chances were slim the lifeline flight would make it in time.

"How did Ash get hurt?" Leo scanned the area.

One of Ivan's men approached and spoke to Ivan. "There's a lot of blood and a dead man on the side of the house. I found a brick with blood on it, looks like he was hit with it trying to save Kassie. The specks of blood lead back to the truck."

"He didn't want anyone seeing him." Leo yelled as the two helos landed in the field behind Jake's house. Grabbing his gun from under the seat and discovering it wasn't there, Leo's eyes roamed Ash's waist to find his gun attached to his side. He nodded for Ivan's man to take over Ash's care, the team wasted no time getting in the air.

Saint, Shadow, Leo, and Chase jumped in the first one and Victoria and Ivan loaded into the second with two men. Somehow, it seemed to Chase, Victoria prepared for this day and there was more to come. Over the coms, he heard Victoria and Ivan issuing commands to men already on the ground. He couldn't think about it right now, he needed to focus on getting to Kassie and Emma.

Chase pinched the bridge of his nose. As the military grade helicopter raced through the sky.

"Ivan has called in some favors; we'll have to stop for refueling about halfway there. We can breach the entry before he gets them back there." Leo spoke into the headphones, "Saint contact Julio and Matthew. Michael stayed to help LJ when I last saw him. He drove to the wedding with Elizabeth. They can care for Samantha and LJ."

Saint placed the calls while Leo and Ivan coordinated men. Ivan's men kicked into gear and plotted how to handle any security on the ground. Leo's team took responsibility for getting into the tunnel. Victoria's men surrounded the estate to ensure no one escaped.

Leo engaged Chase. "What was the promise? What did Kassie make you promise?"

"If it comes down to saving her or Emma. Ladybug's the priority." Chase spoke into the microphone. None of the men said anything at first.

Chase's face showed anger running through him. He wanted to punch something. He wanted to tear something apart. He counted the hours down to make her, his, and he worried he wouldn't get the opportunity.

Shadow sat back and sighed. Saint shook his head.

"She'll sacrifice herself for Emma. I love that woman, damn it. I want a life with her. I'm not willing to sacrifice her or Emma!" Chase felt ready to explode. "She exhausted herself to be the good daughter, the loyal sister, and the best mom. She wouldn't think for a second to lay down her life for her family."

"Doc, calm down. You're thinking with your heart. Think with your head. PITA's changed while we worked on our way back home. Did you catch the bodies in the salon? Your girl did that. Victoria seems awfully sure of herself. Ivan didn't blink an eye at Kassie going with Emma."

"We all knew he'd come for her. We failed her." Chase placed his face in his hands.

A voice came over the radio. "Kassie says love is worth fighting for. Do you think she'll allow James to take away the happiness she found with you? She's trained. She's mentally prepared. Will you treat her like a piece of glass and make her stay on the mountain her entire life?" Victoria's angry voice demanded.

Chase sat back in the seat. Kassie labored to prove she changed from the moment he returned home. Hell, she knocked him on his ass the first day. He was easily twice her weight. Would Stanton underestimate her? Chase felt his muscles relax. Kassie was smart. She tried to tell him she could protect herself. His first job was to get Emma. She didn't say Emma was his only job. She said Emma was the priority.

"Ok Victoria, we have some time to kill. You wanna tell us what you've taught my girl?"

A soft chuckle filled the line.

"I will tell you, Comrade, you don't want to piss her off too often. I will give you some advice. When she gets angry, you make love to her. Make her forget why she was mad. She's like my Tori." A grunt was heard over the coms. Ivan continued, "Redheads make life interesting, yeah? Rest up, because you already have double trouble, and I don't think Tori will be going anywhere for long." Another grunt followed.

Victoria hastened to reassure Chase, "Luv, she knows how to survive. James can't afford to kill her now. He needs Kassie and he doesn't even know I exist, giving us an element of surprise. James won't know what hit him."

CHAPTER FIFTY

The door closed and a lock clicked in place. Kassie discerned her surroundings. While expensive, a fine layer of dust coated the furniture and furnishings. The king of the castle couldn't afford good help.

Kassie checked Emma's pulse. It remained steady and she slept soundly. Knowing cameras filmed the room, Kassie pulled back the heavy drapes and placed her head against the window. Her hand went to her mouth. To anyone watching, she appeared distraught and worried. Yet, she felt calm as she watched the tree line. Her family would come to take her and Emma home. She needed to be ready.

Kassie sat in the heavy chair and briefly wondered if Victoria was held here during her marriage to James. She couldn't imagine Victoria's fear and despair knowing her family died and no one would come for her for years.

A whimper from the bed caught Kassie's attention. She immediately picked Em up and cuddled her in the chair. Still sleepy but scared, Em snuggled in.

"Wake up Em. We need to play Shadow's game. In a little while, I'll have to leave you here. I need you to remember

Shadow's game." Emma's nose scrunched as her eyes grew rounder. Emma sat up and surveyed the room. Shadow taught Emma to play hide and seek in plain sight. Ivan taught her to find cameras and to hit mean men in the balls.

"I think you should go to the bathroom and get a drink of water. It will wake you up. You can play the game with me." Kassie spoke to Emma soothingly. "I have to talk to the adults, and you can play the game once I leave, okay?"

Emma yawned, "Yes, Mama." Emma slid off her lap and Kassie followed her into the bathroom. Washing out a cup, she filled it with water from the sink.

Half an hour later, Emma chattered away and played with the various items on the dresser. The lock clicked and one of James's men motioned for her to come with him. Grabbing Em's hand, she started toward the door.

"The kid stays here," The man gruffly ordered.

Kassie nodded and turned to reassure her daughter. "I might be gone for a bit. So, play our game until I return."

Emma's little arms wrapped around her neck.

"I love you, Em. More than Skittles!"

Emma giggled, "I love you more than Bryanna's cupcakes!"

Kassie squeezed her tight and let her go. Her heart pounded in her chest. It took all her willpower to turn away from her child and walk with the guard. As she walked down the hallway, she let her breath even out and got herself under control. She wasn't fighting for just Emma anymore. She fought for herself, for Chase, and their future.

James sat in a chair like a king holding court as the man shoved Kassie through the office door. James waited for Kassie to take a seat across from the desk before he turned a laptop toward her. "Pull up the accounts," he demanded.

"If I give you the money, what's my assurance you'll leave

us alone?" Kassie sat back in the chair, carefully controlling her expression. Her face remained void of all emotion. Her voice sounded cool as Victoria had instructed.

"If you don't, I'll kill you and take my daughter," he threatened.

Kassie crossed her arms and leaned back in the chair. "A girl won't get you what you need. You needed a son. Why did you shoot Jameson? You could've easily claimed him as Victoria's son. Who would have challenged you?" Kassie watched as the older man thought she paid him a compliment.

"I don't know what you're referring to." James poured himself a healthy-sized glass of wine.

"Really? I swear I was informed you needed a male heir from Victoria's side." When Kassie made no move to touch the laptop, he slid it closer to her.

"Who told you? My son, perhaps? Did Phillip confide in you?" James leaned in clearly wanting to know how she came about the information.

"No. It wasn't him. Plus, he's dead. I don't think his sterility is an issue anymore." Kassie poked the bear.

"I suggest you refrain from talking about my son." James gritted out.

"Did you know Phillip planned a coup against you? He and Roger stole money from you for years. Poor James, the son you pine for didn't give a rat's ass about you," Kassie crooned.

James's fist slammed down on the desk scattering items. "Shut up! You know nothing! Phillip helped kill his mother, do you think he ever tried to kill me? No! Because he knew I could aid him gaining full control of the east!"

Kassie frowned. "No. He didn't want to kill you. He wanted you to feel like he did. He tired of jumping through hoops and taking orders from you. He planned to steal all your money and take control."

"Shut up!" James yelled as he came across the desk and backhanded her, sending Kassie reeling to the floor.

"Sir! The kid has disappeared! I can't find her anywhere!" The guard who escorted Kassie to the dining room came running in. "I've hunted everywhere, and she's gone." The guard realized his mistake as the gun whipped out of James's pocket and fired. The guard slowly sank to the floor.

The nurse in Kassie wanted to run and help. But the mama in her sat still, counting off one more guard.

"Where is she, you bitch?" James turned and swiped the desk, knocking papers to the floor.

"I sat in here with you. How could I know where she went?" Kassie calmly stated.

James raged and called for his men. "Find my daughter and have her brought to me now!"

Kassie prayed Emma wouldn't be found. Shadow and Ivan taught her daughter well. Emma wouldn't come out until Kassie, or the team found her.

James shortened the distance between them. Roughly grabbing her arm, he dragged her down the hall. "It's fitting I took you today. I took my wife on her wedding day. You remind me of my Victoria. You have the same spirit. Between your likeness to my wife and the way you fought me, I knew you suited my plans perfectly."

Kassie fought him as he continued to pull her up a flight of stairs into a large bedroom.

He'll try to break you. At the first sign of weakness, he'll pounce. Draw on the love of your family and know we're coming. Tap down the fear and focus on buying time. Victoria's lessons played in her mind.

Keeping Kassie

"Is this where you tortured your first wife?" Kassie mustered the courage to ask.

James chuckled, "It amused me to watch her suffer. I worked my way up in her father's organization. I carried out jobs for her father and he promised Victoria to me. Another family offered a contract. She was made for me and fell in love with Ivan. Her father made the alliance for his daughter. I came from the streets. Ivan's family wielded power and money. Victoria's father planned to use their influence for his own gain. On her wedding day, I killed her Ivan and her family. I showed O'Leary what his treachery cost him. He died knowing Victoria suffered for his mistakes."

James shoved Kassie's hands behind her back and bound them together before shoving her into the chair.

"If you harm me, there's no place you can hide where Chase and Leo's team won't find you. They'll make you pay." Kassie's chin went up as she glared at him defiantly.

"Ahh, your military friends. They'd have to find you first." James circled her like a shark narrowing in his prey.

Kassie spied the tray sitting on top of the dresser. Several instruments lay on it. Including a long knife similar to the one Roger used on her. Stark terror filled her body. She protested at suffering through the torture again.

"It must've frustrated you I avoided your men for three years. Did you ever wonder where I was?" Kassie knew she held his attention. "All those files... all your money I funneled away from you. My death will keep you from it. The entire world will know everything. If I go missing, the information will go out. There won't be a place on earth you can hide. Daniel O'Leary's sons and the Rostova family will want their revenge. You'll thank your lucky stars if it's only my team hunting for you."

For a moment, James's eyes flared in fear. Standing in

front of her, he yanked her hair back. "What do you know of Daniel O'Leary or the Rostova?" James appeared formidable, yet his voice held a tiny bit of tension.

Kassie laughed in his face. "Three years is a very long time. My presence in the courtroom denouncing my death opened doors for me. In fact, you could say, it brought people back from the dead. I made a few connections."

"I'll disguise it as an accident. After all, I've done it before with Nathan and Abigail Reynolds. Poor Abigail lay there and cried as I killed her husband. I thought for sure she'd fight me. She left twin girls waiting for her at home. She accepted her death. I wonder where you get your strength from. I was positive you'd kill yourself out of guilt over your parents. It's a good thing I threatened to take your sister in your place or I'm sure you would have succeeded in ending your life."

A knock on the door interrupted James. Angrily he stomped over and opened it. A man dragged a fighting, Emma. Her tear-streaked face darkened in terror as she screamed. When the guard let go, she made a beeline for Kassie. She clung to her neck as James attempted to pull her away. Emma's screams echoed in the room.

James focused on Emma as she kicked out and flayed her arms trying to get away.

Kassie screamed, "Leave my daughter alone, you bastard!"

James roughly jerked Emma in front of him while he laughed. "I want those account numbers, or I'll give her to my men."

"You're sick!" Kassie spat. "She's your own flesh and blood. Emma's innocent in all this!"

Her heartbeat sounded in her ears as she felt the blood running through her veins. Would the team get here in time to save Em? "Let her go. Use me if you have to but let her go!"

"What offer do you have in mind? What are you willing to give for her life? I won't let her go, but she'll grow up at my side. She'll be the daughter I never had." James stroked Emma's hair tenderly.

She needed to buy more time. She wasn't allowing Em to get hurt. "I'll do anything." She swallowed the lump in her throat. Victoria told her how brutally James treated her on her wedding night. She knew exactly what James required of her. "Take her back to her room," Kassie commanded.

Handing Emma to a guard, James walked to Kassie and hauled her up from the chair. "Where's your fight now?" He pushed her on the bed. His eyes glazed over her as he held her in an iron grip. Kassie attempted to roll off the bed and he jerked her so hard she thought her shoulder dislocated. Pain flared down her arm.

"Unfortunately, Phillip drugged you the first time. It wasn't as much fun. You put up a fight, yet not even close to Victoria." He untied the rope from her hands. "I like a bit of a challenge." Without warning, he backhanded her, making her fly to the edge of the bed. His weight fell on top of her as he tore at her shirt.

Kassie raked her nails down his face causing James to bellow. When he raised himself up to hit her, her knee shot up, hitting him in the groin. The palm of her hand struck his nose.

James roared with rage as she rolled off the bed. She scanned the room for a weapon. James blocked her path to the tray with the knife. The fury in his eyes promised retribution, maybe even death. Like a bull he charged her. Blood poured from his nose as he advanced. His fist shot out. Kassie dodged to the left as her fist came up and hit his nose again. She heard the sickening crunch as he grabbed it.

His body shook in outrage. Even the pounding on the door didn't deter him from coming after her. Kassie braced her stance as Ivan taught her and as the splitting of wood cracked through the room. Leo and Chase followed by Victoria and Ivan charged into the room.

Shock drained the color from James's face. Two ghosts from the past had come to claim their vengeance. He barely noticed Chase crossing the room with murder in his eyes.

Chase let his fist fly, knocking James to the floor. "You will never touch my family again."

Kassie rushed toward the door, determined to get Emma. A guard dragged Emma into the room with a knife to her throat. Kassie backed up slowly bumping into Chase's chest. Chase placed her behind him. Victoria and Ivan took up positions on either side of the man. Emma's wide eyes conveyed her fear.

James laughed as he walked to the guard and grabbed Emma and the knife. "You played me for a fool, Victoria. Are you willing to risk this child's life or theirs?"

The guard aimed a gun toward Chase. Tears flowed down her cheeks as Kassie tried to place herself in front of him. Unwilling to risk either Emma or Chase, she planned to fight.

Victoria's chin raised as defiance showed in her eyes. "You have committed crimes against the O'Learys' and the Rostova. Our men surround this place as we speak. If you harm one hair on the child, you will pay, James. I promise you. I've kept an accounting for each crime you committed against me. Ivan prefers to take matters in his own hands and promises you a swift punishment." Victoria stared at

Emma's downward head. Her eyes narrowed at James's grip on her arm.

"Little One," Ivan spoke softly. Emma's head shot up as her gaze went around the room and settled on Ivan. "This man intends to do harm. Will you allow him to hurt you?"

Emma's eyes darkened, her nose scrunched up, as her hand clenched into a fist. She stomped on James's foot. It wasn't enough to hurt, just enough to catch him off guard. Emma's fist went directly between his legs. James fell to his knees as Emma ran across the room toward Chase. The guard moved his aim from Chase to the running Emma. Ivan and Leo dove at the same time, taking the guard down.

A shot rang through the room as Chase grabbed Em and rolled to the floor. Victoria kicked James in the stomach making him fall backward while holding his groin. Kassie ran toward the unmoving Chase.

"Chase! Emma!" She dropped to her knees at the sight of blood pooling on the floor. Frantically she turned Chase over. Emma's startled face met hers before she started to cry. Kassie pulled her from Chase's limp hold. Her heart pounded as she searched for the wound. Moving Chase to his back, she found him bleeding from the shoulder.

"Chase! Chase! Why isn't he answering!" Hysteria bubbled to the surface.

Leo dropped beside her. "He hit his head when he went down. He's got a goose egg and a cut on his head from the bedpost. He really needs to stop hitting his head."

A low groan emitted from Chase as Kassie cried out. She tore open his shirt to see the bullet went all the way through. Leo ran to the bathroom to grab some towels to stem the flow of blood.

"Chase," Kassie tearfully whispered.

Chase turned his head toward her. "Emma?" he asked.

"She's right here. She's safe." Tears rolled down Kassie's cheeks as she reassured him.

Leo pressed a towel to Chase's wound and helped him sit up. Ivan secured James as Saint restrained the guard. Victoria picked up Em and moved her to the window, speaking in a soothing tone and distracting her from the scene in front of her.

Shadow walked in holding another man. "Ivan's men are clearing the house. Victoria's men caught a couple who tried to get away. I met this guy trying to climb out the window. He apparently knows what happens to people who cross the families."

Chase pulled Kassie into his arms and kissed her forehead. His hand gently inspected her bruised cheek where James hit her. His gaze hardened as he glanced at the man who reigned terror on his beloved.

Kassie hugged Chase. "What about Samantha and LJ? Jake tried to save us." Kassie's braced herself for the news her friend had died ...and Jake.

"Jameson saved them. He's in critical condition. Jake's in surgery." Chase told Kassie. She didn't miss the worry in his voice.

With Leo's help, Chase moved to stand with Kassie. An all clear came through the coms. Chase walked to Emma and held out his good arm. Emma reached for him to take her as her little arms wrapped around his neck. Her head rested on his shoulder. Kassie gripped his hand. The adrenaline drop came, and her body started to hum.

Shadow and Saint surrounded the little family as they approached Ivan holding James. Victoria moved to Kassie's side. Her arm encircled the young woman's waist.

Chase meant to walk past James and to get his girls out

of the room as soon as possible. A tug on his hand stopped Chase as Kassie stood in front of James.

"You'll never touch my family again. Whatever happens to you, know I plan to use all your money and help those you've harmed. I will put good into this world to counter the evil you've caused. You may have hurt us but we're still here. We won't ever think of you again. By the way, my name is Kaitlyn Abigail Reynolds." Kassie stared at the man who hurt her sister, killed her parents, and felt no pity for whatever happened to James Stanton.

Leo turned to Ivan, "Julio will be here in about an hour. He can take them into custody."

Victoria ran her hand along Kassie's arm. The women exchanged smiles before Victoria spoke. "Leo, thank you for calling Agent Hernandez. I'm sure the men he takes into custody will be more than willing to give him information on James's activities." Turning toward Kassie, Victoria addressed her, "I'm so proud of you, Luv. Now, I ask you to remember your promise."

Kassie slowly nodded. "I do."

"It's too bad James Stanton proved to be elusive to the law again. Tell your agent we will diligently hunt him and will keep him appraised of any new information." At Victoria's words, James began to struggle against Ivan's hold.

"Oh Comrade, I've waited a long time for this day. I tried to persuade my wife you deserved a swift punishment. I always give into my wife's demands." Ivan winked at Chase. "Remember my advice with redheads. This might be a good time to listen to yours."

Kassie tugged at his hand, "It's time to go."

Chase searched her face. "Leo, I don't know about you, but I'm ready to go home."

Leo turned and led the group down the hall and out of the house.

As they climbed into the helo, Emma stayed glued to Chase. Kassie sat beside him and tended to his injury. Shadow and Saint climbed in and sat across from them. Leo waited for the authorities with Julio.

The helo lifted into the sky as Kassie stared out the window. She watched as Victoria and Ivan stood in front of the house. The rest of the men congregated behind them. She could make out Leo in the crowd. As the helo flew further away, a brilliant flash of orange lit the sky. Kassie turned and gently laid her head close to Chase's shoulder. She felt him tug her closer, making her smile. As usual, he thought of her needs.

CHAPTER FIFTY-ONE

Two weeks later, Catherine, Bryanna, and Samantha helped Kassie get ready for her wedding. Maddie buttoned her dress and left her to the younger women. Samantha placed Maddie's gifted sapphire and pearl comb in Kassie's hair as Catherine helped her with the earrings Chase gave her.

"One more thing, Bryanna. In my jewelry box over there." Bryanna returned with the bracelet Chase gave her while she recovered in the hospital. Catherine repeated the old wedding rhyme out loud to check off everything.

"I put a penny in your shoe. Something old is Sophia's earrings and your dress, something new...the comb Maddie gifted you, something blue are the sapphires, now for something borrowed..." Catherine tapped her pink painted nails to her lips in thought.

"Oh, in my bag!" Samantha mumbled with hairpins in her mouth as she held a lock of Kassie's hair.

Catherine pulled out a beautiful lace garter with marigolds embroidered on the blue satin ribbon. Kassie smiled at the thoughtful gesture of her friends.

"The embroidered flowers can be removed, they are gently tacked on, but the garter is Samantha's to borrow," Catherine explained.

Kassie sat while Samantha attached the veil. Catherine got on her knees and began to lift Kassie's dress.

"No! I got it, thanks," Kassie blushed.

Catherine sat back on her haunches. "Don't be silly, stay still so Sam can finish the veil. Leo's waiting outside." She started to go back under Kassie's dress.

Kassie's hands frantically held the dress down. Her face turned redder by the minute. Samantha walked around and studied Kassie's heightened color and a slow grin appeared.

"Cat, I believe our friend is hiding something. Come to think of it, I forgot to provide her with her bridal wear for underneath."

Kassie rolled her eyes heavenward as Catherine's mouth dropped as she finished placing the garter and came out from under the gown.

"I see London, I see France, I see Kassie without underpants! I didn't think you had it in you!" Catherine and Bryanna laughed. "She's naked under there. Our tutelage has paid off!" The three women high fived.

With scarlet cheeks, Kassie laughed. "Chase said he couldn't wait to consummate the marriage right after the ceremony. I'm saving us a little time." Her eyes held her merriment as her three friends plotted on how to make it happen.

Leo, Catherine and Samantha escorted Kassie up the mountain to the wedding spot. Bryanna stayed to lay out the dessert table. Samantha helped Emma walk the path down to where Joe and Maddie waited for pictures.

"You look stunning, PITA. Chase is a very blessed man."

Keeping Kassie

Leo lifted Kassie out of the truck as Catherine grabbed the back of the dress and veil.

Kassie smiled, "Thank you. You're quite handsome in a tux." If she had a brother, she'd want him to be like Leo.

Catherine followed behind. When they entered the opening of the clearing, Joe appeared. He beamed at the sight of his goddaughter.

Leo dropped her arm and placed Kassie's hand in Joe's. Giving a chin lift to Joe, Leo left Kassie and headed toward the front. Catherine went about fixing the veil and adjusting her train before going up the aisle. Confused, Kassie frowned.

Joe patted her hand and started forward. The opening grew wider, and Kassie's mouth dropped in surprise. The team and her friends sat in the chairs. Jake's wheelchair sat on the side of the aisle next to Carol Reese. Emma stood in front holding Chase's hand. Rollo sat beside Chase dressed in a bow tie, tongue hanging out to the side. Kassie turned to Joe. "The ceremony isn't supposed to happen until sunset."

Joe smiled, "I'm following orders, Little Bit."

The music played and everyone stood as Joe walked her down the aisle. Chase's eyes never left Kassie as she made her way to him. Reverend Tinley requested everyone to be seated.

Chase took Kassie's hand in his. His fingers brushed her bracelet. His thumb caressed the Christmas tree as he beamed his pleasure at her wearing it. She searched his face trying to figure out what he had prepared. Chase held her gaze.

"I love you. I want you to know today we celebrate the beginning of our family. You will always have your twin as part of you and I wanted to include her in our ceremony. I finally figured out a way to do it."

The Reverend said a few words and waited for Chase to speak.

"I, Chase Jonathan Winters, take you, Kaitlyn Abigail Reynolds to be my wife. I will love you and cherish you all the rest of my life. I will support you in everything you do. I vow to be a good husband and father—"

So overwhelmed, she skipped waiting for him to finish. He used her real name to ensure she knew he had married her and accepted she would always be her twin. Nothing he ever did would mean more to her. This moment belonged to her and her husband. From this moment forward she was no longer Kassie Stanton. She held his face and peppered him in kisses.

Crying and smiling, Kassie repeated the vows back to him. Reverand Tilley pronounced them husband and wife. Chase pulled her gently into his arms. His hand cupped her cheek as he smiled and leaned down. Their lips touched, sealing the promise of forever. When Chase pulled away from her. He bent down on one knee.

"Ladybug, I'm marrying your mama today. That means we'll officially become a family. I promise to always protect you and be the best daddy I can. Will you please be my daughter?" Chase opened a tiny box in his hand. A ring with a single diamond and tiny pink stones created a flower. "I give you this ring to remind you, Ladybug, no matter where you fly, this will always be your home."

Emma watched as Chase slid the ring on her finger. Her smile went from ear to ear. She leaned in and loudly whispered, "Does this mean I can call you, Daddy now?"

Chase's voice choked up with emotion, "Yes, Ladybug, I'd be honored for you to call me Daddy."

Emma flung her arms around him as Chase lifted her

into the air. They turned and faced their family as they beamed at being introduced as husband, wife and daughter. Emma clapped her hands in glee.

Maddie and Joe surrounded the couple as the others waited their turn. Chase leaned down to tell her in ninety minutes, they needed to repeat the vows and exchange their rings again in front of the town as Kassie and Chase.

Kassie broke through the crowd to find Jake. Carol sat next to him as the disgruntled man rested an elbow on the wheelchair arm and held his chin in his hand. "Hello, Jake."

Jake's head jerked in surprise as he stared at the crowd, he had missed Kassie approach. "You look beautiful, Kassie. Congratulations, I wish you and Chase the best."

Chase tried talking to Jake and assured him Kassie held no ill will. Jake used every excuse to avoid Kassie, unable to forgive himself for how he treated his godson's wife.

"I'll have everything I ever wanted as soon as I get you to understand I love you. People make mistakes. I've made mistakes. But I forgive you because you're family. I want you to be a part of our lives. Please don't keep us away. Life is way too short. We love you."

Jake hugged Kassie tightly. "I love you and Ladybug too. I won't let you down ever again."

"Good. Carol, please push Jake over, we're taking family pictures..."

Kassie kissed his cheek and made her way back to her husband. Now officially married, they took photos so after the next ceremony, they could enjoy the evening with the people they loved.

They were finally home.

❋

CHASE PULLED Kassie close and danced with her in his arms. Kassie raised her face up as he gently kissed her lips as people began tapping spoons to glasses.

Chase leaned in and whispered in her ear, "How much longer do we have to play nice? We cut the cake, they already have us packed, and the jet is waiting. You look beautiful, Princess. I want to drag you away and make love to you as my wife."

"I think we can leave soon. Em's tuckered out from telling everyone she's Emma Winters and shaking their hands. Victoria has a limo waiting for us." Kassie laughed as the tapping on the glasses started again.

"Don't they know all this kissing makes me want to do more to you and I have to be gentle because of your mama's dress and I don't want to rip it," Chase complained.

"I think I can help with that."

"How?" Chase pressed his face to Kassie's.

She tilted her head up and whispered in his ear, "I'm not wearing any panties."

Chase held her back from him to stare into her face. The music played yet he stood stock still. Kassie stifled a giggle as he tried to determine if she meant it. His green eyes turned to dark emeralds as his gaze roamed her face. A slow sly smile appeared on his lips, and he took her hand in his and began walking.

"Chase, what about the rest of our dance?" Kassie practically ran to keep up with him. Seeing her struggle with her heels, Chase swept her up in his arms.

"I'll make it up to you later, Mrs. Winters."

Kassie giggled as Chase didn't stop to let her say goodbye to her family or friends. Their guests laughed as he made a beeline toward the limo. He gently placed her on the

Keeping Kassie

seat and gathered her train before sliding in next to her. Before the end of the ride, she knew her dress might be intact but maybe a little wrinkled. Somehow, she didn't mind.

CHAPTER FIFTY-TWO

Samantha and Catherine cheered and waved goodbye to the happy couple. Victoria conspired with the elder couples to gift Chase and Kassie a two-week honeymoon in Ireland at Victoria's compound. Protected and private, the couple needed the time to themselves. At first, they made excuses. The hospital and Emma topped their reasons for not leaving.

Their family and friends refused to accept no for an answer. They worked out a childcare rotation, and Joe accepted responsibility for the hospital. After all, you only marry the love of your life once.

Catherine watched the happy couple. Thrilled for her friend, she was thankful Kassie fought for her happily ever after. Chase cherished her friend like no other.

Her eyes roamed across the yard watching the reception. Leo held a beer in his hand and laughed at something Taco said. Taco purchased a ticket and was leaving in the morning to see his family. Leo took another swig from the bottle, as he searched through the crowd. His gaze landed on her.

Keeping Kassie

Boldly, Catherine met his eyes. Before he left for the mission, he argued she needed to give him a chance. Then their helo had crashed into the ocean.

Distraught, it took all her willpower to keep from running into his arms when they returned. Leo requested she speak with him on the porch. Thinking he felt the same way, she eagerly agreed.

She closed the door to Chase's cabin and walked briskly toward him. Instead of welcoming her into his arms, his arms crossed, and he stepped back to keep her from coming closer.

"I was so worried. I'm glad you and the team made it home safely." Catherine struggled with something to say. Leo's jaw clamped shut. His mouth set in a firm line.

"I asked to speak with you because I've done some thinking. It's not fair of me to ask you to relive our past when I just survived a helo crash. You have a kid, and she needs stability and a father who can give her everything."

Catherine stepped forward, "Leo, I've had time to reevaluate things too and I—"

"I agree with you. It's not good for either one of us to cling to the past. You'll never be able to get over losing your brother and my part in the mission. I'm focused on getting my company up and running. I won't have time to commit to a relationship. We'll remain friends."

Catherine's heart died that day. Leo walked away and avoided her ever since.

She didn't need a man. Catherine had married once before; it was doomed from the start. Ash made her life miserable. His mental games when he returned from missions tortured her soul. She breathed a sigh of relief every time he left. He paid men to follow her when he deployed. She wasn't allowed to see her mother or her friends. All she had left was Melody.

If Derrick "Leo" Strong thought she'd cry over him, he had another think coming.

Samantha sat down beside her, yanking her back to reality.

"It was such a beautiful wedding. I swear Kassie practically glowed." Samantha sighed as she watched Maddie and Joe slow dancing on the makeshift dance floor. "Bryanna's packing up. We thought we'd share a bottle of wine, you in?"

"Sure, that sounds great. Elizabeth asked if we'd bring over the stuff Kassie ordered for the hospital. Wanna drop it off tomorrow?" Catherine picked up her fork and took a bite of the almond cupcake. Her tastebuds did a happy dance. "Bryanna's a genius."

"I know, I think between Ty's food and her cupcakes, my butt has grown two sizes," Samantha sighed. "Look at them." She nodded her head in Maddie and Joe's direction.

They watched as Joe held Maddie close and kissed her on the head. Maddie lovingly caressed the man's cheek. The love in their eyes, evident to everyone around them.

"I miss that." Samantha said forlornly. "I miss Liam holding me as we danced in the kitchen. I don't think I'll ever meet a man like him ever again. My mom keeps pressuring me to date. I swear, I set my mind to it, and then I get a glimpse of Liam in LJ. My heart refuses to let me."

"Liam?" Catherine asked.

"Oh, you know him by what the team called him, Whiskey." Samantha explained as she played with her wine glass, lost in her thoughts. "He spoke with an Irish accent that I swear made me want to drop my panties when he walked into a room."

Catherine giggled and Samantha laughed.

"Don't we make a pair! Come on, let's go help Bryanna, then we can open another bottle of wine," Samantha suggested.

"Let's go," Catherine agreed.

❄

THE FOLLOWING morning Samantha pulled into the circular driveway of the hospital and opened the trunk of her SUV. She started pulling out the bags of homey items Kassie purchased for the hospital.

Catherine grabbed the comforters and posters marked for the teen area. Kassie wanted the teens to be able to decorate their rooms. A box of double-sided tape sat on the floorboard.

After several trips between their cars, the last four bags sat in the trunk.

Samantha inspected the items. "These things are for the cabins in the subdivision. Did Kassie say why they stopped building them?"

"No. I guess we can leave them here at the hospital and when they finish, Kassie can take them down when she gets back," Catherine suggested.

Samantha checked the other bags to confirm the items went to the same area. "Let's head down and put them in one of the finished cabins. That way they don't get lost among the other stuff."

"Good idea, I'm sure one of these keys open them." Catherine pulled the keys Joe gave her from her pocket. "The view is totally worth the walk."

Samantha grabbed the bags and closed the trunk. Catherine took a couple from her as they headed down the path leading to the subdivision.

"Which one should we leave them in?" Samantha asked as they neared the log cabins.

"Let's leave it in the middle one. It's the last one built so we'll remember where we put the bags. Plus, the view from the balcony slays. We should've brought a bottle of wine and some snacks." Catherine checked the keys in her hand.

When she found the correct one, she slid it in the lock and opened the door. Using her back, she held it open for Samantha to go in first.

Samantha made her way through the hallway and stopped. The bags dropped to the floor as Samantha gasped, catching Catherine's attention.

"Samantha?" Catherine closed the door, grabbed her load, and headed to find her friend.

Catherine entered the living area where she skidded to a stop.

Two men sat at the kitchen bar playing cards. The shocked expressions on their faces mirrored the women's.

"Liam?" Samantha whispered.

Catherine stared at the man who resembled her dead husband. Fear settled at the base of her spine. The need to drop the bags and run as fast as she could to rewind what she saw in front of her beckoned.

For one woman, her most fervent prayer had been answered. The love of her life stood before her.

The other woman's worst nightmare walked in front of her. The life she made, free of her tormentor, just turned to hell.

EPILOGUE

Victoria nodded to her men as she made her way down the chilly corridor and into the large cell housing James Stanton.

The doctor reset his arm and he sat in the corner whimpering in pain. A beard marred his face, and his hair needed a cut. James lost some of his bulk. The once formidable man became a shell of his former self.

"Good evening, James," Victoria greeted the man who terrorized her for years.

The doctor walked over to his bag one of her men held. He dropped in his supplies, closed his case, and exited the cell.

"I heard you showed a bit of a temper last night." She tsked as she walked outside of the boundary of the length of chain connected to his ankle. The riding crop tapped against her leg, making James wince as he held his arm.

"It's time, James. Will you walk to the table on your own or shall I have my men help you? Today, I want to talk to you about Kassie Reynolds. The young girl who reminded you of me. You know I met her a long time ago. I confronted and threatened her to get her to leave my son. I thought she was blinded by all your wealth and couldn't see you and Phillip for what you were." Victoria paced the floor as she spoke.

"Kassie adamantly refused to leave. You and Phillip threatened her twin and her child. You killed her parents to get her to agree to marry our son all because of my father's will. She was so young, James." The crop tapped harder against her leg.

"Victoria…" James weakly whimpered her name.

"Now James, how many cuts do you think destroying an innocent's life is worth? I think one for everyone in her family, who you hurt, seems fitting to me." The crop flew across the room.

"Were you aware she carried a child the day she died? It was Matthew Cartwright's. You killed another innocent, James. Shall we count?" Victoria tapped on her fingers as she listed each one of Kassie's family members. "The total of cuts come to six. I think we need to count Matthew. You destroyed his life by sending those men to kill her twin. Poor Matthew spent three years searching for that sweet girl."

"She was a worthless bitch just like you," James spat. Then, realized drawing Victoria's ire wasn't a good idea, he pressed his body further into the corner.

Victoria watched as her men filed in behind her. "The count is up to eight. Oh, I almost forgot. Remember the agent your men killed on your orders while he protected Emma and her mama? That's nine, James."

The men took a step closer to James and he began to kick and scream.

"I didn't hurt her by killing an agent! He doesn't count, Victoria!" James struggled as the men dragged him to the table and placed his wrists and ankles into the attached cuffs.

"Oh, I disagree. I think he counted to someone very much. You hurt his three girls and a very lovely wife. Come to think of it, this puts us at thirteen. Must be your lucky number." Victoria pulled out the ivory handled knife. "Do you remember this knife, James? It's the one you threatened to hurt Emma with."

James warily watched Victoria as she bent to his thigh and made the first cut. His screams echoed and bounced off the wall as his blood dripped onto the pristine floor and down the drain.

"Twelve more to go," Victoria counted.

"Please, Victoria. I beg you to stop. I'll do anything." James pleaded.

Victoria felt no remorse for the man in front of her. She made a cut on his broken arm. James struggled against the restraints as he screamed bloody murder.

"Eleven, James." The knife twisted into the loose skin on his side.

Victoria stood in front of him. Making sure he got a full view of her. She waited until he calmed down before beginning again.

"Do you remember our wedding night, when I told you I refused to help you rape me?" Victoria watched James's face crumble as he cried like a child. She ran her gloved hand through his hair as if to soothe him.

"Don't worry, James. It's a punishment for another day. Do you remember what I told you? When you touched me, I told you for everything you did, I'd keep a list." Victoria bent down to see his face as he shook his head furiously. "My record is long, James. So very, very, long..." She sighed, letting him mentally calculate how many things he'd done to her throughout the years.

"Don't forget you turned my son into an animal and

shoved me down the stairs while I carried our daughter. I haven't forgotten all your transgressions against them."

James's body heaved heavily as he sobbed in his misery.

"Ten James. I need to finish up as Ivan and I are going home to Serenity."

"Victoria...Victoria...Please I beg you..."

The knife slid like butter across his back. James moaned knowing pleading for his life was futile. Victoria would take her pound of flesh.

"Why James. I know you don't mean that. After all, you only ask once..."

SNEAK PEEK COVETING CATHERINE

Chapter One

"Derrick, promise me. You'll watch over him. I don't know... I have a bad feeling about this. I can't explain it." Catherine pleaded. Leo and her brother, Eric "Olaf" Reese, returned home from their last mission on edge.

She felt the tension radiate off both men as they readied themselves to leave again. She sighed, resigning herself to the life of a soon to be wife of a Navy SEAL.

Leo wrapped his arms around her waist and gave her his self-assured smile. "Don't worry, Kit Kat. I got Olaf's back. In a few months, he'll be my brother for real. I'm not going to let anything happen to him." Leo proceeded to make slow love to her, making the dread disappear from her mind. His confident and strong hands held her tightly, as he commanded her body to do his bidding. The next morning, she said goodbye to her fiancé and her brother, not knowing it was the last time she'd hug Eric.

Two weeks later a Navy chaplain knocked on their door with another officer to tell her family, Eric, died and was lost to them, forever. Leo was nowhere to be found. He didn't show up for Eric's funeral. Texts and calls remained unanswered. For every day that passed, Catherine became angrier, confused, and lost. Where was the man who professed to love her family when they needed him the most? Surely, he had access to a phone.

A couple of team members showed up for the funeral

looking haunted and claimed they didn't know the whereabouts of Leo.

A knock at the door sounded throughout the house. Once full of

laughter and love, it felt like a tomb of dismissal silence. Catherine walked down the staircase to see her mom greeting someone. The flash of a dress white uniform caught her eye and made her stop on the stairs as her mom called for her dad. Henry Reese practically ran toward the door hearing the tone of his wife, Carol's, voice. The door opened wider. Catherine walked down the remaining steps to witness her parents hug Leo and her mom burst in fresh tears. Rage enveloped her. She stomped to the entryway and pushed the screen door open sending it crashing against the house.

Startled, her parents pulled away from Leo.

"We'll leave the two of you. When you're done, we'll have dinner."

Carol soothingly told Leo as she rubbed his arm in passing.

Catherine waited until her parents walked back inside. Her blood

raced through her body. The pounding in her ears got louder. She clenched her fists at her side as she waited for the door to close. As soon it clicked shut, she shoved Leo.

"How dare you! You promised me Leo, you'd keep him safe!" She hit his chest, her frustration bubbled to the surface and exploded bringing simmering emotions over the edge. Catherine pounded on his chest with her fists. Leo stood straight, his arms hanging lose at his sides, not attempting to stop her. "You promised!"

His red rimmed eyes pooled with unshed tears as he swallowed hard and nodded his head. His easy-going, relaxed face appeared tired and haggard as he started to speak.

"Kit Kat, I'm sorry—"

"I don't want your apology! I want Eric back," she demanded.

Catherine refused to imagine a world where her brother didn't exist. Eric took the role of her big brother seriously. He allowed her to tag along to the movies with his friends, he drove her and her gaggle of friends to the mall, and always gave her the peanut butter cups from his Moose Tracks ice cream. The day he introduced Leo to her, he laughed as Leo's eyes bugged out of his head as he stuttered his name. Eric winked at Catherine as she put Leo at ease as if he knew some grand secret.

Eric and Leo started a lifelong friendship, and the Reese family adopted the scrawny kid with holes in his T-shirt and sneakers. Under Carol's mothering, Leo packed on weight, and she always conveniently found clothes meant for Eric. When they didn't fit, she never seemed to find the receipts and suggested Leo keep them. Henry Reese provided the stability of a father and encouraged Leo to check into the military. His grades improved and he became a small-town hero. At graduation, the Reese family cheered for the two boys as they accepted their diplomas and planned to enlist in the Navy the following week. Leo's family never cared or showed as Leo left for training. The young men cemented their futures as Navy SEALS and stayed in contact as their career paths led them in different directions. Leo visited every chance he returned and when he asked Catherine out, his father called him into the study and lectured him on his expectations for dating his daughter. When they announced their engagement, her family wasn't surprised.

"He was my best friend." Leo whispered. Guilt radiated

from his body as he allowed Catherine to take out her wrath on him. The confident SEAL appeared lost and confused.

"You weren't even here when we had to put him in the ground."

Katherine twisted the small diamond on her left hand until it fell into her palm. Gripping it tightly until it left an imprint in her hand, she shouted

"You didn't bother to come to the funeral to console my mom or watch my dad shake as they handed him that damn flag. I don't want to marry you, Leo. I refuse to marry the man who let my brother die."

Leo stepped toward her, his hand reached out, and his thumb brushed the tear running down her cheek. Catherine jerked back, as if he scalded her with his touch. His face crumbled as his eyes squinted shut trying to hold the pain inside. Catherine didn't care. Leo made his bed when he broke his promise.

"Take it." Catherine shoved the ring at him. When he refused to

accept it, she threw it at him. "Go Leo. You aren't welcome here anymore."

"Kit Kat, I know you're hurting. If you'd listen to me for just a

moment—"

"I don't want to hear excuses! My brother is gone!" She sobbed.

"Nothing will bring him back. It's over, Leo."

She turned and headed for the house. She barely registered his agonized whisper.

"I love you, Kit Kat. Till my dying breath, you'll always be mine." She slammed the door. Her parents stood in the hallway completely stunned as they heard Leo's truck start and pull away.

"Catherine Ann Reese, what have you done?" Her mother exclaimed.

"That boy is hurting. Our Derrick needs us—"

"He's not ours, mom! He promised to watch over Eric! I can't believe you're on his side. Eric was your son, not Leo." Catherine exasperatedly

replied. "You welcomed him with open arms. You should be mad! You should've refused him at the door! You...you should have..."

"Honey, that boy felt guilty enough as it is. He can't tell us what happened because that's his job. Erik knew when he became a SEAL what he signed up for. Don't blame Leo," Henry Reese tried to be the voice of logic.

"I can't believe you right now. It's like I don't even know who you are..." Catherine backed up, grabbed her purse and keys and walked out the door. She needed a drink to get Derrick "Leo" Armstrong out of her head and most importantly out of her heart.

ABOUT THE AUTHOR

Cassie Colton is an award-winning romantic suspense, military, and contemporary romance author. Always an avid book reader and storyteller, she moved from Illinois to Florida to one of the happiest places on earth. It was there she found her love for making magic and happily ever afters.

She lives in Virginia with her wonderful family and amazing Golden, Leia. She enjoys gardening, flowers, cooking, and learning about beekeeping.

The Serenity Mountain Series is the beginning of her author journey. Detailing the lives of former military men and women who have lost their way and have found peace on Serenity Mountain. Like every story, her characters have to fight through their adversity to find their happily ever after.

Like life, Cassie writes about character struggles that sometimes become dark before they see the light, but she always provides a happy ending. She believes everyone deserves to find happiness and love because it is the only thing worth fighting for.

https://www.cassiecoltonbooks.com/

ALSO BY CASSIE COLTON

Finding Kassie

Chasing Kassie

Keeping Kassie

Coming Soon

Coveting Catherine

Made in the USA
Columbia, SC
30 August 2024